"The truth is the MacDonnarts set out to usurp Camville holdings centuries ago for only God knows what reasons," she said with a small, tight, angry smile.

The accusation stung. Frowning, Ross struggled with the anger only the Camville feud could draw out of him. "The truth is the Camvilles were cattle thieves."

Leonora faced him silently, her gaze level, her chin tipped at a resolute angle. "Well, they certainly haven't been for the past fifty years. That's over now, right?"

"Is that what you believe?" Ross caught her arm and gently swung her around to face him. Boldly, he cupped her chin in his hand, unable to take his gaze from her ripe lower lip, glistening from the mist. To his surprise and pleasure, she did not pull away from him. "You think centuries of bad blood can be ignored, can be wiped away and forgotten because you've decided to return a cup?" he demanded.

"Why not? Forgiven if not forgotten," she said toe to toe with him, prideful and unyielding.

"You think there should be no price to pay for the past?"

"What pri—"

Her mist-jeweled hair and her pride were too much for him. His mouth descended on hers. The truth was, the Camvilles had been defeated. He was not about to allow them to quit the field without surrender . . .

From "The Bridal Cup" by Linda Madl

BRIDE AND GROOM

Deborah Johns
Linda Madl
Patricia Waddell

ZEBRA BOOKS
Kensington Publishing Corp.
http:www.kensingtonbooks.com

CONTENTS

The Knight
de la March

Deborah Johns

One

Ginevra Venier always knew that, once she found the Knight de la Marche, he would be forced to marry her. How could he not? He was a knight and a warrior lord and thus his chivalric code would compel him to honor his word, especially to her. So when she fled the Venice of her powerful parents, she packed few clothes and no jewels, but she brought her wedding dress. Silk itself, it lay carefully enfolded within a white silk envelope that was strapped close to her heart beneath the drab home-spun of a mendicant pilgrim, a disguise that had served her well. The only other thing she carried was a sumter filled with the unguents and tisanes she had ferreted from the abundant stores at Palazzo Venier because Gatien de la Marche's wounds were said to be quite grave.

Not that he looked particularly indisposed as he towered over her; gray eyes snapping out like light-ning from within his thunderclouded face. Ginevra had to mobilize all of her not-inconsiderable energy to keep from trembling like a leaf before his storm. Still, with his fair hair and fine features, he was the most beautiful man the Maid Venier had ever seen. She had loved him from first sight.

"Ginevra Venier, I have a mind to put you across my lap and paddle some sense into you and, indeed,

I would gladly do this, mark my word. But you are so disgustingly dirt-covered that disturbing you in any way would mean encasing the whole of Signora Margaretta's well-cleaned cottage within a mountain of foreign dust."

Ginevra blinked her blue eyes and wrinkled her freckled nose. These were not exactly the first words she had expected to hear from the man who was soon to be both husband *and* lover. (She hoped in that order, but she was prepared for the inversion.)

The Signora Margaretta in question, a rosy cheeked, abundant little woman, hastened to intervene. "Indeed, my lord de la Marche, you must not say the poor child is quite that dirty. Why . . ."

Gatien silenced her with a slight shake of his head. Ginevra noted, with no little satisfaction, that not even such a seeming stalwart as Signora Margaretta was proof against Gatien's dudgeon.

"I cannot imagine what could possibly have induced you to come here." Gatien splayed the fingers of his functioning left hand on the trestle table that separated them. "To undertake a journey from Venice to the very tip of Calabria in this year of Our Lord 1397—what in the name of St. Bernard were you thinking? The roads are filled with brigands and robbers. You could easily have been killed, or worse. Your parents must be frantic with worry. What in God's name were you thinking?"

"The journey here was actually quite uneventful," Ginevra replied lightly, though in truth she was beginning to worry just a bit. Sir Gatien had not been expecting her. He did not, indeed, seem pleased to see her. Was it possible he had forgotten? She took a deep breath, began again. "Not bad at all. I came to you as soon as I learned that you were still alive and that you were here in the village of Badolato."

She hesitated. She could not yet bear telling everything that had happened in Venice on the night she ran away.

"Oh" was all the Knight de la Marche replied to her declaration. Sunlight streamed through the small open window and touched gold to Gatien's fair hair without softening his stern face in the least. He seemed much older than when Ginevra had last seen him in Venice. In the year since they had separated, the Burgundian knight had been to war and come back again to Italy. He was safe but not the same.

"And how did you manage to 'come to me,' as you so succinctly phrase it. If I am not mistaken in my geography, it seems that practically the whole of the Italian peninsula separates Badolato from Venice's Grand Canal." He waved his good arm once again making her uncomfortably aware of her grimy clothing and her mendicant's coarse veil. "I can only imagine that Lord and Lady Venier have quite taken leave of their senses."

"Actually," began Ginevra. Her voice broke. She tried again. "Actually, they have no idea that I am here."

"Why does that not surprise me?" The Knight de la Marche looked at her for a very long time and then motioned her to a small wooden chair. "I think, Givvy, you'd best tell me everything. Start at the beginning, if you please. And you, Signora Margaretta, please join us. I imagine I will need a witness later to assure me that I have not dreamed this fascinating intrigue."

The woman curtsied and bustled herself onto a small stool. Ginevra sat down beside her. She was actually glad to be off her feet. She had already walked the long pathway that snaked from the sea to the hilltop village and the day had not as yet even reached its midpoint.

A hen with two chicks paraded through the low stone doorway and settled down nearby as if they, too, had come to hear the Maid Venier's interesting tale.

"I like this place," said Ginevra, looking about at the snug whitewashed walls and simple wood tables neatly set with pewter dishes and baskets and food-stuff. "But it is so far up the mountainside. Are you even able to see the sea from here?"

The Knight de la Marche nodded toward an open window where light-flax curtains fluttered in a breeze. "You can see straight to the Ionian Sea from the whole of this side of Badolato, but you can smell its freshness all through the village. The people who live here would not have it otherwise."

"Indeed?" replied Ginevra, happy to buy even a short sand's span of relief time before the Knight de la Marche's full wrath descended upon her once again. "But if the folk here are so sea loving, why did they place their thorp high upon the hillside? Would it not have been better to place the city walls near the sea?"

"Not when the sea is infested with pirates,"

Ginevra shivered delicately. "I had no idea there were Saracens nearby. We came by land, not by sea, you know."

"No, Givvy," said Gatien, using the pet name he had given her in Venice but not saying it in the way he had said it there. "I know nothing. Why do you not now inform my ignorance? I was the most amazed man in this world when Signora Margaretta informed me that I had a visitor—a certain Lady Ginevra Venier from Venice. *She*—Signora Margaretta—was amazed as well. I must say, Givvy, you do not much resemble a lady. Your elegant mother would have you immediately converted should she see you now."

"My mother has other worries." Ginevra looked quickly away, but when she turned back to Gatien she was smiling once again. "And it is understandable that I should be so tattered. I have been upon the Pilgrim Road for three whole weeks and four days. I set off as soon as I learned where you were."

"Where I was?" Gatien shook his head. "I cannot imagine why you would search me out at all. But we had best save the whys and wherefores until later. Now just tell me calmly of your adventures so that I, in my turn, can detail them in writing to your parents."

Nothing would have pleased Ginevra more than to tell the Knight de la Marche of her adventures. During the time that France had built its coalition with Venice against the Sultan Bayezid, Gatien, the Duke of Burgundy's personal emissary to Italy had stayed for months on the Grand Canal at Palazzo Venier. Ginevra was the youngest of Count Luciano Venier's four daughters—the others were either profitably married or handsomely betrothed. Ginevra was somehow different from the rest of her strong-willed family, something that Gatien had remarked but could not quite understand. In any event, for some reason or other she had become his particular pet; the younger sister he had never had.

This was a friendship the Knight de Marche was just now starting to heartily regret.

"Oh, Gatien, you would not believe the adventures I've had in searching for you." Ginevra sat eagerly forward in her seat. "It was enough even to hear where you'd gone. My father was reluctant to discuss what had happened at Nicopolis, and of course, my mother is too frivolous to be interested in the battle. Once she found it would not disturb her access to fine cloth and spices from the East, she had done with the matter. The others thought that I was too young to hear. But I was determined and I waited. I could afford to do this because I always knew that I would see you again."

She favored Gatien with a smile so radiant that it

drew forth a sigh from the depths of Signora Margaretta's ample bosom.

"Proceed, Givvy, if you please," remarked the Knight de la Marche.

"Though it was hard to keep faith on account of the rumors," continued Ginevra. "You cannot suppose the stories that were carried to us from the battlefield at Nicopolis. Horrible tales—thousands and thousands dead or captured. The whole of France's army exterminated, as well as a large part of Hungary's. Everyone was frantic with worry.

Gatien said nothing. What was there to say about the horrors? Thousands and thousands dead, Ginevra had said. Friends of his, relatives even—but he himself had been forced out of the war just one battle before its terrible ending. At Rachowa, just short days before Nicopolis, a stray arrow had caught his right arm. There had been grave damage; he had almost lost it. The duke's son, Jean of Nevers, had insisted he be shipped back to Italy where an excellent surgeon, Yacopo Moscato, had managed to save both his arm and his life—but neither was as it had been. Now his arm ached and he longed to rub it. But Gatien de la Marche, a First Knight of France, would not allow himself to do that until Ginevra had finished and was gone.

He was a warrior, descended from a long line of warriors. What had happened had happened. Now he must go on.

"It was November before we in Venice heard of the defeat," continued Ginevra softly, "though they say the battle was fought on St. Michael's Day, the Twenty-ninth of September. In France, they did not hear until Christmas Eve. A runner brought the news directly into King Charles as he sat at festive table. They say that the cries of the women in Paris reached up and echoed off Heaven. Through the whole of France, bells tolled the news from city to village and from village to hamlet. It was terrible. They say the pealing continued day and night. My sister Domiziana said that not one of the noble families escaped the loss of someone they loved."

"Peasants died as well," said Gatien, "and plenty of them. But that is neither here nor there. Will you not tell me how news of Nicopolis got you here?"

"Because I had to find you!" Ginevra exclaimed. She dropped her hands into her lap and, true to Gatien's fear, a cloud of dust billowed forth to settle amidst the floor-thyme at her feet. "The count of the Ducci Montaldo brought us the news—or rather I should say he brought it to Venice because he was in service to the ruling *Signoria*."

"Which your uncle heads," remarked Gatien.

Ginevra turned to Margaretta. "*Zio* Antonio is the Doge of Venice. He is the head of our ruling oligarchy."

"Now you see where the Maid Ginevra gets her penchant for command," Gatien remarked. "Tell us what happened next, Givvy."

"Mother and the others were glad enough that Olivier Ducci Montaldo had been spared. He is, after all, my sister Domiziana's betrothed. Did you know that he was chosen to bring back terms of ransom for the few others who escaped the slaughter? He is livid with rage at what happened. He thinks there was treachery involved in the defeat."

"I had heard," said the Knight de la Marche. He looked down at his useless arm and then back to Ginevra once again. "Both about the suspicion of betrayal and Count Olivier's anger over it. But this still does not explain your being here."

"Oh, but indeed it does," replied the Maid Venier with alacrity. "It explains everything. I was worried sick about you. I had heard no word from you since you set sail and the rumors were fearsome—though less fearsome than the truth as it turned out. By the time Count Olivier reached Venice, I had been in San Marco every day for weeks lighting candles and praying for your safety. He was the first to sit with me and tell me you were safe; that you had been seriously injured in an earlier battle and shipped home with the Black Fleet when they returned for provisions. Oh, Gatien, why did you not send word?"

For a long while Gatien said nothing. He just stared at her through the light that filtered into Margaretta's snug chamber—a light that continued to turn his fair hair golden but now shaded his light eyes to darkness.

"It was a bad moment," he said finally, "not only for me but for many others—more so for others. Quite frankly, I did not think you would mark my absence. I thought your parents would have well betrothed you by now."

"Not mark your absence?" echoed Ginevra. Her clear blue eyes widened to saucers of incredulity. "Betrothed me to another? But how can that be, Gatien, when I have pledged my troth to you?"

The Knight de la Marche shook his head emphatically.

"Givvy . . ." he began.

"But that is neither here nor there," Ginevra continued, ignoring his warning tone. "As soon as I heard the news, I knew immediately what I must do. Mother and Father were useless; they were both so distracted. There is so much hatred and suspicion in the city. You would not know it as the same place where I taught you to dance the tarantella at *Carnevale* or where we rode out together along the marshes of the Veneto. The people of Venice are beside themselves with rage and frustration at what happened. They are looking for scapegoats. There was a true witch-hunt within the city. They dragged an old woman from her bed. They . . ."

She stopped abruptly. She could not tell him who

this old woman had been and what she had meant to them—to the Veniers. At least she could not tell him this now.

"I can readily understand the chaos and the grief within the walls of Venice," said Gatien, "but what I absolutely have no grasp of is why you are here and not there. Surely your parents, distracted as they may be by their responsibilities to the city, cannot possibly have allowed you to dress in pilgrim clothes and travel through Italy without an escort."

"They would never have allowed me to come to you had I told them my intentions. Things may be in great upheaval, but my mother is a Venier only by marriage; this makes her painfully aware of the conventions. She would have sealed me alive in my chamber before she would ever have allowed me to set off to seek you—at least until we were satisfactorily married or, at the very least, officially betrothed."

"A wise woman," mused a rueful Gatien, still not quite sure he wished to pursue the exact reason young Ginevra had formulated such strange ideas concerning her future with him. Best to stick with the adventure itself; the reasons behind it had best be put off a bit longer, after this child had had a good rest. "You would be wise yourself, my dear Givvy, to follow your mother's stable reasoning. Or to have followed it, perhaps I should now say. But tell me the rest of your tale. Then I will leave you in the capable hands of Signora Margaretta and go off to my ink and my parchments so that letters, which may perhaps rectify this singular situation, may be sent."

"There is really no 'rest' to tell you," replied Ginevra. "After Lord Olivier told me where to find you, I laid my plans. With the times in such disarray, I knew there would be many pilgrim bands traveling to pray at the shrines in the south. I had but to slip away and join a group that was heading along the

Via Pellegrina. Actually, reaching you was easy. It was waiting those months for news of you that was quite the hard part."

Gatien said nothing. He glanced at the silent Margaretta and then walked toward the window, pulling wide the casements, looking out at the sea. He stood like that for a long time while Ginevra watched him.

She loved him so much. Even when his back was turned to her, he seemed beautiful. It had been so long since she had been able to look upon him that everything about him seemed sweet to her: the long, slender line of his body beneath the simple dark blue tunic that he wore; the crisp curl of his hair against the nape of his neck; the way he gingerly touched his good arm with his bad when he was deep in thought. This last was new, however; he had never rubbed his arm during his carefree days in Venice. Of course, he had not yet borne this wound when she had known him there.

"Does it give you much pain?" Ginevra asked him softly. "Because if it does, I've brought medicines. Lord Olivier's ward once pointed me toward the best tinctures and elixirs to use again affliction. I can help you get well again; that is, if you like."

Gatien turned from the window and gazed at her with a haunted look that was new to him as well.

"Yes," he said simply. "Sometimes my arm troubles me. I am sure the pain will pass without assistance. Tell me, Givvy, is there a particular reason you have gone to such pains to find me? Certainly it was not to carry medicines that I could easily have found myself."

Ginevra looked at him incredulously. "Indeed, that was not the only reason. I've come to marry you, of course."

"*Marry* me?"

The two words thundered out of him. Ginevra was sure she heard them tumble down from the top of this hillside and Signora Margaretta's trim stone house, past the astounded, upraised faces of the villagers to finally fall like lead into the sea.

"You needn't act as though you did not know this," she added.

Without another word to her, Gatien turned to Margaretta Mulino who still sat transfixed and interested upon her stool.

"Madam, I know this is against all the laws of good behavior, but would you please leave me alone to speak with the Maid Venier? I promise that she will be in no way compromised by my unchaperoned proximity."

Signora Mulino scurried to the door.

"Marry you?" he repeated.

"Don't tell me you forgot!"

"I seem to have," said Gatien, making a small bow to Ginevra—a courtesy that was abundantly belied by the cheerless and fulminating look on his face. "Perhaps you might acquaint me with the circumstances."

"Oh, gladly so," Ginevra replied, "though, I must say it is more than a little crushing that you so have so easily forgotten what happened. But, of course, with the battle . . ."

"Continue," barked Gatien de la Marche, who had not a small reputation as a great leader of men.

"It was near the Bridge of Sighs," said Ginevra immediately, "on the night of *Carnevale* right before you set sail to the Nicopolis. I told you that I loved you and asked you to marry me. You said that you would surely do so, if when I turned eighteen, I was not yet betrothed and still would have you. You ruffled my hair as you said it; and remarked that such a cute child as I—and that is exactly what you called me—would surely be spoken for within the next full moon's time. But I wanted no one else. Indeed, I am eighteen now and not betrothed to another. Neither have I forgotten you. And that is why I am here."

She looked at him with wide, expectant eyes.

"But, really, Givvy." If anything, her explanations had only served to further confound the Knight de la Marche. He shook his head back and forth as though to clear it, and then began again. "But really Givvy. It was only . . . surely you did not think . . . Truly, you are so *young*.

"I am but ten years younger than are you," retorted Ginevra. The she narrowed her eyes and stared closely at him. "What is it? Do you love another? Is that the problem? They say the women of the East are quite beautiful and perhaps . . ."

"No," said Gatien, a little too quickly. "It is just . . . but enough of this talking. Whether you were right or wrong to make this voyage, you are surely tired from it now. I will fetch Signora Margaretta to care for you, while I send word to your family of your whereabouts. Afterward, we will think this thing through and calmly discuss it. But first you must be cleaned up and well fed. You will love Margaretta. She and her husband, Pietro, have a habit of making people welcome. I stayed in this house when I first arrived here in Badolato; in the very chamber in which you are now placed. Of course now I have petitioned for hospitality at the Monastery of San Francisco, which is just a little beyond the village walls. It would not do for me to remain here now that you have come."

"But you will come back, won't you, Gatien?"

For an instant Ginevra felt like the child the Knight de la Marche still imagined her to be.

"Of course I will." Gatien's stern face softened. "This is a small village. You cannot help but see me in it. But first you need your rest. I will send in Signora Margaretta to help you. She is probably lingering just outside the door."

* * *

"My goodness, you are a wonder," exclaimed the merry Margaretta as she energetically rubbed the last of the water from the abundance of Ginevra's auburn hair, "to have walked all the way from Venice to the tip end of Calabria. And you a noblewoman and all."

"I don't see what being a noblewoman had to do with it," replied Ginevra, who naturally held a democratic view of life, "anyone could have walked that distance if they'd had reason enough."

"And you did!" exclaimed Margaretta.

"Certainly I did." Ginevra shrugged herself into the clean white tunic Margaretta had found for her. "I had to find Gatien. I had to see if he had need of me."

Margaretta stood back to stare at her handiwork. "Well, you are clean enough, my lady, but that tunic could fit two of you. Still, 'tis all I had for now. Let me think . . . There is a peasant good with a needle near the main piazza of the village. Her name is Luisa. Perhaps she can make something else for you, though I must say, we have no fine silks or linens here about. We are a mightily plain village."

"Badolato is such a beautiful place that one does not need silks and fine linens to parade about its streets. These simple clothes are perfect for me, and I thank you for them."

"You are like no noblewoman I've ever met!" replied the forthright Signora Mulino. "They all would be moaning about their bright colors and their laces and their pearls."

"But I've brought my pearls with me!" said Ginevra. She bounded over and rummaged through her discarded mendicant's clothes——raising another cloud of dust in the process—until she found her silk sumter. She opened it reverently and withdrew the fine-stuff of the pearl-embroidered wedding tunic she had carried close to her heart through her travels.

"I've never seen such a beautiful thing. Never in my life," said Margaretta breathlessly. "I dare not even touch it."

"Of course, you much touch it," insisted Ginevra. "It is to be my wedding dress."

"Oh," said Margaretta. The Knight de la Marche had taken her aside and told her that in no way had he ever compromised the Maid Ginevra and Margaretta believed him. He had convalesced four months within her household and she respected and liked him. But she found herself liking Ginevra as well and wondering how such a mixed pottage might end.

"You brought this with you all the way from Venice?"

"Hidden beneath my tunic," whispered Ginevra. "No one suspected at all. But then, of course we were lucky enough not to have hit brigands and robbers on the trail."

"By St. Helen's bones, all you did was walk up to this group of traveling Franciscans and ask to join them? You are a bold, bright one indeed!"

"Well, first I naturally made sure they were coming southward. 'Twould not have done at all had they been set upon crossing the Haute Savoie to the shrine of St. Bernard in France."

She enjoyed telling her adventures to this jolly woman. While they were in Venice, Gatien had praised her exceedingly for her enterprising spirit, though he seemed a bit less taken with her initiative now that it had brought her to his doorstep once again.

"Well, they could not turn me away," replied Ginevra, eating an apple while perched on the edge of the bed. "I said that I was going to the shrines to pray for my husband. This was true enough. I have prayed night and day for Gatien since the very moment that he set sail from Venice."

Margaretta nodded at this but wisely said nothing as she began working a wide wooden comb through the thick mass of Ginevra's long curls. "And did he set sail long ago?"

Ginevra turned to the woman, and Margaretta was astonished by how dark and deep had eyes had become. For the first time, she thought the Knight de la Marche was mistaken in thinking this woman a child.

"A lifetime ago," said Ginevra. "When the stories started coming from the east. When we heard the horrible numbers of those who had been killed . . ." She let her voice trail off.

"Indeed, the Knight de la Marche was fortunate," said Signora Margaretta. "At least, that is, in his own way."

"Though I imagine he does not realize that now," said Ginevra. "He did not mention his wound except once when I asked him if it pained him. He replied, very briefly, that it did. That was all."

"Sir Gatien is a man very much in pain," replied Margaretta. She hesitated and then turned to Ginevra. "Pain from both inside and out. Though, of course, he will not talk about it. He says that all is well. He is anxious to get back to Burgundy and the people who are under his care. But neither my husband, Pietro, nor I are fooled by his heartiness. His life was soldiering. He said he took his first paging at seven, just as had his father and *his* father before him. The de la Marche family has fought for France for hundreds of years, since the time of Charlemagne. Now that life is over for him, and I think he has no inkling of how to construct another. Did you know him well in Venice?"

"Only well enough to love him," Ginevra replied with a smile.

Margaretta looked over at her, sitting on the bed, her hair curled around her head and tumbling midway down her back and her blue eyes turned deep and dark with some sort of special knowledge.

The Maid Venier has a kind face, Margaretta decided, a face that belongs to a woman perhaps much wiser than her years.

She made a quick decision and pulled a three-legged stool close beside the bed.

"You may call me Retta," she said. "Margaretta is quite the mouthful. Much-too-much name for all the backing and forthing we will be doing in the days ahead. You seem to be such a little thing. The Knight de la Marche told me that you were a child, but no child could have walked half of Italy to reach him."

For a moment Ginevra said nothing, just studied Retta with her lovely eyes. "I love Gatien de la Marche," she repeated. "I have loved him since the first day I saw him stride into my father's house."

"It is good that you love him," whispered Retta, "because he will need that love if he is once again to become whole."

They sat in silence for some time, listening to a robin sing just outside the chamber window.

"He was brought here after the first battle," continued Retta. "November. They brought him here because the snows had already started falling on the mountains and there was no hope of getting him home to his main fortress in Burgundy. His wound had reduced him quite badly. We are lucky in having a good surgeon—a lay doctor trained at Salerno, not a monk. Yacopo Moscato. Sir Gatien has already spoken to you of him. But even he thought it would be impossible to save the Knight de la Marche's life, much less his arm. He has surprised us all. Still . . ."

"Still what?" urged Ginevra.

"Dr. Moscato insists that motion may still hide within the arm's inertness. He says that if the Knight de la Marche would just try some simple exercises, there might be hope for movement. Of course it would never be as it was before—he would never be able to swing a sword with it again—but some improvement might be possible. At least this is what the doctor says."

"And Gatien will not do this? He will not try?"

"Not at all," replied Margaretta softly, and there were tears in her eyes. "He becomes angered if this hope is even mentioned."

Again she stopped speaking and bent over from her stool to make a great show of folding the linen bathing towels and pulling the lump of rose soap from the cooling water in the beaten-lead bathing tub. Then she made another great show of her silence.

"Perhaps the Knight de la Marche has been waiting for you," she said finally. "Perhaps that is why he has lingered so long at Badolato. And perhaps that is the true reason you have come."

Two

Ginevra, who had grown up among the marshy islets of Venice, had never seen a sea like the one that stretched out before her now. From her chamber window in her parents' grand palazzo, she had grown to womanhood looking out on a silver city that merged gradually into a gray sea. This in turn disappeared just as slowly and majestically within the mysterious foggy swirl that lead to the East, where the city maintained great and providential trade relations. None of it bore any resemblance to what lay before Ginevra now. Calabria was so bright and colorful that it could have come from the stars.

From her perch on the white stone wall of the village, she looked down on a hillside alive with a riot of summer flowers. She counted shades of yellow and gold, red, blue, violet, and an incredible number of oranges before her senses began to drown in the colors.

And the sea! Ginevra splayed her fingers, reaching out to touch it, although she knew its closeness was only a mirage. Only that morning she had walked the steep path that led from the shore to Badolato and her feet still ached from the journey, which had taken many a sand-span of the hourglass.

"One would not think that anything so beautiful could be infested with violence," said Gatien coming up behind her. "But the Ionian Sea is filled with pirates."

"Saracens?" asked Ginevra. "Or French?"

"Both," replied the Knight de la Marche, "and also Venetians. In fact, the Venetians themselves are rumored to be the most ferocious of them all."

He smiled as Ginevra turned toward him.

"Then that rumor is a lie," she retorted, "because we Venetians are known for our peaceful and calm docility."

The boom of Gatien's laughter scattered birds from the treetops.

"And you are the sterling example of the docility of your city?"

She straightened her back and stared at him with what she hoped was a show of at least calmness, if not docility. "Indeed I am."

"Then no wonder your city has been at war since the first inhabitants fled Genghis Khan and claimed it clear of the marshes. If not for land, then for trade routes, Venice has always shown itself determined to go on."

"With the Veniers in the thick of the battle?"

He looked at her with his dove gray eyes. "In the forefront of it, I should think."

Ginevra did not like the turn of this conversation. She had journeyed to Badolato to become a de la Marche, not to be reminded of her history as a Venier. After what had happened to the *strega* Elisabetta—after what her family had allowed to happen to that poor woman—she had turned her back on them forever. She would have fled to the ends of Marco Polo's Silk Route to be away from them. But instead, Providence had finally pointed her to her love, the Knight de la Marche, instead.

"Gatien, I've something to tell you."

"I imagine you have, Givvy, but first you must hear me out."

She knew exactly what he would say to her.

"Later," she whispered, "there is still time. I have just arrived from a painful voyage. Tell me where I find myself. Tell me of this sea."

He paused, as though considering. Then with some effort, he used his sound arm to lift himself onto the wall beside her.

"It is beautiful, is it not?"

Ginevra nodded. "More than beautiful, it is magical. I have always thought of the sea as one color. Instead this one is alive with shades of green and blue. One can make them out quite distinctly."

"As night falls," the Knight de la Marche said to her, "you will see these same greens and blues slowly shade to pink and violet in the sunset. It is an extraordinary sight. I have never seen water so. It is not so beautiful even in the south of France at Aquitaine."

"What I wonder," said Ginevra, wrinkling her small nose in thought, "is why the villages in Calabria are built upon hillsides. How can these people stand to be so far from their beautiful sea?"

"Because of the pirates, as I mentioned earlier," Gatien reminded her. For a brief instant he was once again a First Knight of France and a warrior as he gestured with his sound arm toward the flatness of the white shore. "The people of Badolato would have had no defense against incursion if they had remained hugged to the sea. Now they are snug and happy upon their hillside and have been for some hundreds of years. The sea has become only a vision to them. They rarely visit it, at least after sunset."

"But don't they fish upon it?"

Gatien shook his head. "You will see, Givvy, that although the food here is quite tasty, it is based more on mutton than on fish. Sheep, pigs, and goats can be raised on the hillside. They are a much safer choice than fish."

Ginevra sat quietly for a moment, listening to the swell of the sea that echoed from below them. It was hard to imagine that anything so peaceful looking and so beautiful could have inspired a terror that had lasted for centuries.

"And how did you come here?" she asked him at last. Margaretta had already told her part of the reason, but she wanted to hear the rest from Gatien himself.

Gatien smiled over at her and for the brief radiant duration of that smile he was the man Ginevra remembered from Venice. The man she had loved at first sight.

"Through what could only be described as happy circumstance," he answered. "Venice's Black Fleet has a healthy respect for all the pirates hereabouts. When they got wind that the Saracens were near us, they put off both passengers and commerce at the very nearest port. Badolato was that port."

"Lucky, indeed," said Ginevra. She turned her small face up to the light. "I have never seen such a beautiful sea. And the sun! Can it be the same one that shines on Venice? Never in my life have I seen anything quite this bright."

"That's because you are not wearing veiling against it!" scolded Gatien. "Your nose is already liberally sprinkled with sun dots. Your mother, Lady Claudia, will be most upset when she sees you. You know how meticulous she is about such things."

"I've never cared a fig about protecting my complexion. In Venice you told me that you liked this. You said I looked healthy and real among all the artifice that is Venice!"

"I didn't say *I* didn't like your sun-dots," Gatien explained with great patience. "I said that your *mother* wouldn't."

Ginevra wryly wrinkled her sun-dotted nose. "Believe me, Sir Gatien, the last thing that would worry my lady mother at this time is the state of my complexion. She has many other things with which to be preoccupied."

"Such as what?"

But the Maid Ginevra had turned once again toward the sea.

Gatien answered his own question. "Such as the state of your virtue and your reputation," he said.

"I have done nothing to compromise my virtue," said Ginevra.

"Of course I believe that," replied the Knight de la Marche softly. "I know you—or have you forgotten? Your virtue was never under question.'Tis your judgment at issue. But I have written to Lord and Lady Venier to tell them of your presence here. I am sure they are quite frantic with worry. I imagine you left no clue as to where you were going and to whom?"

"Of course not," replied an incredulous Ginevra. "They would have stopped me had they known."

"As well they might have." Gatien had once again taken on his scolding tone. "I cannot even imagine the perils you must have gone through on your journey—and probably without realizing that you were going through perils at all. But don't tell me of them, at least not yet. I don't know that I am strong enough to bear the recitation. I'm sure you know, Maid Ginevra, that your father could easily have you convented for the silliness you've done. In Venice, your reputation is bound to be rag-tattered. You have heaped nothing but dishonor upon your family's good name.

"I was accompanied to the very foot of this hillside by a company of nuns," protested Ginevra. "In no way have I abased myself or my family. And I resent being treated as though I were still a child."

"You are being treated like a child because you have acted like a child, but perhaps amends may still be made." He paused to consider. "Undoubtedly, you will need to marry and marry in some haste. I have a nephew, the youngest son of my youngest sister. He is a nice, presentable fellow from a family that is well respected in Burgundy. Indeed, at twenty he has already earned the golden spurs of knighthood. It has occurred to me that perhaps I might dower you to him. That is," he added hastily, "if your own father refuses to accept financial responsibility in this. I will write to my sister. Perhaps she can persuade her son in this."

"You want to marry me to another?" Ginevra's bright eyes grew round with incredulity. "When you know that it was always you that I would wed?"

"I want no more talk of marriage between us," replied an angry Gatien. "We played silly games in Venice—games that I had no idea you were taking seriously—if indeed you were. For whatever reason, you have now determined to hold me to a joking promise. But you need to be married to someone your own age, Ginevra. Someone who has his whole life still before him. Not someone old, as I am now old, and broken."

"Fie!" retorted Ginevra. She was righteously angry herself by now. "A nephew indeed! I have no intention of being bargained about as though I were a child. You make yourself into an old man, Gatien, because it suits you. We both know that you have but ten years more than I. Is all of this because of your wounding? Because I can assure you that I would rather have you broken and at home than whole and wielding a sword on some strange battlefield. I am heartily sickened of war!"

She stopped suddenly and reached out a hand as though to catch the words and stuff them once again back into her mouth. But they were out there now, frozen in the open. They had quite turned the Knight de la Marche to stone.

"The fact that the wound I bear leaves you unimpressed only points to your immaturity," he said. "It is obvious that you have a young girl's idea of marriage. One that has been formed of marzipan tales sung by troubadours. You have a midge's idea what it would actually be like to live with half a husband."

Ginevra's remorse melted at his words with the rapidity of frost beneath the sun.

" 'Tis you, Gatien de la Marche, who seem to have a head full of romantic notions. I came to *knowing* you had been injured. It is not something that I learned on the road. Indeed, in Venice they lamented that your injury was graver. And I still came. Nothing could have stopped me from coming. Nothing in this world."

He looked at her closely for a long while. Ginevra did not flinch beneath his stare.

"Then we must marry," he said finally. "As you are still a virgin and came to me with neither parental permission nor chaperonage, it is my duty to wed you. I took a vow of chivalry toward women, and this must be honored. I was a guest within your family home when this unfortunate misunderstanding occurred, and now I cannot leave you to face the consequences of your actions alone. I will write again to your parents requesting permission and then have the banns called from the altar. We should be wed within six weeks."

With that he turned on his heel and left her to the mercy of the sun and the sea.

We will be wed, he had told her.

Ginevra had gotten what she came for, but she had never had so little reason to feel triumphant.

"I should have invited Dr. Moscato as well," said Retta as she bustled about with a pottery bowl of preserved and sugared oranges. "We are very fortunate indeed to have such a learned man in our midst. He did marvels with the Knight de la Marche. But he was busy. For one reason or another, summer has always been a great birthing season here in Badolato. For such a small town, it certainly replenishes itself well."

"It should be a great birthing season," boomed her husband. Pietro Mulino was quite a small man, gray bearded and simply dressed, but with the same daunting energy as his wife. "The town itself was birthed in summer. On the very eve of the Virgin's birth to be exact—that would be September seventh."

"Or so goes the legend," adjoined his wife.

"What legend?" barked an indignant Pietro. "We are speaking here of historical fact!"

"Signore Pietro is the unofficial historian of this village," Gatien whispered to Ginevra, though quite loud enough so that both the Mulinos could easily hear him. "But officially he is its able schoolmaster."

The four of them—Margaretta and Pietro Mulino and Ginevra with the Knight de la Marche—were gathered around the long trestle table that dominated the main room of the Mulinos' sturdy village house. The board was set with brightly polished pewter ware and bowls of flaming, scented geraniums. Roasted meats, cheeses, and fruits lay heaped in pottery upon it.

Pietro Mulino laughed. "I don't know how good I am at schoolmastery. But I was born in Badolato more than fifty years ago, and the history of this place has always intrigued me. We are as yet still a young city—founded less than four hundred years ago by Roberto Guiscardo, the first duke of Calabria. Not nearly as old as your native and splendid Venice, my lady Ginevra—but already we have our first ghost!"

"Shhh about that," replied Retta, shaking her

wimple-wrapped head. "You will frighten the Maid Ginevra with your foolish talk of ghosts and such likes. She might become afraid to walk along the paths at night, though heaven knows nothing exciting ever happens in Badolato. We are too safe and snug upon our hillside."

"You must tell me" protested Ginevra. "Nothing frightens me."

"To say the least of it," replied the Knight de la March, though his words were pitched so low that only she could hear.

"Ah, the ghost," said Pietro Mulino, obviously eager for his tale.

"Well, go on with it if you must," scolded Retta, throwing up her hands.

"Perhaps 'tis not really that interesting a story," replied her husband, modest now that he was sure his audience was well captured. "And it is not that the ghost is bloodthirsty or anything along that unsettling line."

"Get along with it, then," prompted his wife, "and let the Knight de la Marche and his Lady-to-be decide."

Pietro looked toward the window where a clear evening breeze ruffled the flax curtains at the glassless window. "The ghost in question is a Templar knight. Do you know anything about the Templars, Maid Ginevra?"

"Only that they were thought to be warlocks or worse," replied Ginevra with a shiver. "They were reputed to have done terrible things and King Philip the Fair of France burned them all to save civilization from their wicked ways. Or so he said."

"You don't believe this?" urged Pietro.

"I cannot know the truth of those accusations. I was not alive a hundred years ago when they were posted. I do not live in France. But I think it wrong to burn souls on witchcraft chargings. I think it is very wrong to do this at any time and to anyone."

"There were fearsome stories told about the Templars during their last days," agreed Professor Pietro. "But these were greed-fueled. Whether this was the Templars' greed to enrich themselves or the king's need to enrich the coffers of France with the order's gold——well, who is to know this now?

"Hugh of Payns began the Order of the Temple to protect the sacred places of the Holy Land," continued Pietro. "He saw it as a means of marrying the best of both the monastic and the warrior stations, creating a troop of knight-monks who would be disciplined and would help bring a sorely lacking harmony and method to the European Cause. Robert, duke of Calabria, had a son who was prominent within this order. It is his son, Bohumond, who haunts this place."

"Have you ever met him?" asked Ginevra.

Pietro looked across the trestle at her with dancing eyes. "Only once. I only *needed* to meet him once. It was enough."

"Because he was so fearsome?"

"He is not fearsome at all. Quite the opposite." Pietro barked a short laugh. "But I have a feeling, Lady Ginevra, that you will one day learn this fact about him for yourself. He will have something of interest to tell you. Something that may change your life as completely as mine was changed by what he said."

Out of the corner of her eye Ginevra saw him quietly cut sugared fruit into small pieces and place it before the Knight de la Marche.

So this is the reason for this diversion.

The two women exchanged a quick glance.

"Certainly I will then hope to encounter him," she said brightly, effectively calling attention to her-

self. "God knows that I have much need of his services."

She laughed, while keeping covert watch as Gatien
picked awkwardly at his food with his left hand. She
reached for her goblet and accidentally spilt drops of
water down the front of her linen tunic.

"Ah, water!" exclaimed the ever-ready Pietro with
typical rapture. "Badolato's water is said to be the
sweetest in all of Italy. Why, they say that for lovers . . ."

"That is quite enough, Pietro," said his wife, playfully rapping at his knuckles with her steel spoon.
"You will have the Lady Ginevra thinking that we are
all bores and provincials here if you continue pump-
ing up the glories of our little village."

"Retta, how can you say such a thing," began her
husband indignantly. "Why the whole of Calabria
knows that I—"

A loud clattering interrupted them. Ginevra
looked over to see a stony-faced Gatien bend over to
pick up his dropped knife and plate from the floor.
Sugared oranges lay strewn among the thyme and
rushes. For a moment there was no sound, and then
the Knight de la Marche laughed.

"I seem to have turned these oranges into quite a
quatrain," he said. "I spear in circles at my food and
become a menace so those around me. I hope I've
not caused too much damage."

"To the floor?" scoffed Retta prettily. "But perhaps you should join us again tomorrow evening for
the meal. I will inspect the rushes carefully and give
you my opinion then."

They all laughed at this and the embarrassing moment passed. But Ginevra did not forget.

Neither did the Knight de la Marche.
He lay thinking on his hard cot in the monastery,
long after his young page had drifted off to sleep.

How could he possibly marry this woman? How could he possibly carry her off to his estates in Burgundy and the life that now would await them there?

He was a wounded warrior with a useless arm. And yet he had both priests and peasants dependent on him. He was guardian to vast lands and to many people's interests. How could a useless man see to these things, especially if he were encumbered with such a wife?

Ginevra.

Imagine that child of class and privilege walking half of Italy to meet him—and without care and proper chaperonage! What a muddle she had made of everything! What a muddle she had made of his life!

He set his mouth into a stern line and then unwittingly smiled at her enterprise.

She'd been like this in Venice. Different from the other Veniers, a strange duckling who paddled her own away amidst their sea of swans. Not that Ginevra was disagreeable looking. In many ways with her lovely blue eyes, fine features, and truly spectacular auburn hair, she was the loveliest of the family. Much better-looking than her stern sister Domiziana who was thought to be the beauty of the bunch. It's just that Ginevra did not care for beauty; she cared for doing as she wanted.

He had loved this about her in Venice. Had loved her enterprise and her life and her smile. It was the reason he had kept close company with her—and this was the reason he was in such a devilish mess right now.

He had loved being with the child Ginevra. But he did not love her.

No, not at all.

* * *

Ginevra's small chamber lay at the very front of the Mulinos' snug stone four-roomed house. Through its windows she could hear the soft whooshing of the surf breaking on the sand of the seashore. This had been Gatien's room before he'd gone to the monastery and left it to her. But she could still feel his presence in it. Could still smell the clean French soap and leather and Gatien-ness that she remembered so well.

Margaretta had rapped upon her door and then come in to sit upon a low stool. She came right to the reason for her night-visit; she did not bustle about.

"You know Sir Gatien well. I saw this tonight in the way you looked at him and didn't. In what you said and in what you left unsaid. You know him just as surely as I knew my own Pietro when we plighted wedded troth," said the older woman, "and as your mother must know and love your father as well."

Ginevra frowned at this mention of the Veniers. "I imagine that she does, though we have never talked about it."

"Did you ever tell her about your feelings for the Knight de la Marche?"

"I couldn't tell her anything like that," said Ginevra, pulling her bare feet up beneath the billows of another of Signora Mulino's enormous white linen bed tunics—the kind that made Ginevra feel safely tucked inside. "She would never have understood my feelings for Gatien. Marriage is something else for her. It is more like a business, a family enterprise. You have a daughter. You dress her up, teach her all manner of pretty and decorative nonsense, and then you sent her forth to see what profit she can make of what you've done. The idea that she find someone who loves her and whom she loves does not constitute a successful conclusion to this venture. We are taught to look to people for what they can do for us. When they can do nothing—or nothing more—then we are encouraged to let them drop."

Retta looked at her through the soft light of a tallow candle. "The Knight de la Marche said that your family is one of the most important in Venice. He said that you are directly related to the ruling *Doge* himself."

Ginevra laughed. "It is like Gatien to make much of my origins, as though it would be a sacrifice for a Venier to troth herself to a de la Marche. He thinks this forms part of his code of chivalry; instead it is intrinsic to his particular charm. I imagine you know that not all knights are as good and as kind as the Knight de la Marche."

"Calabria has seen its share of invasions," replied Retta wryly. "I have good reason to realize that not all warriors are as goodly natured as Sir Gatien."

"He is a First Knight of France," said Ginevra softly, "and one of the premier warriors in all of Europe. At least he was. His family have held their estates in Burgundy since the time of Charlemagne. There are many women—royal ones as well—who would have considered themselves singularly blessed to bear the simple title of Lady de la Marche."

"I don't think I understand."

"You would have to know my family to understand clearly," replied Ginevra with a sigh. "My sister Domiziana—my mother's favorite and the oldest—is betrothed to the count of the Ducci Montaldo. Indeed, by now she has probably managed to wed him. She was determined upon this marriage, as was my mother."

"I have heard of the count of the Ducci Montaldo," said Retta, wrinkling her brow in thought. "Is he not a famed *Condottiero,* a warrior-general?"

"Indeed, he is. Though not so famed as my Gatien," replied Ginevra stoutly. "The Knight de la

Marche is the most famous knight of his generation. He once held the lists at Paris for three straight days. They say that when he was so grievously wounded in battle that even the duke of Burgundy's son, who commanded the enterprise, came out to do him homage as he sailed away."

"Sir Gatien did not tell us this!" exclaimed Signora Mulino.

"Oh, he would not," replied Ginevra, her eyes shining. "He is too modest and noble to talk of himself and his achievements, which is probably why he was never quite popular with my mother or my sister."

She paused for a second, remembering the witch-fires before the Cathedral of San Marco and hearing the screaming. She longed to bring her hands to her ears; she longed to block out the screaming. But it hadn't been possible to do then, and it was not possible to do now. Elisabetta's dying cries would always be with her.

"Yet," said Retta, "I cannot understand why, if the Knight de la Marche is so famed and well situated, your parents would not have wanted him as your suitor."

"They may not have liked him, but they would, indeed, have wanted him," said Ginevra, "and exactly for those reasons. But they were not the reasons that I wanted Gatien for myself. Quite simply I wanted to be with him and to be his wife because I loved him. That is the whole of it. From my first sighting of him—wholly and completely—I have loved the Knight de la Marche."

Retta nodded. "I don't doubt that. But perhaps you do your parents a disservice to see them as being so mercenary in this circumstance. Sir Gatien has sustained a grievous wounding. Our Yacopo Moscato was able to work wonders; that much is true. He trained under the Arabs, who are master physicians, and at Salerno, where the university is famed for healing work. He saved Sir Gatien's arm and has assured us that there could be even more improvement. It is just that . . ."

"What?" urged Ginevra. "Please tell me."

"Perhaps it is that the Knight de la Marche does not want to improve." Retta shook her head. "No, that is not it either. Perhaps he is just frightened by the idea."

To her surprise, Ginevra did not argue this idea. She did not haughtily remind Margaretta that they were discussing a First Knight of France, a man who had held the Paris lists for three days and had conquered far and wide.

"Because," said the Maid Ginevra softly, "he knows that no matter how much he might get better, he will never again be what he once was. His life will never again be the same. What is behind him is over and yet what is to come is still unknown."

Retta's hands played softly with the stuff of her voluminous night tunic. "He does not complain, much less spend his time pitying himself for what has happened. Sir Gatien is quite lucky to be alive and he knows it. Thousands with whom he fought are now dead. It is just that he has lived the whole of his life in one manner and now this must all change. The change will not be easy for him—has not been easy. I'm certain that he considers himself useless to both the peasants who work his land and the duke of Burgundy who is his liege lord. How can he defend them if he has not the use of his sword?"

Ginevra nodded. "This belief that manhood is somehow intricately involved with a man's ability to wield a weapon and sit a horse is a common and silly fallacy among knights. What rubbish! Gatien has lost the use of his arm; he has not lost his ability to be Gatien. He has not lost the grace and the power and the wisdom that I have always seen and loved in him.

Certainly these qualities are still amply needed by the peasants of Burgundy and the duke himself. Nothing has changed intrinsically with Gatien. The problem is that he does not himself know that this is so."

"Perhaps you can help him to learn this. Perhaps it is part of the reason you have come." Retta smiled. "And, of course, to marry him."

"Yes, to marry him," agreed Ginevra with a small, shy nod of her head.

"So it seems, indeed, that we must marry," said the Knight de la Marche to the Maid Venier one morning not many days later. "I trust you have not changed your mind?"

"No, no!" said Ginevra eagerly.

"Somehow, I had not thought you might," answered Gatien wryly. "I have not heard yet from your father, but I doubt he will post much opposition, at least under the circumstances."

"Under the circumstances," echoed Ginevra equably, though her cheeks were rosy with belated embarrassment. "It is kind of you, Sir Gatien, to take me as your wife."

They were seated on a wooden plank beneath an orange tree in the Mulinos' tidy courtyard, and for a second Ginevra thought she saw Gatien's eyes light with amusement. But then she decided she was mistaken.

"As though I had a choice," he said.

Ginevra opened her mouth and then closed it once again. She did not especially like what he told her, but she also realized that it was true enough.

"The banns have been given to the Church of Santa Caterina," he told her. "We should be free to wed within six weeks' time. That is well enough. I had been planning to leave then for Burgundy. We will get across the Haute Savoie well before the snows begin."

Ginevra nodded and kept her eyes lowered. She had made a much-belated vow to be demure.

"It is only fair to tell you that I have no idea what is awaiting us in Burgundy," Gatien continued. "I am crippled now. It remains to be seen if I will be able to uphold my lands, much less add to them, as is the bounden duty of every knight. I am sure Count Luciano set higher sights than these for his youngest daughter."

He might as well be lecturing a schoolchild rather than his future wife.

"It does not matter what my father wants or does not want," replied Ginevra, "as it is not he who intends to marry."

She reached over, picked a peach from her basket, and began the delicate work of peeling it.

"And does it matter to you what I want?" asked Gatien softly. "Are you so much a Venier, so much like the rest of your family, that you give no thought for the desires of others?"

Ginevra's heart iced at his calm words. But she did not stop peeling the peach. She would not show how much he had hurt her. It was only after some seconds that she thought herself able to look directly into the dove gray eyes that she loved.

"But can you truthfully say you do not want me?"

Sun broke through the sheltering leaves and threw its dappled light on her, but Ginevra did not look away from the Knight de la Marche. It was as though she willed him to look at her, to see the woman she had become. Nor did she flinch as his gaze took their quick tour of her body; she did not blush or look away. She let herself feel the heat of their gaze as it touched her cheek and her temple and the heartbeat at her throat, as it lingered for an instant at the rounded curve of her breast. And she, too, continued to stare at him, both remembering and memorizing once again the way his golden hair curled crisply at his hairline; the scar along his cheek, a remnant of some early blooding; the light that still lay hidden in the depths of his clouded eyes.

"Since you went away, I have seen things. Things have happened to me," she said softly. "They did not leave me where they found me. I am no longer just a rich man's child."

A small rivulet of juice ran down between her fingers as she drove her nails into the delicate skin of her peach.

"Can you tell me that?" she whispered. "Can you say that you do not want me? That you could never desire me?"

The world around them seemed to hold its breath, waiting for the Knight de la Marche's response. The robins, hidden in the branches above them, stopped their merry singing; the bees ceased buzzing in the grass at their feet. Even the sun seemed to shift on its axis in the heavens and cock a listening ear to where Ginevra sat close beside Gatien, waiting to hear the words that would change her life on earth.

"No," he said at last. "But desire is not love. We had no time to fall in love, to build a rooting for our life. In Venice, you were just a girl to me. The Maid Ginevra. Now, because of my thoughtless joking and your equally thoughtless actions, we are forced to marry. Yet already it is too late for us to build a life together. My wounding has changed everything. You are too innocent and much too determined on your own way to see what life will hold in store for you, married to a knight who no longer has the use of his sword arm. You have lived a very privileged life; but in a few weeks' time, we will leave for my fiefdom and I have no idea what will await us there. The de la Marche family has maintained its lands for hundreds of years, but only hands firmly trained to the sword have made this possible. Burgundy is a duchy rife with intrigue. We will not find the quiet there that desire needs if it is to grow into love. I thought you different, Ginevra, but in truth you are very much like the rest of the Veniers. Determined to have your own way, no matter the cost."

"Perhaps," replied Ginevra softly.

She rose from the wooden bench and then, quite unexpectedly, lobbed her peeled peach to him.

Without thinking, the Knight de la Marche reached out his sword hand and neatly caught it.

"What you don't understand, Gatien," said Ginevra, "is it is only because we were wounded—both of us—that we are able even to 'desire' each other today."

Three

"And he caught it," whispered Ginevra, "with his sword hand."

Retta paused with her hands deep in bread dough. She and Ginevra were in the tidy kitchens behind the main house and their cheeks were pink from the hearth's heat.

"I don't think he even knew he had caught the peach until the juice from it began to seep through his fingers," added the Maid Venier.

"The doctor said there was a chance that the muscles could gain some movement in his hands and arm. He urged the Knight de la Marche to exercise his arm, but he would not. At least until now."

Retta stopped her industrious kneading long enough to smile.

"He showed me the exercises that might help Sir Gatien," continued Ginevra. "He said he learned them when he studied medicine under the Arabs in the East. He said that it is still uncertain whether the Knight de la Marche's situation can actually be bettered. We will not know that until he is willing to help himself in this. But at least there is—hope."

"And many times hope is enough," replied Retta, going energetically at her bread dough once again. "But how will the doctor persuade the Knight de la Marche to do the exercising? He has not been able to do this in the past."

"I will persuade him," said Ginevra sadly. "Indeed, I can do anything I like now. He can hardly despise me more than he already does."

"He does not despise you," said Retta with a stout shake of her head.

"But then neither does he love me," replied Ginevra. "He told me this on the very day he decided to marry me 'for necessity's sake.' Indeed, if he were not such a gentleman, I imagine my father would have speedily consigned me to the nearest convent. I have brought nothing but disgrace upon myself and upon my family name—at least this is the lecture I hear repeatedly from my afianced."

Ginevra turned away but not so quickly that Retta did not see the tears that shimmered in her eyes. She wisely said nothing; but had the Knight de la Marche been near, she would gladly have thrown a gauntlet at him, injured sword arm or not.

"Perhaps I was wrong to come to him," said Ginevra, "but I knew that he was suffering. We were so close in Venice. He hung the world for me. I tagged behind him everywhere, and there was his joking promise that we should marry. So when I heard that he was injured and when . . ."

Her words stopped abruptly.

"Obviously he is right," she continued. "I am just like the rest of my family—strong-willed, selfish, determined to have my own way. Well, if I am a Venier, I will be a Venier to the end. I will challenge the Knight de la Marche to his exercises—for his own good of course. In the end, it does not matter how angry he becomes at me. It does not matter if he loves me or hates me—or merely desires me. In the end, he will marry me no matter his feelings. Nothing can stop our wedding. Very soon now, I will be the Lady de la Marche."

She paused again. "I have gotten exactly what I wanted. I am a very lucky woman indeed."

Ginevra busied herself with helping Retta finish her simple kitchen tasks and so it was almost dusk before she found her way to the steps that fronted the little stone church dedicated to Santa Caterina. This was her favorite church among all those in Badolato and this was her favorite time of day. Except for a stray bantam rooster, Ginevra had the small stone piazza to herself.

It was a lovely place, rich with the scent of roses and the sea. Below her, sheep bleated upon the hillside as the sun sank slowly over their heads. Ginevra had discovered this singular place quite by accident during one of her solitary roamings through the village's narrow cobbled streets. Suddenly she had rounded a corner, and this tiny church had gleamed before her. It was so lovely that at first Ginevra had thought it an enchantment, meant for her alone. Immediately she had decided that this was the church from which she would wed her knight. Not the ornate chapel at the Palazzo Venier with its frescoes and bright gilding; even less the huge Cathedral of San Marco, which was Venice's pride and joy. No, she wanted this simple stone structure with its plain whitewashed walls and wooden cross. She wanted so special a day to be framed by cliffs and ripe roses and a hillside that stretched endlessly to the sea.

She wanted to be loved; but since that was not to be, she would settle for the simple savage beauty that surrounded her. Perhaps it would make her wedding day memorable enough for her, when nothing else could.

Santa Caterina had become her great comfort. She told no one about it but came regularly to sit on the stone steps before the church or on a small wooden stool in the very back of the nave. She loved to sit here, quiet and alone and thinking; now she took her customary or just watched the light from the small white candles glow against the plain white walls.

And she loved the feeling that she got within it, as though a presence were near who understood what she had gone through and still promised her love.

"Because Gatien would never understand."

Yet when she had set out from Venice she had been convinced that the Knight de la Marche was the only one in this whole world who might possibly understand what had happened. She had come to nurse him, but she had come to confide in him as well. The thought had warmed her and given her courage. It had sustained her as she tramped her way through Italy. Indeed, it was comforting—at least, as far as delusions went.

For she had discovered that Sir Gatien was the last person who could help her; the last person who would be able to forgive what the willful Veniers had done.

Just like the rest of your family.

Indeed, perhaps that was true.

But it isn't. Deep within, you know that it isn't. At least not in the way that you think.

"What?"

Ginevra whipped around, expecting to see someone or to hear again that whispered voice. She could have sworn that a man had spoken those kind words directly into her ear. But there was no one. It was eventide; the simple folk of Badolato were busy preparing for their evening meal and closing down their village for the night. There was no one beside her, no one even near.

Yet she had been so sure.

Ginevra laughed aloud. "My mind is so filled with Gatien that now I think scolds me even when he is not near."

But the voice had been neither chiding nor scolding. It had been soft, coaxing, as though it wanted

desperately to be heard. Ginevra shivered in the
warm night air and drew her flax shawl closer.

" 'Tis but my imagination," she whispered, "but I
cannot allow it to tarry me. I have unpleasant work
enough to do."

Upon leaving his chamber at Margaretta Mulino's,
Gatien de la Marche had taken lodgings within the
cloistered confines of a small monastery dedicated
to St. Francis that lay just outside the main village
gates. Ginevra recognized the dark green and white
of his standard, which had been hung upon the
wicket as a signal that he had taken shelter there.

The sight of his colors fluttering in the breeze
brought Ginevra up short. In the village, the Knight
de la Marche dressed simply, in white linen tunics
and light calfskin pants. But the sight of his standard, the flash of his colors against the tranquil sky
reminded her of the Sir Gatien she had known in
Venice. More than his words of remonstrance, this
banner reminded her that the man to whom she was
betrothed was a knight, a warrior. Badolato was just
an idyll, a place for healing. In the end both she and
her wounded husband would find their true lives in
France.

"Gatien," she whispered into the stillness, "you
are a man used to battling. Now you must try one
more time, because if you don't . . . if you don't, it
will mean the end of hoping. And if we lose our
hope, what will we have left?"

She shifted the small package she carried from
one hand to the other and then knocked with reso-
lution on the porter's door.

The wooden spy upon it was opened just the tini-
est fraction. Ginevra caught the quick glimpse of one
lone eye staring out at her before the latch was
slammed once again into place with such force that

the whole of the great gate shuddered from the impact. Alarmed, Ginevra jumped backward, but then she raised her hand to knock again upon the wicket. This time, however, she pressed her lips upward into a bright smile.

"I come for the Knight de la Marche," she called out brightly.

Silence.

Then after a second the spy moved and the one brown eye appeared within its framing a second time. Ginevra willed herself to beam.

"No women allowed," declared a voice so gloomy that Ginevra decided it could only be connected to the person who bore that baleful eye.

"I have not come seeking entrance to your cloister, Padre," she replied. "I come in search of the Knight de la Marche."

"The Knight de la Marche?" echoed the voice. Behind the spy, his eye moved first upward and then from side to side as he took in the simple blue tunic that Ginevra had borrowed from Rita, who was more amply built. Indeed, she thanked every saint in heaven that she had had the foresight to pull her light shawl up over the tumble of her red hair. This man could very well be Gatien's confessor; and if so, then he had heard tales aplenty about her wantoness and lack of responsibility. He probably thought the very fact that she could be present on his doorstep at all an indication that the Latter Days were soon to start.

"I am his betrothed," she added quickly, when it looked as though the small spy might be shut in her face once again. "I have important news for him."

"His betrothed?" There was still distrust in the voice but the word *betrothed* worked its magic. His response, though grudging, was at least encouraging.

"I will see if the Knight de la Marche knows anything about having a 'betrothed.' "

"Whatever are you doing in those ghastly clothes," said Gatien striding out from the main gate. "You look like some sort of deranged penitent. Take that veiling off your head immediately."

"I came dressed appropriately to the circumstance," replied Ginevra, but she reached up and gratefully struggled out of her veil. "You know that monks are notoriously prejudiced against women. And God alone knew what you had told them of me."

"I've not told them anything," replied Gatien. "How could I? Where would I possibly begin?"

"But you told them we were betrothed?" she said, stopping with her hands tangled amidst the snarled webbing of her veiling and her hair.

"Yes, I told them I soon planned to marry. I said that my bride-to-be was Venetian but that she had recently joined me at Badolato—I did not tell them *how* you had arrived."

" 'Tis just as well," replied a stoical Ginevra. " 'Twas enough of an enterprise enough just to have the Father-Porter fetch you. Imagine his reaction had he known how much of a sinner I truly am!"

"A true Jezebel!"

"Though still as yet a virgin one."

Silence cracked between them for an instant as Ginevra stood before Gatien, with her fingers still entangled within the flow of her hair.

"You make me nervous with your fiddling," he said hoarsely. "Here, let me help you."

Ginevra had forgotten how gentle his fingers could be. For a warrior, he had a surprisingly gentle touch. She had also failed to remember the care he could take with small things. Or how the tip of his tongue edged through his lips as he concentrated. In her rush to get him, she had started to forget Venice, started to forget the very things about Gatien that had made him her great love.

The memories flooded back now as his hands worked at unraveling the jumble she had made. She remembered walking with him along the bridges that laced the small islands of the city into one great whole. She remembered seeking him out with her troubles because he would listen patiently and understand them when no one else could. She remembered his promise to marry her on the Bridge of Sighs.

A joking sport, he had called it. A troth plighted to a young girl who would soon grow into womanhood and forget the feigned promise he had made.

Will you marry me, Sir Gatien? Will you wait for me?

"There," he said, finally turning her toward him. "You look like yourself again. I never could abide veiling on top of fine hair."

He has such beautiful lips.

Ginevra thought them a revelation. They were chiseled but just enough to mark him as the aristocrat that he was. But they were also full enough and slightly open so she could see the flash of his white teeth and the tease of his tongue. She was so close to him that she could smell the clean smell of lavender and thyme from the soap he used; the same scent that still lingered in the chamber at the Villa Mulino—in the chamber that once had been his and now was hers.

"Gatien," she whispered.

She wanted nothing more than for those lips to come down upon hers. Wanted nothing more than to wrap her arms around his broad shoulders and lay her head against the promised safety of his sturdy chest. He was so close. And he wanted her. She could smell the want upon him just as surely as she smelled the lavender and the thyme. Ginevra watched his eyes narrow and darken; she heard the breath catch in his throat. He may not love her—he'd made this clear enough—but he did want her. That should be enough for her. He had never kissed her, and she wanted so desperately to be kissed by him.

What was he doing? Had he lost all reason?

These thoughts diligently pecked at part of Gatien's mind, but they did not stop him.

Nor did the idea that this was Ginevra he was so determined to kiss—and that it was wrong to give her false ideas. Who knew where this kissing might end? Ginevra was still so young and innocent. She might think her husband-to-be would possibly grow to love her.

And he wouldn't. He couldn't. He didn't dare.

Gatien bent lower.

Ginevra held back.

Just for an instant, but it was long enough to see the question in her eye. Long enough for him to see the masking of her hurt.

Then she was reaching for him; drawing him close.

"Gatien," she whispered.

And as strange as it might seem to the Knight de la Marche—a warrior born, a legend to men—his own name had never sounded so sweet and so pure and so young. It had never sounded so whole.

"Have you no interest in why I braved the dragons to reach you?" Ginevra queried mischievously, purposely pulling away from him at last and breaking the spell.

"I lay everything you do to your native perversity," replied Gatien as both his hands fell from away from her to rest once again at his side. "You know that monks do not want you near, and so this guarantees that you will come."

His heart still beat wildly; his reason still rebelled, but at least his voice was light when he spoke. The Knight de la Marche was grateful for that.

"The monks had nothing to do with my decision. It was predicated by something that Dr. Moscato said."

"Dr. Moscato?" For the first time he noticed the small flax parcel that she carried. His eyes had narrowed considerably when they looked at her again.

Ginevra's lips still burned from his kissing, but she was already woman enough to know that this one strange, tender kiss would not be proof against what she had to say.

"I've come to ask you to do your exercises, Gatien," she said softly. "The ones that might give you some usage in your arm and your hand."

His face changed immediately. Thunder flashed into the darkening sky.

"Take your exercises and be damned with them. Will you always and in everything be determined to have your own way? You wanted to marry me. I have agreed to marry you. Must you run everything else in my life as well?"

Gatien and Ginevra stared at each other; both shocked by the words he had used and the vehemence behind them. Both shocked by the unexpected kiss they had so recently shared.

"I am sorry. Truly sorry," said Gatien hastily. "I had no call to speak to you in that way. You are a lady; I am a knight. There are laws of chivalry that should be in force between us. I forgot both myself and my station and I do sincerely beg your indulgence, Maid Ginevra. You must not fear that I will raise my voice to you again. It is just, perhaps that you are a Venier and this means . . ."

"Just what does it mean to be a Venier?" Ginevra whispered. "Tell me, Sir Gatien. What exactly does it mean?"

Her question took Gatien by surprise. "It means to be a member of the ruling oligarchy of Venice. It means to have both the power and the money to do as you please, and with whom. It means . . ."

"It means to have blood on your hands," Ginevra finished for him, "to be soaked in it."

"Blood on your hands?" Gatien smiled down at her indulgently. "You are undoubtedly a spoiled child, Ginevra, but I doubt anyone could seriously consider you capable of murder in order to get what you want."

She looked at him steadily for a long moment. The moon was dark; the stars not yet risen; and there was no light from the monastery walls. Still, Gatien could feel the change in her. It was as though something gathered around them and whispered and shuddered very near.

"Come, let us sit on the village wall," said the Maid of the Veniers to the Knight de la Marche. "I want to gaze upon the sea as I tell you just what my family means."

His fingers were cold upon her warm ones as he handed her up to the ledge. Ginevra gathered her legs together and wrapped her arms around them while Gatien hoisted himself beside her.

"Do you remember Elisabetta, the *strega*?" she asked him.

"The witch?" Gatien's brow briefly creased as he thought. "Wasn't she the peasant always with your sister?"

"Yes, always with her," replied Ginevra. "At least in Venice. She was Domiziana's constant companion from the time my sister first set eyes upon her at the Castle of the Ducci Montaldo, where she had journeyed to join Count Olivier, her betrothed."

"Now I recall the tale," said Gatien. "Your sister had some slight illness. Elisabetta was the village Wise Woman and she was called in for her help. As I recall, she did in fact heal Domiziana."

"She *cured* her," whispered Ginevra. Her own clear eyes clouded with the memory. "Domiziana could not be healed. What ailed my sister went far beyond the reach of effigies and boiled herbs."

Gatien shook his head at this. "I cannot imagine that your sister wanted for much. She was—she is a singularly beautiful woman. She was betrothed to one of the most illustrious knights in all of Europe. By now I am sure she is his wife."

"But Count Olivier did not love my sister," said Ginevra.

She did not add: *Just as you do not love me.*

"Love her or not, he was willing to wed her," replied Gatien. His gaze was leveled on her. "He cared enough for her to maintain his word in that."

"The promise of marriage had consoled her at the beginning. Theirs was considered a brilliant mating; and this was enough. But then, somehow, she became determined to make the count love her. This object became her life's obsession. She planned and she plotted for it day and night. But Lord Olivier was already heart and soul in love with someone else."

"With his ward, the Lady Julian Madrigal," finished Gatien for her.

"Totally in love with her—though I don't think that either Julian or he knew this, at least at the time. But my sister certainly knew of their love. She sensed it the first time she ever saw them together and determined to have Olivier Ducci Montaldo all to herself."

Ginevra waited. She expected Gatien to chide the Veniers for their selfish waywardness.

Instead, he said nothing.

"My sister suffered a slight indisposition during her first days at the castle. Once this was so speedily cured, Domiziana saw potential in the witch. She brought her back within our caravan when we journeyed home to Venice. Elisabetta was a simple woman. She was old and ugly and considered to be the poorest person within a village that was itself poverty-stricken. She marveled at our family's palazzo. She ogled the glories of Venice and thought herself in some paradise on earth. My sister took advantage of her dazzlement and made sure that the *strega* slept upon a clean bed with bright linens and that everyday she feasted well. Poor Elisabetta, she gave her life in forfeit for these trinkets."

Gatien surprised both of them by reaching over to smooth back a lock of hair from Ginevra's forehead.

The Maid of the Veniers wanted to lower her eyes with shame at what she was about to tell him, but she could not. Her family had done a grave thing, an evil thing; and she was part of that family. It would not be fair to marry him until she told him the scandal that surrounded them, even though that scandal had remained a secret. And she wanted to tell him. *Needed* to tell him. It had been one of the reasons she had walked half of Italy to come here. Gatien was the grown-up friend in whom she had confided her childhood's secrets. Now she needed to tell him how that childhood had come to an end.

"At first the whole thing seemed but a joke," Ginevra continue, never once taking her eyes from Gatien's, "and Elisabetta some sort of household pet. At least to me. Domiziana was deathly serious. She knew what she wanted. And what she wanted was for Elisabetta to cast spells and enchantments for her. She knew she could claim Count Olivier's body, but she wanted his soul as well."

"And your mother?" prompted Gatien. "What did the Lady Claudia say to all of this."

"Nothing." Ginevra stopped and then corrected herself. "Or rather I believe she regarded the situation much as I did in the beginning. It was a game and a plaything. Something that kept my sister contented. Domiziana has always been my mother's favorite child. She had been given dolls to play with when she was younger. As an adult, if she wished to play with a poor old woman—Why, what harm could there be in that? This is the way my mother reasoned."

"And your father?"

Ginevra shrugged. "My father was busy with his own affairs as usual. Plus he had the extra burdens of a warring Venice. Besides, my mother had always been given full rein in her household. She did as she wanted."

A flock of night birds swooped out from their daytime hiding. All about her, Ginevra heard the rush of wings she could not see.

"All went well for a time. The wedding was set; my sister was radiant," Ginevra went on, "but then came the war and its losses—and losses there were aplenty in Venice. We had sent our Black Fleet to aid France, and we had commissioned Lord Olivier to take his mercenary army to the service of the duke of Burgundy. With the collapse of the Burgundian endeavor, our trade routes were perilously endangered. All through the city prominent people were denying their part in the endeavor. And so scapegoats were needed—and they were needed quickly."

Ginevra paused. "Of course, since time began, a witch has always been the perfect prey. A witch is thought to be old and without consequence and poor. Unless, that is, she is the Lady Domiziana Venier. There had always been rumors about my sister. She had buried two husbands before plighting her troth to Lord Olivier. When she passed through the marketplace, many of the peasants gave the sign against the evil eye. There had been incidents of this type even before Elisabetta came to us, but our family's position was proof against them. Suspicions and accusations came to nothing. But that was before the defeat." She paused, shrugged. "One day a maid, going through some clothing chests, discovered two effigies carved of pig soap. They had been deeply secreted beneath the Lady Domiziana's linen. One imaged a woman with blond hair; the other a man, dressed in a tunic upon which had been crudely stitched the arms of the Ducci Montaldo. The maid immediately cried witchcraft. She crossed herself and then presented the images to the ruling *Signoria*. Domiziana was brought before it on charges of sorcery."

Gatien could not hide his shock. "The Lady Domiziana was tried before the rulers of Venice. The *Doge* allowed this?"

Ginevra smiled at him sadly.

"Perhaps you do not know how rigorous my family is in such matters," she replied. "My uncle, Antonio Venier, who is the elected *Doge*, had an only son. His parents doted on him; he was the child of their old age. My cousin Eugenio was both rambunctious and fun-loving. It happened one day that he infracted one of Venice's smaller laws. He was ordered to prison for this and carried across the Bridge of Sighs. There he took ill. Nothing serious. A little medicine and a good sleep in his own bed would have easily cured him. But his sentence had not run its course and my uncle would not release him. Eugenio's mother begged and pleaded with her husband, but it was no use. It was a bad example for the city should a Venier be released before his time. Eugenio grew worse. Eventually he died. My uncle allowed this to happen to his only son and his heir." Ginevra paused. "Do you think Domiziana, who is a woman, would have found mercy from such a family connection?"

"No," replied Gatien. He found that he was holding his betrothed's hand.

Again came Ginevra's small wry smile. "Neither did she. But Domiziana is more than capable of taking any situation well in hand. When called, she threw herself upon the mercy of the *Signoria*. She blamed everything on the *strega* who had done nothing more than my sister's bidding. Domiziana swore before God and all the angels and saints that she knew nothing of the effigies. She said she had been duped by the witch's vile machinations, just as had everyone else."

"And they believed her?"

"She is a Venier," said Ginevra simply, "and unlike my cousin Eugenio, she had not actually been caught in any suspect act. On the other hand, Elisabetta is—was—a poor, quite illiterate woman. Wise Women had been revered for centuries in Tuscany. She did not understand that times had changed and that the Inquisition had begun. And so when she was asked a direct question, she answered it directly. She had made the effigies? What harm was there in causing love? She proudly chatted on and on about her herbs and her healing. Without understanding what she was doing, she took the entire blame onto herself."

Ginevra paused. By now, the stars had come out and the moon. By their light, she and Gatien could glimpse the sea stretching out, violet and alive, beneath them.

"I tried and tried to make my sister and my mother do something," the Maid of the Veniers said at last. "Tried to make them see the wrong in what they were doing. Elisabetta used her skills at my sister's urging. Domiziana was just as guilty as she was— even more so. They laughed at me. My mother asked was I so jealous of my sister that I would see her dead. And I didn't want that. I didn't want to hurt Domiziana, no matter what she had done. The *Doge* would not see me. I had no place I could turn."

"Givvy, tell me what happened to Elisabetta." Gatien reached up with his warm hands to wipe away the tears that were flowing freely down Ginevra's cheeks.

"They burned her," was the soft reply, "on a pyre before the Cathedral of San Marco. My whole family was there along with all the other members of the ruling oligarchy. All of them were looking quite stoical about this doing of their duty, almost as though justice had been done. My father and my mother wanted me to attend the spectacle as well. They insisted that this was my duty. I must show my support for my sister. I could never have done this, no matter the threats. But the count of the Ducci Montaldo had already told me you were alive and where to find you. I set out at first light."

"Why did you not tell me this before?" whispered Gatien.

Ginevra shrugged. Pursed her lips. "I wanted to. I meant to talk to you immediately. I always had in the past. It was part of the reason that I came."

"But you didn't."

"I couldn't. You were so different from the good friend I'd known in Venice."

"Wounded?"

"Yes, wounded." Again she paused. "Inside and out."

Now it was the Knight de la Marche's turn to stare out toward the sea. One by one, he lifted small stones and tossed them down in an effort to break its smooth surface.

"Perhaps," he said finally, "I have used my injury as an excuse to grow progressively selfish. Perhaps I have let it rule my life; let it make me afraid."

He tossed one last smooth pebble over the hillside's ledge. "You shame me with your courage, Givvy. I am proud that you stood up to defend a woman who could in no way stand up for herself. Now be the good friend you've always been and demonstrate those exercises that Dr. Moscato is so determined I should learn."

The Knight de la Marche lay awake for long hours on his narrow, lonely bed. His arm still ached from the working Ginevra had inflicted upon it; his mouth still burned from her kiss. But he knew the pain of both—if pain it was—to be constructive. He was a veteran of many battles and as many woundings. He knew the difference between aching that would lead eventually to healing and a pain that had just turned more deeply into itself. He had just forgotten this.

Until Ginevra had come to remind him.

And now within the span of but a few short days, this same Ginevra was to be his wife. Her father had sent a brief and hurried letter, explaining that he was quite involved with some unexpected occurrence but was glad that Ginevra had been found and that the Knight de la Marche planned to do the right thing by her. Gatien had not asked for dower trothing and this had not been mentioned. A cursory letter, Gatien had thought. No inquiry had been made as to the Maid Ginevra's happiness or health. But now this omission did not surprise him.

And so he was about to wed.

Gatien had not thought much of marriage. An early and proper betrothal arranged by his parents had ended abruptly with the girl's death from plague. Since then, he had found his life more than filled with the needs of his estates and the demands of battle. No one could live a boring life when Jean the Fearless, duke of Burgundy, was his liege lord.

But still he'd always known that someday he must marry. In fact, it was inevitable that this would be so. He had his duties and his people. They looked to him and his family for leadership and defense. Marriage, yes; but to Ginevra?

Ginevra was a child.

Gatien threw back his head to laugh outright. Beside him, on the cot, his page snuffled in his sleep.

Could the kiss of a child have affected him as strongly as Ginevra's had done? Or had the Maid of the Veniers, his small friend, grown into womanhood while he was away?

Before the war, he had spent three months with the Veniers in Venice. It had been an active time in which he was kept busy drumming up support for the war France, and especially Burgundy, was determined to mount. In truth, he had not liked the family. It was old and prestigious, but Gatien had always believed that Count Luciano and his wife represented the weakest of their strain. Of course, the Lady Claudia was not even a born Venier and there had been gossip—to which Gatien had refused to listen—that concerned itself with her birth. He had thought that their three eldest daughters were much like their parents, highly decorative on the outside but with something dark and cunningly dangerous within.

He had never thought Ginevra like the rest. There was a candid, clear light about her that the others did not share. *She* was a true Venier, a member of one of the families that had wrestled Venice from the marshes and made it into the greatest city in the world. He had seen this difference in her, even as he had casually played with her and ruffled her hair. That she would be the lone one in her family to stand against the powerful *Signoria* did not surprise him.

My changeling. The Lady Claudia had often described her daughter and then laughed the brittle affected laugh that reminded Gatien of the scratching of glass shards.

Indeed, she was different from the rest of them.

"Will you marry me?" she had asked him with forthright earnestness. "I know already you are the only man I will ever love."

"Yes, Givvy," he had answered, ruffling her hair. "If, when you turn eighteen, you are still determined to have me, I will marry you without a doubt."

He had not reckoned on the war. He had not reckoned on the troubles this war had obviously caused for Ginevra's father. He had not reckoned on Ginevra's determination.

Most of all, he had not reckoned on her kiss.

The Knight de la Marche paused and considered the feel of the Maid Ginevra's flesh beneath his fingers. He ran his tongue along his teeth as though searching for a last taste of her warmth in his mouth. It had been a great while since he had so thoroughly enjoyed a kiss.

"Ginevra."

He said her name with wonder. He did not allow reason, with its whys and wherefores and why-nots, to push aside this strange contentment and peace. It had been too long in the coming.

"Ginevra," he repeated, as he drifted off to sleep.

Ginevra Venier lay quite still upon her maiden's bed in the cozy back chamber of Signora Mulino's house. She was thinking about the kiss. Reliving that extraordinary moment when Gatien had drawn him to herself and she had held back, breathless, just an instant and then had reached up her arms and drawn him near.

"Gatien," she whispered. The smile upon her face was shy and secret.

And troubled.

Lying alone on her bed, Ginevra could not understand exactly what it was that bothered her. Certainly it was not the kiss itself; she had never been kissed before, but she had three married sisters. In the afternoons, over their tapestry work, they had not left much of the relations between men and women unsaid. She had expected that the Knight de la Marche would kiss her. She had not been frightened. She had known just what to do.

Perhaps that was the problem.

Ginevra wrinkled her brow as this and similar disturbing thoughts began their swift invasion of her mind.

In its strange way the kiss had snatched Gatien from the realm of her fantasies and made him flesh-and-blood—a man filled with his own reasons and his own desires. More than that, he was a man who still thought of her as a child; and he was now, more than ever, a man who needed much more than a child beside him as his wife.

Perhaps he was right about her, and she was wrong. Perhaps, indeed, she was little more than the capricious, spoiled daughter of a very rich and powerful parent.

Ginevra's heart skittered at the thought. Still . . .

She had been so busy—first, in loving the Knight de la Marche, and then, in escaping her parents to find him—that she had not even stopped to think that perhaps he had been merely playing with her. Not in any bad sense—Gatien would never do anything against his honor or her own—but as a fond older brother would humor a younger sister. Smiling at her hero worship and carrying her along in his wake.

Indeed, when she thought of Gatien, she thought of sweetness, not of passion, picturing their life together as one long walk through tranquil flower-filled valleys and high plains. Even his wounding had not changed the fantasy that played within her mind.

Only his kiss had.

It had changed everything. It had taken her breath away. It had shattered the smugness of her own small piece of earth, and then brought it back together again around a different core.

He had accused her once of paying too much attention to jongleur tunes. He had been right.

"But kissing him only made my situation worse," whispered a thoroughly confused Ginevra into the lonely night. "It made Gatien real to me. It made him a man."

Indeed, she still felt the force of his desire, of his need and his want. She could lift her wrist and smell his passion on her; its musky scent still lingered on her, as though it had already seeped deep and found a home within her skin.

She held her wrist to her nose for a very long moment, taking a woman's exultation in the smell of the man she loved.

Her small room was already filled with bounty for her wedding. The whole of the village had been invited to the church and to the celebration and so the overflow filled the Mulinos' small house. Baskets of fruit lined the far wall along with flaxes of marzipan and stored cakes and other sweets. Ginevra smelled the herbs that had already been blessed. Everything was as she had left it earlier; and yet everything fundamental had changed.

"Gatien." She whispered once more into the gloaming.

The Maid of the Veniers had no idea what tomorrow would bring her. But she knew that for right now—for just this moment—it was enough to hold that name close as a talisman against the dark.

Four

" 'Tis strange I've had no further word from your father," said the Knight de la Marche, as he alternately clutched and loosened his hand around a rag ball. "Just that brief message consenting to our marriage and then nothing else."

"I think you should grasp just a bit harder," Ginevra said, and then she blushed. "Perhaps he has decided to disown me. You never know. I have thoroughly disgraced the name of Venier; or at least he might think so."

"Nonsense," scoffed Gatien. "I've told you over and over, Givvy, that you cannot base your life upon troubadours' singing-lies. There is no reason for Count Luciano to 'disown' you, as you so dramatically put it. Certainly he has reason to be annoyed. But that is not the same as disowning you or wishing you ill. We are, by no means, star-crossed lovers. I am wounded, that is true enough, but my name is an old one and my lands well able to provide for a wife, even if that wife is a Venier. Besides, you are but the youngest in your family."

Ginevra wrinkled her brow. "And what does that have to do with anything?"

She was looking down at the flax rag ball in her hands and so did not see the Knight de la Marche's eye twinkle.

"I mean, my love, that younger daughters are generally worth less to their parents in the great market of matrimony. Count Luciano and Countess Claudia would probably have been well content to see you settled with a nice shepherd who had but one small hectare of grazing to offer them in exchange for your hand."

"You don't know my parents," replied a serious Ginevra. "They would surely never have conceded such a marriage for me. They would have seen me convented first!"

"But Ginevra," said the Knight de la Marche, his eyes quite wide with innocence, "did you not tell me of your determination to have me even if I had only one goat to bring to the matrimonial dinner?"

"I said that because you are you," replied Ginevra earnestly. She looked up, saw the mischief twinkling, and laughed, but only shortly. She turned back to her work of guiding Gatien through the series of exercises Dr. Moscato had prescribed.

Gatien's kiss had opened a Pandora's box of doubts and fears that she found not easy to close. She had always thought herself so different from her sisters, different from her strong-willed mother and her weak father. But was she really?

Was she not, instead, just like them?

"Indeed, I am no better than Domiziana," she muttered.

"What did you say, Givvy?"

Ginevra forced a smile. "I said that you have smashed that poor ball into a puddle. Perhaps it is time to work with the hemp rope?"

She chattered merrily as he took it and worked at putting strength again into his weakened hand. She called to Retta and Pietro Mulino, as they chatted about in the little garden beyond the tiny outdoor kitchen. She laughed at the children who played in the piazza and the peasants who trudged up from their fields in the late afternoon sun.

But most of all she made sure that her feelings were well hidden and that she smiled.

"You are making excellent progress, my lord," said Yacopo Moscato, as he examined the arm of the Knight de la Marche. "One can see a difference in circumference in just the short time you've been at work."

He held up a measuring string that had been marked, in two distinct places, with scarlet dye. "And we have not as yet passed the new full moon," he added.

" 'Tis because you have given me such a competent nurse," replied Gatien. "You were wise to enlist the aid of the Lady Ginevra. She is a determined woman and would not give me an instant's rest until I did as I was told."

Yacopo Moscato nodded. "Indeed, she is remarkable. To think that I have tried since last December to put you through these movements and it was not until the Lady Ginevra came that you did them—and she has been here but six weeks. I could use her help with others of my healing projects."

"Then you had best be quick," replied Gatien, shrugging once again into his tunic. "The village priest has already started publishing the banns for our marriage. As soon as we are wed, I will be taking my wife back to my own lands."

Moscato looked genuinely distressed at this. "I don't understand why you cannot rest longer with us, my lord. Life is good in Badolato, and at any time we might again stand in need of protection, especially with the pirates that prey upon our coasts. Since Norman times, many French have found a safe home in the south of Italy. Why your own Robert Guiscard became our first duke of Calabria . . ."

A furious clanging of the parish bells interrupted his discourse.

Gatien reached for the sword he no longer carried.

" 'Tis Saracen pirates," cried Pietro Mulino, running from his house into the piazza, his wooden shoes clattering against the stones. "They have been on the beach during the night."

Gatien walked to the low stone wall and squinted down the little trail that cut through olive groves, leading to the monastery and then onward to the sea.

"I've never heard of pirates willing to attack a walled city during sun hours," he said mildly. "And I've never known them sending a messenger to announce their attack."

"A messenger?" Pietro came to stand beside him.

The Knight de la Marche nodded and pointed down the mountain. "On a small donkey, no less."

"But all this noise! All this clamor!"

"Probably means," said Gatien mildly, "that the monks believe his message to be important. Undoubtedly, at least, it comes from an important person."

"So Count Venier is on his way to our village," said Retta, as she and Ginevra laid the trestle for dinner.

"Not my father," replied Ginevra, balancing a pottery platter of goat cheeses against her hip. "It is my lady mother on her way to Badolato, along with my eldest sister.

"The Lady Domiziana?"

"Who by now should be the countess of the Ducci Montaldo," replied Ginevra with a sigh. "My sister was determined to marry Lord Olivier and I'm sure that by now she has."

"I say well enough to that," replied Retta, as she arranged the four wooden bowls. "At least as long as she loves him."

She gave an exaggerated, heartfelt sigh.

"Loves him?" Ginevra's shrug was weary. "I wonder if she even knows the meaning of the word. I wonder if I do myself."

"Goodness, these are serious words," Retta replied. "Especially from a woman who is soon to be a bride."

"Indeed," said Ginevra turning away to make much of arranging a small bowl of sweet geraniums. "She has gotten the man she wanted. Just as I have."

Retta very wisely said nothing until Ginevra turned back to her and said, "What is marriage really like?" Color touched her cheeks. "I love my parents and I miss them—something I never thought I would say when I ran away from Venice. It pleases me mightily that at least my mother has come to see me wed. But coming to this village, living in this house; these things have been a revelation for me. Seeing your marriage to Pietro—why, the two of you fit together as snugly as spoons."

Retta laughed. "Of course we do. We're married and have been together so many years. Sometimes it is hard for me to recall my life before Pietro." Retta shook her wimpled head in bemusement. "But you will know the feeling yourself after you have been wedded for a while. Especially because you love the Knight de la Marche."

"I thought I loved Gatien," replied Ginevra, turning away. "I was sure that love for him was my only motivation. Now I am not quite so sure."

They worked in silence for a few moments more, putting the finishing touches on the simple meal, lighting the few fragrant beeswax candles, putting the one torch into its iron sconce on the wall.

Finally Ginevra asked, "How did Pietro ask you to marry him? Do you remember?"

Retta stood with the jug of scarlet flowers in her hands and a bright faraway look in her eye. "I remember it perfectly. How could I not? It was springtime in the fields just below the village. You could clearly see the tower of St. Catherine from the point on which we stood. Pietro said, ' 'Tis time we were married.' And I said yes, that it was time."

"Were you not hesitant or nervous?"

"Oh, not at all," said Retta, still with that dreamy look in her eye. "You see I *knew* it was Pietro the first time I saw him, when he was still a young boy and still pulling at my braids. I knew from the first time I saw him that he would ever and forever be the only one for me."

"But were you certain of this? Were you *sure*?"

"Oh, more than certain. More than sure." Retta came to wrap gentle arms around Ginevra. "Has something happened to trouble you? Has the Knight de la Marche done . . ."

Ginevra shook her head. "Gatien would never do anything to dishonor me. Indeed, he is not the problem at all."

"Not the problem?" repeated Retta. "Little one, it is normal, right before a wedding, to have jitters. After all, you are taking a step that will change the whole of your life."

"My problem has nothing to do with bridal jitters," replied Ginevra. "My problem is what I've come to learn about myself."

"What have you come to learn? That you are a kind, sweet girl. That without you, the Knight de la Marche would not . . ."

"Without me, the Knight de la Marche would not be getting married," saidGinevra. "Of his own accord, he would never have chosen me. He told me this himself at the beginning and from there nothing has changed."

"But I am sure . . ."

"Nothing has changed," Ginevra insisted. "How could it? I have brought this unhappiness upon myself. I gladly condemned my sister Domiziana for her machinations and her selfish ways, only to find that I am no better than she is. It was I who decided that the Knight de la Marche would marry me. I who searched him out and held him to his promise, a promise given only in passing to amuse the notions of a young child."

"Ginevra, I think you are too hard upon yourself. You are not your sister."

"Perhaps not, but I will have my sister's life. Married to a man who has been forced to marry me. Living that lie day after day."

"But he will be yours," cried Retta. "You love Sir Gatien and now you will have him all to yourself."

" 'Tis exactly the problem," said Ginevra wryly. "Unfortunately, like all the Veniers, I've managed to get exactly what I wanted. I have forced this man I love to marry me and this has turned my life into a living hell."

Ginevra tossed and turned upon her bed, balling her hand into the soft down pillow and bunching the linens beneath them. Starlight poured into her small chamber. In the distance, very softly, she heard someone calling to her, telling her to get up. She ran across the herb-strewn floor to the doorway, throwing the scent of thyme into the night air.

No one moved within the piazza. A bright moon, full and fat, beamed down benignly on the village where the people of Badolato slept the snug safe peace of the just.

She longed for that peace, yearned for the harmony she had found here, as her steps carried her higher and higher to the very top of the walled village and the Church of Santa Caterina where she would wed.

The doors to the sanctuary had been left open to the night air. From a distance, at the far edge of the piazza where she had stopped, Ginevra could just see the flicker of candlelight against the simple white walls. She walked on very quietly and then paused for an instant near the stone stairs that led into the church, but she did not go in. Instead she turned to the wall that looked down the hill and into the valley and from there to the swelling sea below. It was that hour just before sunrise when the earth was at its darkest but, paradoxically, already held the first faint promise of dawn. Ginevra stared through this; her eyes going directly to the huddled monastery that sheltered Gatien. Looking for him. Just as she always had, and probably just as she always would.

A presence whispered all around her even before the man began to speak.

" 'Tis most lovely the way that monastery clings so close to the hillside," he said. His voice, the underlay of accent, reminded Ginevra of Gatien. Even before she turned to him she had decided that he must a Burgundian soldier come to serve the Knight de la Marche. She felt no fear.

"Indeed, it is," she answered, smiling, "at least to me."

"It is named for San Francisco," the man continued. "Strange tales are told of him, that he could talk to birds and that deer and squirrels would come to eat from his hands. Do you believe them?"

"From all I've heard, he was a kind and gentle man," replied Ginevra, "the kind of man even small creatures would easily trust."

"But did you know he started life as a warrior? He fought mightily for Assisi in its war against Arezzo, so mightily that he was grievously wounded. And this wounding changed him totally. It was only this that enabled him to discover the true life that he was meant to live."

"Which was to learn to feed birds from his hands?" Ginevra asked.

"Gentleness and kindness are no mean feats. Would not you agree, Maid Venier?"

The knight's voice was amiable and low, almost hypnotic. Ginevra could barely make out his features in the gloaming but he was tall—even taller than Gatien—and with the same cropped hair and beardless face. His tunic was white, however, with a crimson cross slashing boldly across its front.

"How did you know my name?" she asked him.

"Everyone in Badolato knows of the Maid of the Veniers and the courageous way she tramped through Italy to come to the aid of the Knight de la Marche," replied the stranger. "This tale will soon become the stuff of troubadour's singing. Mark my words if it will not."

Ginevra smiled ruefully and turned once again toward the sea. "So said the Knight de la Marche," she whispered, "but tell me, sir, do not troubadours' tales generally end in happily ever after?"

"Not always," said the knight as he too turned to the sea. "But yours will. At least from what I've heard of the story."

"Have you been long in Badolato?" she asked. "Did you accompany the Knight de la Marche.?"

"Oh, no." His laugh was as soft as the night around them. "Badolato is my home. It is my—how can I best explain? It is my duty to guard it and to keep its secrets alive."

"What secrets?" asked Ginevra.

"There are many of them, so many that it would take a lifetime to tell them all. But there is one that might interest you especially . . ."

Below them, the lone bell in the monastery began the call to terce prayers.

". . . And might even prove useful," continued the warrior, once the pealing had stopped. "It concerns the night of the falling stars."

Again Ginevra turned to the stranger.

"The night of San Lorenzo," he continued. "It happens each year on the tenth day of August, or rather on that night. The sky is filled with shooting stars then—stars that fly each year on that night to take up their new watch in heaven. You can see them beautifully from the hills in Badolato. In fact, it is probably the best place in all the world from which to see them."

He drew nearer. "That is why the legend is special to this place. If, from Badolato, you look into the heavens and see a star skirt across its surface, then wish upon it, believe me, Maid Ginevra, your wish will be heard."

"Really?" queried Ginevra. "Truly?"

During these last few weeks she had come to doubt in love and wishes and happy endings.

"Really," assured the knight, "and truly. On the tenth of August, you must only remember to hold the secret sacredly in your heart and then send it onward to the stars in heaven. They will hear it. Look there, toward the east. Even now with dawn coming, you can still see him standing guard."

He lifted a hand and pointed. At first Ginevra saw nothing. Then, gradually, she glimpsed a merry twinkle in the sky.

"I see it! I see it!"

She clapped her hands and then whirled back once again to the knight, but he had disappeared. Only one lone, early rising rooster swaggered through the piazza, eager to crow in the new day. Ginevra craned to look over the wall and down the winding dirt road that led to the monastery gates.

She ran to the church door, but there was no one there either; she watched as the last burning candle sputtered out in its iron rack.

There was no one.

"I even forgot to ask his name," she said aloud, turning back toward the house of Margaretta and Pietro Mulino and the swift dawning of a new day.

"August tenth," she muttered sleepily. "Why, 'tis only one day away."

Five

"Your mother has taken hospitality at the monastery of Santa Prisca," said Gatien to Ginevra later that same day. "It is but an hour's journey. I will set off immediately to provide them safe escort."

"You do not know my mother," she said to the Knight de la Marche, "if you think she needs escorting. I have never known her to leave Venice without ten caravans at her disposition and the protection of ten men-at-arms."

"She requested escort," said Gatien softly, "and she requested that you form part of it."

Ginevra was surprised how happily her heart beat at the thought of once again seeing her lady mother, and even of seeing Domiziana, though she and her sister had never been close.

"Indeed, I wish to come, my lord," she said. "That is, if you will not be inconvenienced by my presence."

"Such subservience!" exclaimed Gatien. "You parents will not recognize you, miss, if you continue with such submissive manners. 'If you will not be inconvenienced by my presence,' indeed!"

From her doorway, Retta muffled a giggle at the Knight de la Marche's cogent mimicry.

"But you cannot go like that, my lady!" she cried. "You are dressed in my old tunic and you have berry juice upon your hands! Lady Claudia will think we made you work to earn your keep! Good heavens! And your tangled mass of hair . . ."

"My mother will think me well cared for," replied Ginevra, hugging her. "And she will be right."

"If I were you two, I'd be on my way swiftly," Pietro mouthed in an elaborate whisper. "Before my lovely consort remembers that the elegant Lady Claudia Venier will soon be at her doorstep—and that she should stop this worry about Lady Ginevra's demeanor and start to worry a bit more about her own appearance and that of her house!"

"Oh dear!" cried Retta.

They set off late that morning: Sir Gatien, the Maid Ginevra, and the young page who carried the green-and-crimson standard of the de la Marche knights. Their horses carefully threaded a way through the village wicket and down the meandering road that led to the valley and eventually along the white sands that fronted the sea.

"I must confess," Gatien said, "that I did not expect to see your mother come to bless our wedding."

Ginevra shook her head. "Nor did I. 'Tis not like my mother to journey so casually through Italy. Nor is it like her to accept hospitality from the monks. She always complained in the past that their guesthouses were devilishly uncomfortable, especially for women. 'They hate us,' she would tell me, 'and they take the opportunity of feigning cordiality to sneak lice amongst our beds.' "

Gatien laughed. "Indeed, that sounds more like Lady Claudia. Perhaps she has developed a new interest in religion?"

"I doubt that. My mother would never allow religion to interfere with what she would consider a mortally serious endeavor: to stay in as many fine castles of the dukes of Calabria as she could possibly manage. Or, failing that, to be the guest of other high-ranking Angevin or Norman nobles. She would be able to make much of such connections in Venice with her friends. I am afraid that not many of them will be interested in her stories of Santa Prisca. There is a dearth of interest in religious pilgrimage among the people she frequents."

Gatien whooped with laughter at this. "Ginevra, you have the happy capacity for saying the most devastating truths in the most innocent of voices. But perhaps your mother has changed in the wake of the tribulations that have lately engulfed Venice."

Ginevra wrinkled her brow thoughtfully at this. "I don't think my mother truly cares for Venice. I don't think the city has ever really made her happy. Perhaps my father has but not his city."

She guided her horse expertly around a tangle of briars that encroached onto the narrow road. "Still, 'tis fully three months since I left Venice and many things might well have changed."

Retta had insisted Ginevra wear netted veiling, but the Maid of the Veniers pulled it off, held her head back, and lifted her face to the salt air and the sunlight.

"You will get more sun dotting if you do that," warned Gatien.

"It does not matter to me," replied Ginevra, "do sun dots bother you?"

"Not at all," he said. "I think them healthy looking."

"As do I."

But she lowered her head and soon lapsed once again into silence.

"Will you tell me what you are thinking?" Gatien asked.

"Nothing," Ginevra said quickly, but then changed her mind. "I was thinking about Venice. I was thinking about Badolato. How different I am now from what I was before."

"Different in what way?" he asked her softly.

Ginevra shook her head. "I don't know—or at least I cannot exactly name the change, although I know it is there. Perhaps I am too close to it to see it. My father always told me that if you could not put a thought into words, it meant the thought was not yet clear to you. I always thought that was nonsense. In the past it seemed I had a thousand million feelings, but I could always put a name to each. Now I see that my father was right. No longer are things as clear as they once seemed. I have no idea what I am thinking or feeling." She paused. "I have no idea what it is I really want."

She shrugged and then smiled over at him. "I met the strangest man this morning in the piazza at first light."

Immediately Gatien became his scolding self. "You were out in the piazza without chaperonage this morning? Ginevra, you will be the death of me! Has no one told you of the pirate threat? I myself explained to you . . ."

"This man was no pirate," Ginevra calmly replied. "He was kind and benign. I felt no fear of him."

"In you, Givvy, courage is a defect. But who was this man? I know of no other knights this close about the neighborhood."

"And yet he was a knight," she replied, shifting a bit in her saddle to face Gatien. Sunlight enveloped him, turning his hair golden and lighting up his face. He held the reins to his destrier in his sword hand. Still gingerly, Ginevra noted, but well enough that he was able to keep the powerful animal on a tight rein.

"I know he was," she continued. "He carried the jeweled sword and he wore the golden spurs. It is his duty to protect Badolato; he told me this."

"I know of no other knight," insisted Gatien, "but look. There is the Monastery of Santa Prisca. We will speak of this later, when we are once again alone."

"Thank goodness you have come for us," Claudia Venier whispered, as she enfolded her youngest daughter into a vice-like embrace. "Of course I always knew that you would. No matter what has happened, we are your family. And you were always like that, Ginevra, very quick to get angry and just as quick to forget about it again."

"I have not forgotten what happened to Elisabetta," Ginevra replied. "But I have worried about you, Mother. I am especially worried now that you wished to see me without the presence of the Knight de la Marche and that you have hidden yourself in such secrecy."

She glanced around at the darkened room whose air was heady with her mother's perfume—and with fear. Ginevra had sensed this dread immediately, as soon as the monk had opened the door to this stark chamber.

Ginevra squinted into the darkness. "And where is Domiziana—or should I now address her as the Contessa Ducci Montaldo? Why is she not here? Your letter said that the two of you were arriving together."

Claudia turned away, but not before Ginevra caught the gleam of tears within her eyes. "Your sister will join us later. She—*we* thought it best that I should speak alone with you at first."

Again a shiver of fear ran through Ginevra. She looked at her mother and noticed with dismay that the normally fastidious Contessa Claudia had inadvertently latched her tunic inside outward and that short dark hairs grew along the edges of her fashionably plucked hairline.

These two small things shouted to Ginevra that something was grievously wrong; something terrible had happened.

"Why has not the count of the Ducci Montaldo accompanied you?" she asked so softly that she could barely hear herself. "If he were occupied, he would certainly have arranged an escort of soldiers from his Gold Company. It is not like Count Olivier to leave his new wife to travel unescorted."

"They are not married," replied Claudia. She had gotten hold of herself. The tears were gone and the once famous Venier hauteur was again evident upon her face. "He would not have her—not after the scandal."

Ginevra felt her own blood run cold at this.

"Scandal?" she repeated. "My God, did I cause him to turn away from Domiziana because I ran away?"

Her mother snorted derisively. "My darling, you underestimate your mother. Within an hourglass's sand-span, I knew that you had hidden behind nun's drab and joined a pilgrimage on its way to Spain. Your small escape was nothing. It is your father who has brought disgrace upon us."

"Father?" exclaimed Ginevra.

"Indeed," Tears threatened again as Claudia turned away. "It seems that in the weeks leading up to that wretched battle at Nicopolis, the count of the Ducci Montaldo and Count Olivier had the strong suspicion that someone in Venice was secreting information about the French plans to the Sultan Bayezid. Naturally all suspicion was centered on the rulers of Genoa; they have always been great rivals of Venice and every defeat for us would be to their gain. But Olivier Ducci Montaldo was never quite convinced of this. When the French were crushed so decisively at the battle, he determined to leave no stone unturned in his investigation. He had lost many men to the sultan's rage and he did not want their deaths to have taken place in vain." Claudia stopped and her laugh was bitter. "In the end, it was the witch-burning that focused his attention upon us. Is this not ironic? Domiziana had been the one originally accused of the sorcery. Unfortunately these suspicions did not die as easily as did the witch."

"Domiziana urged Elisabetta onward," Ginevra said. "Even well beyond where Elisabetta chose to go. You know this yourself. We are guilty as well because we all allowed Domiziana her head in this."

"Not you," replied the Lady Claudia. For the first time she smiled, though sadly. "Not you."

"But how did this affect Father?" Ginevra asked. "He had nothing to do with the witch. He allowed you to do as you pleased with Elisabetta, just as he . . ."

She stopped, out of respect for her lady mother.

"Just as I was always allowed to do whatever I wanted?" Claudia laughed bitterly. "This was the fiction of our marriage. The poor, weak yet still noble husband; the demanding, scheming, upstart wife."

Again that bitter laugh.

"The burning of the witch brought the eyes of the city upon us at a time when your father would surely have wished them diverted elsewhere. In particular, he would have wished the attention of Lord Olivier focused on anything or anyone other than himself. The count of the Ducci Montaldo had taken a pledge at the Shrine of San Pellegrino to discover who had betrayed the Venetian plans to our enemies. It did not take him long to remember that your father had been at all of the important meetings where his cousin, the *Doge,* and the other rulers of Venice planned their participation in the attack."

"But Father would never have done such a thing. He is a Venier. They are bound to the city."

"More so than I—is that what you meant to say?" Claudia's smile lost its rancor. "That is what most people would say. He was a Venier born; I was lucky indeed to be one by marriage. And a true Venier would never betray the trust that had belonged to the family since Venice itself began."

Tears welled up in Lady Claudia's eyes, as Ginevra reached out to draw her near.

"We can talk about this later mother, if it distresses you to speak of these things now."

"No, I must tell you. I have not much time left, and it is part of the reason I have come," said Claudia. "Though his suspicions were strong, Lord Olivier would never have openly accused your father of such treachery. No proof existed. And although there was never any doubt in anyone's mind that he did not love Domiziana, neither did he hate her—at least not then—and his code of chivalry would never have allowed him to betray her father without the most explicit evidence."

"But how could there be proof? My father would never have done anything that would have caused so much loss of life and so much maiming."

"Including that of your own Sir Gatien? It seems that Lord Olivier had a friend, a certain Bulgarian spy who had been captured early-on. Eventually this man died from the wounds he received at Nicopolis; but before he did, he indicated your father as the serpent who had betrayed the Venetian interests. He told where letters were hidden, and money as well. Olivier easily found both."

"There was no mistake?"

"None whatsoever.

Ginevra had not heard her sister Domiziana enter but she turned to her now, and it was like seeing someone she had never known before. She could barely recognize her sister, though Domiziana had been the idol of her youth.

The young Maid of the Veniers remembered how she had always admired her sister; how she had loved the sheen of her silver-gold hair, the quickness of her gray eye, the elegance and hauteur that she had inherited from their mother. And she had been envious as well. She had always felt that the perfection Domiziana possessed was anything she would ever grasp. Now it was as though a candle had been extinguished within her sister and everything about her had dulled with the passing of the light. She was swathed head to toe in black, almost as though, within the riot of color that was Calabria, she wanted to hide herself from the threat of sunlight.

"Oh, Dommi," whispered Ginevra.

"It was Zio Antonio who had Father arrested," Domiziana said very softly, as she walked into the room. "He would have been the one to do it. Do you recall cousin Eugenio?"

Ginevra nodded. It was a famous story; she had told it to the Knight de la Marche.

"If Zio Antonio was so ruthless as to let his own son perish in prison from fever for a young man's indiscretion, you may well imagine what our father will face from him. Already he is in prison. We accompanied him to the Bridge of Sighs, but then they turned us back. The soldiers told us we must return to our own palazzo. Of course they laughed when they said it. 'Twas already well known in Venice that the palazzo had already been confiscated and that the family of Luciano Venier had no home left.

"Once the count of the Ducci Montaldo made public his disclosures and the *Doge* gave credence to the charge, they asked for Luciano's confession," said Domiziana. She sank down onto a simple three-legged stool. "The *Signoria* thought this better than to inflame the city with a public trial. The nobles rule only because the people allow. That a member of oligarchy had so betrayed them would only have led to trouble for them all. Father understood the meaning behind his words exactly. He could sign the confession and live—albeit for the rest of his life in prison—or he could refuse to sign and—who knows? Perhaps we would have all been quietly poisoned. It was already too late to save the property. It had been confiscated on the first day of the inquiry. It was sold shortly thereafter to a wealthy importer, someone who had recently bought his own way into the nobility. Venice donated the proceeds from the sale to help with the ransom of the Duke of Burgundy's son, Jean of Nevers, who had been captured after the battle. Do you not find this ironic, little sister? It was the House of Burgundy that enticed Venice into this disastrous encounter. And yet we paid for the heir's release. We have not a florin left."

For an instant she was the old Domiziana—witty, bold, determined—and then that brief light died once again. Ginevra longed to hug her as well, just as she was now holding on to their mother—but they had never been the type of family to which expressions of emotion came easily. They were, after all, Veniers.

"Have you come then to seek shelter with me?" she asked. "I live a simple life, yet I am sure Mistress Margaretta would find room . . ."

"And the Knight de la Marche?" Domiziana's gray eyes fastened upon her. "He is a First Knight of France and key to the duchy of Burgundy. Do not tell us that as his wife . . ."

"We have not yet married," replied Ginevra, "and now we will not."

This time it was their mother's turn to intervene. "We need no aid from the Knight de la Marche. Nor are we to stay here with you, at least not for long. We will be sailing to Picardy on this night's high tide."

"We are being convented," said Domiziana shortly. "And lucky we are to be so handled rather than thrown into prison. The *Doge* sentenced us to this himself. We might do well, he added, to spend our lives praying for the redemption of Father's soul—and of course restoration of the Veniers' good name."

"Even this did not come easily," whispered Claudia.

Domiziana shrugged. Two deep bitter lines etched their way along each side of her mouth. "We had no money, and no convent in the Veneto was willing to take two women without dower money. Especially two women who were no longer young."

"In the end it was the count of the Ducci Montaldo who dowered both of us," said Claudia, "to a convent in Picardy that he knew well."

"Because of course Olivier would not have me once the truth came out. There was no question that I could besmirch the name of the Ducci Montaldo with that of a disgraced Venier."

"He could well have left us on the street," snapped her mother. "After what happened. After what your father did. After what *you* did to the witch Elisabetta. Indeed, perhaps we deserved to be sent to the streets."

Domiziana's cheeks flamed. She turned away.

Ginevra stared at her mother for a long time through the dimness. It was as though she had never really seen her before, as though she had really known no one in her family—even though they had surrounded her for the whole of her life and she had loved them.

She still loved them.

"Now you will come with me to Badolato," she said. "We can sail from that safe haven just as easily as we can sail from Santa Prisca. After all, we will have plenty of time to stay within our French convent. You will love the village. It is a sanctuary, a place of healing. For this last day, let us breathe the clean fresh air of our native land."

The lady Claudia nodded at this, and she smiled. She had always been a tiny creature but now, in her simple dark flax tunic, she stood quite tall. Without jewels or ornamentation, and with her hair tied simply back, she looked the picture of nobility. In truth she looked the noble Venier she had always longed to be.

They had gathered their simple sumters and were at the door before Ginevra thought to ask, "But why, if you were on your way to Picardy, did you come so far south to begin your journey? 'Tis just past midsummer. Would you not have been better to trust yourself to the mountains of the Haute Savoie than to risk a sea crossing? You have always hated the thought of a sea voyage."

"I still do," replied her mother quietly, "but you are my child, my beloved youngest daughter, and I could not have gone into the convent's silence without seeing that you were happy with your good knight and to wish you both God bless."

The Knight de la Marche had never liked Domiziana Venier and his feelings toward the Lady Claudia and what he considered to be her affectations bordered, at best, on indifference. He could accept Ginevra as his bride, was even secretly coming to enjoy the thought, but he could quite happily live without the rest of them, and had cheerfully made up his mind to do so.

He was unprepared for the change that had come over them. The lady Claudia no longer complained about the major inconvenience of their journey back to Badolato, where before her prattle had been a continuous lament about the inconvenience. The lady Domiziana even managed to half-graciously thank Mistress Margaretta for laying out an extra cot and clean linens in Ginevra's chamber, the one that they would all now share.

"We have no money with which to pay you," said the Lady Claudia, "but we are willing enough to work to earn our keep."

"Indeed, ma'am, there is nothing that needs doing. The lady Ginevra has been more than a help. She has shown a fine hand for bee work and for baking. Here, taste some of the Sicily marzipan that Givvy—I mean, of course, the Lady Ginevra—rolled. My husband says it is quite the best he's ever eaten, and he is an expert on sweet things, which you will notice once you see him."

"Expert enough to pick you, my honey," said her husband coming up in the courtyard behind them, "out of all the busy bees."

Retta made her introductions and everyone laughed and smiled, except Ginevra and the Knight de la Marche.

Something has happened, thought Gatien. *I must get Givvy to talk to me.*

He looked up to find the dark eyes of the Lady Claudia upon him. She did not look away.

"Mistress Margaretta," said the countess Venier. "My daughter has told me of the special waters you have in Badolato. She says they are sweet and healing. Is there not a well nearby we may visit?"

"Indeed, there is," replied Retta with great alacrity. "Come, Pietro, we will take the Lady Claudia and her eldest daughter to the Piazza."

"But I've just come home!" protested her husband. "I've not had time . . ."

"Now," said his wife meaningfully. "You can attend to whatever your need is when we return."

* * *

"They've left us alone on purpose," said Ginevra Venier to her betrothed.

"That much is obvious," replied Gatien. He eased himself down beside her on the weathered wooden bench beneath the orange tree where they had spent so many summer days. Above them the first green buds were already beginning to form, though it would yet be many months before the fruit would ripen.

I will not be here to eat it, Ginevra thought.

But then she had never planned to remain in Badolato. This had always been a healing time, for the Knight de la Marche, she had thought. Now she realized that she was the one who had been healed as well.

"Gatien," she said quietly, "I've something to tell you."

It was night once again as Ginevra finished her tale. They sat side by side in silence for a long moment, listening to the sounds from the piazza as children swooped about and played before their mothers called them home.

"Is this supposed to make a difference?" Gatien said into the silence. "Because I assure you, Ginevra, it does not. I have promised to wed you—indeed, I have given you my oath as a knight to do so—and we shall wed. There was never any discussion as to dowry. The changed circumstances of your family have nothing to do with my maintaining my word."

"That is just the point." For an instant Ginevra looked much older than her eighteen years " 'Tis not just for the question of the scandal, though by itself that should be enough to halt any marriage between us. It is I who have changed as I daily watched the Mulinos and saw the life they share. Theirs is not a commitment that comes because one is obeying his honor-promise. It has nothing to do with chivalry or family duty. It has everything to do with love."

"Ginevra, I have no idea what you are saying," replied Gatien irritably. Though in fact he did have an idea and this was at the back of his irritation. "It might help if you would just speak your thoughts plainly."

"I mean to say that I will not have you in marriage, Gatien," she said. "I mean to say that I have made a mistake."

"At least you are right on that count. You should never have attempted such a treacherous journey. Journeying unescorted through half of Italy . . . Coming here . . ."

"You don't understand," Ginevra said with grave quietness. "Coming to Badolato was exactly what I should have done. Only here was I able to realize how wrong I was for insisting."

"For insisting?"

Ginevra looked right into his soul with the clearness of her bright eyes. "That I must have you."

"If this is a joke," said the Knight de la Marche wearily, though in fact his heart skittered and for some unaccountable reason he was growing alarmed, "then it is certainly in the worst of taste. The church is ready; the preparations are made. You carried your tunic with you from Venice! Why, tomorrow is the very day. You cannot . . ."

"Change everything? Give you up?" Ginevra rose from beside him. "Indeed, I can. Because the church and the preparations and the wedding tunic mean nothing, if there is no love."

"Love?" echoed Gatien, looking quite perplexed.

"Love," repeated Ginevra. "This is the reason that I truly came to Badolato, though I did not know this myself until now. I came to learn of love, to see it. I have seen it in the care Margaretta shows to Pietro, and in the care he shows to her in his turn. It exists in the peasants laboring in the fields each day so that the village and its children can exist through another winter. I see it in these same children at play and on the edges of the piazza where the mother hen cares for her young chicks. Love is all about me in this village. It is everywhere, except in my own life."

"You never talked of love before," said the Knight de la Marche darkly. "At least you never spoke of my loving you. You wanted marriage. That was enough."

She shook her head and looked over at the Knight de la Marche. "Whether or not you loved me did not matter to me then. But it matters to me now. I have changed here in this village. I am no longer a child who *must* have what she wanted. I have grown up."

"Certainly you are behaving like a child in this" Gatien exclaimed, uncomfortably aware that he might himself be behaving like one. "You should honor the vow you made me take to you! We should marry on the morrow as you said!"

"I have discovered what love is, Gatien, and now I will not settle for anything less. And you don't love me. 'Tis that simple. I would rather not have you at all than to have your body and lose all the rest."

Gatien, already amazed by his racing heart and his actions, surprised himself still further by jumping up from the bench. "After all this, you are now telling me that you *don't* love me?" he demanded. "After walking half of Italy? After braving my wrath? After . . ."

"I will always love you, Gatien. I know that more than ever. And I will continue to love you every day of my life. For as long as I live. 'Tis only that I will no longer marry you."

"But why, Givvy? Give me your reason."

"Because you do not love me, Gatien. That is my only reason. And it is enough."

* * *

The Knight de la Marche did not even attempt sleep that night; he did not go near his cold monk's bed. Instead he dismissed his page to sleep with the novices and paced back and forth in his chamber. Remembering the rest. Remembering what they had then said:

"I've never thought of loving you," he had told his betrothed finally. "You were from a good family. I gave you my word and had to honor it. That was enough."

"It was for me, too" said Ginevra. "It isn't anymore."

"But where will you go? What will you do?" Gatien had caught at these scant twigs of rationality and logic with the focused determination of a drowning man. "Your father has been disgraced and imprisoned. Your mother and sister . . ."

"I have already discussed my decision with my mother. I am to sail this night with her and with my sister for Picardy. I have no desire for the convent and no money with which to dower my way there, but there are pearls upon my wedding tunic. I will sell these and the money from them will sustain me until I can find decent and useful work."

"*Work?*" Even now, hours later, Gatien could hear his own exclamation ringing in his ears. "What can you do? You are a lady. You will starve to death."

Ginevra had looked with meaningful silence at the arm with which he gestured his frustration. It was his right arm—his sword arm—that slowly and painfully had been brought back to life.

"I doubt I will starve," said the youngest child of the Venier. "There are ways in which I can earn a small living. Ways in which I might help. Yet that is something I must cope with by myself and in the future. Now I should go and help Retta with the

evening's meal. You will live through this change in
your plans, Gatien," she added with some irony. "We
both will."

"Not if you love her," said a voice right beside
him.

Gatien jumped.

"Love her?"

He turned to the tall knight who had somehow
materialized in his chamber. The man was dressed in
a white tunic emblazoned with a large crimson cross.
He looked quite kind.

"A Templar knight," mused Gatien. But this did
not alarm him; he did not automatically reach for
his sword.

"We were speaking of the Lady Ginevra," said the
knight sternly, "and of your love for her."

"I love Givvy?" Gatien said and then repeated. "I
love Givvy."

"Well, of course you do," said the strange knight.
"Indeed, you have loved her from first sight. But you
had better hasten. She is leaving. I would not be
surprised to find that she is already at the sea. You
are lucky, Sir Gatien, that this is the Night of San
Lorenzo. The Night of the Falling Stars. Anything
can happen under its magic. And if you hurry, it
will."

"Look up, Ginevra," said her mother. "And you
will see the most beautiful falling star."

Ginevra paused at the water's edge, one foot already within the small boat that would carry them to
the ship that would soon sail for France.

The star shot directly over her head, full and
bright and coming straight toward her. So close she
felt she could touch it with her hand.

And she remembered the strange knight at the

Church of Santa Caterina; she remembered what he had said.

Wish on the star. Believe that it will happen.

"Please help Gatien to be happy," she said, looking directly up into the brightness. "Help him to find a woman he can love and want as a wife."

"Then marry me, Givvy," said the Knight de la Marche close beside her. "Because 'tis you I love. You only that I want, and will ever want, for wife."

As she turned to him he raised his sword arm and tossed her the rag ball they had worked with so many long hours. It was worn now and tattered, and the hand that held it still weakened and unsure.

But the Knight de la Marche tossed it and the Maid Ginevra caught it as she looked at her beloved with tears of joy in her eyes.

"Life has changed for us," he said softly before gathering her to him, "and it has changed us. Things will never again be as they were before, but I think, Givvy, they can be better. In some strange way they can be better."

"Because we are better?"

"Yes, because we are better," he said as he gathered her to him. "My dear wife."

And so early on the morrow, the Maid of the Veniers dressed in the tunic she had carried with her from Venice, and with a crown of wildflowers woven through the cascade of her long auburn hair, walked confidently to the small Church of Santa Caterina. There, before its plain altar, she plighted her troth to the Knight de la Marche. Afterward there was feasting and dancing aplenty in the village with Margaretta crying copious tears and with Pietro regaling:

"Did you not see last night how the stars shot through the heavens? They say at such times the ghost of Bohumond the Templar is active, busy granting wishes and changing lives."

"Go on with you!" exclaimed his wife, "with your legends and your stories."

"But 'tis true," insisted Pietro.

And above it all, Bohumond the Templar himself smiled and looked on.

The Bridal Cup

Linda Madl

Prologue

Boston, 1896

"Cease your fussing, lass, my time has come, and there's an end to it," Uncle Grant rasped from his bed. With a feeble gesture, he pushed Leonora and her stethoscope away.

Bewildered and frustrated, she sank onto the edge of the downy mattress and removed the stethoscope earpieces. Uncle Grant had never scolded her, never refused her anything. And now, feverridden with pneumonia, he refused to listen to her best medical advice.

Instinctively she noted the blue tint to his fingernails. A bad sign. Her gaze shot back to his face. He was gray as a dingy sheet, and his eyes were sunken and bloodshot. The smell of illness hung heavily in the room. Her heart ached, and her gut rebelled against her helplessness. But she knew there was little more she could do.

"We need to get you to the clinic, Uncle Grant, where I can better help you," she said, with as much confidence as she could muster. "At the clinic I can—"

"Nonsense, you can't do anything for me at that clinic and you know it. Bring me the box, I say." In his agitation he attempted to raise his head from the pillow. "Time is short. I have secrets I must tell you before it is too late. Bring me the box."

Secrets? She exchanged a puzzled look with her younger sister, Janet, who was standing on the other side of his bed. Dear Janet, devoted mother of three sons and another baby on the way, and a busy hostess for her railroad tycoon husband. She'd been an uncomplaining nurse to their favorite uncle throughout his sudden illness.

"The rowan wood box, Uncle Grant?" Janet asked, stepping closer.

"Aye, Janet, you know the one? With the brass corners."

"Yes, now I know." Janet went to the cupboard and brought out a box about the size of a hatbox trimmed in brass hardware hammered with Celtic designs. "Don't argue with him anymore," she whispered to Leonora as she set the box on the bed.

Leonora stared at the unfamiliar object. Surely she would have remembered such a unique item if she'd seen it before.

Uncle Grant lifted his head again. When he saw the box, he fell back against the pillow. "Yes, that's it. Now, before you open it, you must promise that you will forgive me. Leonora. Promise. Your father, God rest his soul, and me. You must forgive us."

Pale and weak as he was, his dark hazel eyes glittered with urgency and anxiety. She touched his hand to comfort him. She'd never seen him like this. Uncle Grant had always been so sure of himself, confident, a carefree bachelor. He'd been her hero, the man who'd taken her to the opera when she thought she wanted to be a prima donna. The man who'd taken her to the county court when she thought she wanted to be a lawyer. The man who'd seen her as Leonora when her father saw her only as his daughter—and as the next woman surgeon when she wanted to be a doctor for babies, new mothers, and grandmothers.

Uncle Grant went on. "Your father thought he was doing the best thing, not telling you about this. But it has never set easy with me. I always thought that one day I would set it aright. Now, before it is too late—"

He began to cough.

She'd had enough. Whatever he had to say could wait. Leonora stood up. "You're going to the clinic. When you're rested, you can tell me about whatever this is."

"I'm not going anywhere," Uncle Grant choked out in gasps. "Take your blinkers off. You're a good doctor, Leonora. But your blind stubbornness does you no credit. Sit down and listen to me while there is time."

Without looking at Leonora, Janet reached across the bed and touched her arm. "Listen to him, Lennie."

"What—"

"I don't know, just sit," Janet said, tugging on Leonora's wrist.

She sat, silently struggling with the knowledge that she had not recognized his nausea as an early symptom of pneumonia. If she had recognized the symptom . . . if he had not refused to take care of himself . . . if she could have . . . or maybe . . . but now he was dying. Saving him was beyond her skills.

"Open the box, Leonora," he said, his gaze resting on her face. "Take out the cup."

With a frown of puzzlement, she did as he asked. Obeying his wishes was all that was left to do for him. Unwrapping layers of a dark plaid that she knew was the Camville plaid from around the mysterious object, she could feel that it was a sizable thing, but light in weight. Polished metal gleamed as the last of the wool fell away. She held up an intricately worked goblet.

The silver was surprisingly warm in her hands. Two stems fashioned like vines emerged from the base and twisted upward round each other to join at the bowl of the goblet. Glowing rubies wreathed a clan crest. Celtic swirls undulated to life, dipping and flowing over the graceful cup's contours as she held it up to the weak winter sunlight.

Astonishment hissed from Janet. "What a beautiful thing," she said, her voice full of the same wonder Leonora was feeling.

Chalice was the word she would have used to describe the cup, a silver chalice on a graceful double stem that twined upward to join in one bowl. She'd never seen the like before. The workmanship was exquisite, and the design had to be ancient.

"This is the MacDonnart bridal cup," Uncle Grant said, his voice little more than a whisper now. "See the MacDonnart crest?"

She gaped at him. "MacDonnart? But how—where?"

"We Camvilles stole it from them centuries back," he said. "The MacDonnarts bragged it was a wedding gift from Queen Margaret in return for a favor. It was intended for The MacDonnart to use in sharing the first toast of his married life with his bride."

"Saint Margaret?" Janet stammered. "You mean the Scottish queen who was mother of King David I from the eleventh century?"

"I knew you'd appreciate it," he said, his eyes drifting closed.

Leonora studied the cup closer. For an instant, the beauty and antiquity of the goblet stole her thoughts from Uncle Grant's condition.

What Camville warrior had had the audacity to steal this beautiful heirloom from a MacDonnart bridegroom—from a man anticipating sharing it with his bride? The maliciousness. The indignation. The insult.

An angry dark, kilt-wearing MacDonnart warrior loomed in her mind's eye. Powerful sinewy muscles and a grim set jaw. In swift pursuit of the Camville thief clutching the cup, the warrior swung a shiny claymore. The Camville ducked. The steel sang against stone castle walls. Labored breathing echoed and the smell of hatred filled the cold air. The Camville vanished into the darkness, elated with his victory. But the MacDonnart's fury lingered, black and chilling.

The chill sent a shiver down Leonora's back, but she clung to the cup. "So there was more to the feud than the vague tales of injustice whispered by Aunt Fiona when she thought Papa was out of hearing?" she said.

"Indeed, lass," Uncle Grant was saying. He reached out to touch her hand as he talked, pulling her away from her images. His voice was surprisingly steady and his words lucid. "Your father was chief of Clan Camville as was our father before him."

"And you are the last Camville chief, Uncle Grant," Janet said, the cup suddenly forgotten and tears glimmering in her eyes. "My sons, good boys all, but they are Fairfields."

"That's of little importance now," Leonora said, casting aside fantasies about the cup. She wanted to deny all the evidence of her uncle's deteriorating condition and to battle for his life. There had to be something more she could do. "Let's get you to the clinic."

"Listen to me." Uncle Grant gripped her hand with surprising strength that made her freeze on the edge of the bed. "The Camvilles, your grandmother and grandfather and your great-uncles and aunts, left the Highlands because the clan lands were gone—the last taken by the enclosures. The clan seat at Camville Castle had been usurped and pulled down by those bloody MacDonnarts and the Roundheads long ago. These things you know."

She and Janet nodded in respectful silence. Every Camville, lad or lass, had grown up knowing about the feud with the MacDonnarts. Every Camville knew that from the beginning of time—Scottish time at least—the Camvilles and the MacDonnarts had warred against each other, betrayed each other to the English, and stole each others' cattle, land, and sometimes even their women. Aunt Fiona had made certain they knew even as Papa had discouraged the telling of the tales. The origin of the feud seemed lost in the mists of time, but even a Boston Camville knew never to trust a MacDonnart.

"So you hold in your hand a part of this story," Uncle Grant continued.

"But we live in America now," Leonora said, her fear and impatience growing. What mattered a feud when her best friend was dying? He had to give this up. "Papa may have been The Camville, but he did not want the clan looking to the past. You know that. We are in a new place. This is a different time."

"But the past is still with us." Uncle Grant pointed a trembling finger at the cup. "You hold the past in your hands."

Leonora glanced down at the goblet she'd forgotten she held. Before she could say more, Uncle Grant rasped on.

"Listen to me, lass. I've been living a lie. I am not the legitimate chief of the Camvilles. You are."

Janet drew in a sharp breath and glanced in her direction.

Leonora stared speechless at the man she thought she'd known so well. What was he telling her?

"I took the title when your father died and swore your Aunt Fiona and the others to secrecy. I knew your father never told you that the true Camville clan chief is the chief's body-heir. No bloody English traditions for us. The Camville heir is not the male heir, but the body-heir, male or female."

"Then Leonora is Maid of the Camvilles, then," Janet said, comprehending what Leonora could not make herself grasp. "Papa never said anything about it to us," Janet said.

"Kenneth was proud to be a Camville and he was a good chief, fair and evenhanded, but he had little use for the clan ways," Uncle Grant said, looking into Leonora's eyes. Truth weighed heavily in his gaze and his words. "I am telling you, lass, that you are the true Camville chief. Your father didn't want leadership to pass to you. It can be a heavy burden. He was so proud of you and in so many ways you have been his heir in temperament and intellect. You're as fine a doctor as he ever was."

At the moment she didn't feel like a fine doctor. "Papa wanted us to be Americans."

"That he did, lass." A weary sigh whistled from him. "When I was younger, I didn't understand what he meant, and why he was so adamant about forgetting the past. I didn't understand his wisdom. But now, it is clear to me. What you must know is in the five years since your father's death, I have usurped your rightful place."

With eyes wide, Janet stared at Leonora with new respect, respect that Leonora did not feel she deserved. She knew that in Scottish history there had been women heirs, women who led the men when leading needed to be done—often when fighting was necessary. But who was she to take on the leadership of a clan? She was no fighter; she was a healer—one incapable of saving her uncle.

"Now, about the cup." Uncle Grant stirred in the bed. Leonora feared he was in pain, but he was gesturing at the cup. "I'm asking you to return it to the MacDonnarts, lass. Take it back. Declare the feud at an end. It's what your father wanted. He asked me to do it, and I refused. Foolish man I was. I thought it a fine thing to possess another clan's treasure, but it is not. Often it is that I've regretted letting your father down, lass."

"But who does Lennie return it to, Uncle Grant?" Janet had the presence of mind to ask.

"Why, to The MacDonnart, of course," he muttered, his lips barely moving.

Leonora hardly heard what he was saying. She seized her uncle's wrist and took the pulse. Thready. Weak. Her heart sank.

"Go to the MacCages first," he murmured, without opening his eyes. "Loyal always, the MacCages. There's an address on my desk. They will stand at your side, if need be."

Suddenly, he opened his eyes, his gaze resting on Leonora. In a firm voice he said, "Do this for me. Do it for the Camvilles, for the future. Promise me, lass."

"I promise," Leonora said. Who could refuse a man on his deathbed? He smiled at her and closed his eyes again. She clutched his hand hoping to find the same powerful grasp he'd exerted earlier, but his grip had weakened.

"Don't leave us, Uncle Grant. Don't leave us," she pleaded, panic rising in her at last. She had so many questions for him, now that she knew the truth.

Uncle Grant never heard her plea. He'd slipped into a coma. Nothing she did could bring him back.

Within the hour he was gone. Numb with shock and defeat, she closed up her black bag and walked from the room.

Later Janet found her standing against the wall in the back hallway still reeling from the loss. Relatives had been notified. She could hear the muffled comings and goings of those who wished to say good-bye before the undertaker came. But she was too hollow inside to face them, to receive their condolences.

Her neck ached and her legs were stiff from the deathbed vigil. Clutched in her hand was the silver goblet. Strange how its weight and shape felt familiar to her as though she'd held it before, as though it had been hers once.

"You're not blaming yourself, are you, Lennie?" Janet asked, touching her arm. "You did everything you could."

Leonora shook her head. "But one always has to wonder. He was only forty-eight. If something had been different . . ."

"I know." Janet nodded. "But don't think of what could have been. It's an impossible task. You're exhausted from delivering three difficult babies this week."

"And I lost one of them, too," Leonora said.

"You know that was a difficult case and it couldn't be helped," Janet scolded. "You've been a doctor long enough to understand these things. And Uncle Grant, him always refusing to wear a hat in the rain and to get himself into dry boots when he should."

"That's no excuse," Leonora said, grief and weariness settling over her. There should have been something she could have done for the ones she lost.

"Still, you've got a cup and a title, Dr. Camville," Janet said. "You're Maid of the Camvilles. What now?"

"Is that who I am?" Leonora asked. She didn't feel like a clan chief. She felt like a helpless doctor, fatigued and lost. Uncle Grant had uttered a few words and died. The world she knew was altered, forever. "I'd always assumed that we—the Camvilles—had come here to leave everything behind. For a new start. That's what Papa always wanted us to believe. And now we find this. Do we know who we are, Janet?"

"We are Camvilles," Janet said, eyeing Leonora as if she'd feared she was slipping into madness. "A proud Scots family who depends on no one and takes care of our own. Nothing changes that."

"But here is the proof the past is still with us, as Uncle Grant said." Leonora held up the cup.

"So?" Janet braced her hands on her hips, a challenge in her eyes. "And what are you going to do about it, Lennie?"

"Keep my promise to Uncle Grant, the one he made to my father and never carried out," Leonora said, astonished once more by the beauty and the warmth of the silver goblet in her hands. "I'm going to Scotland to return the MacDonnarts' bridal cup. Returning it is the only way to put the past behind us."

One

Perthshire, Scotland

The steam-powered wood saw hissed, belched smoke, and hiccuped thunderously. Gears locked and belts quivered. Distressed gears whined. The saw blade never moved.

"Adjust the other valve," Ross MacDonnart, Lord Glenalder, shouted over the cacophony of noise he knew was all wrong.

The operator stared at the gauges, hesitating to make a move.

Impatient and without a twinge of guilt about his obligation to be elsewhere, Ross thrust his coat at a millworker and climbed the ladder of the monster machine. He had learned that few had his talent for hearing or visualizing a mechanical problem, even trained operators.

"This valve here." He pointed it out to the perplexed man.

The Hampshire lumberman, whom Ross had persuaded to travel north to teach the millworkers about the new engine, immediately did as Ross said. The belching and hiccuping of the engine smoothed. Belts whipped into action and gears meshed.

"That's an improvement," Ross called over the

low rhythmic hum that promised productivity. Victory.

"Aye, my lord, that's the right sound of it," the operator agreed with an embarrassed grin, sweat dripping from his brow. "We'll have you running this thing in no time."

The heat at the panel of gauges and valves was stifling. But Ross was too pleased with the operation to notice. He laughed. "I'll leave the operating to you," he told the lumberman. The millworkers gathered around the machine and shook their heads in amazement. This engine was considerably more powerful than the one they had worked with before, and it would be more productive. Grumble as they might about making changes, Ross knew they would come to appreciate the new equipment.

He grinned at them, glad to see in them, even the old-timers, a glimmer of the enthusiasm he felt when he'd purchased the steam engine and hired the operator. That morning, when he had seen the equipment was assembled and the operator had arrived, wedding or no, he had been unable to resist starting it up for all to see. Millworkers and wedding guests.

Glenalder and the MacDonnarts were putting the old ways behind them. He had made that decision several years ago when he'd become The MacDonnart. As soon as he'd decided the course, he'd put his law books aside, gladly said farewell to London, and returned to the Highlands. He had begun to educate himself about the future of animal husbandry and forestry—and pick up his old fascination for mechanical things.

At the age of twenty-eight with the twentieth century only four years away, it wasn't difficult to see that the new technical developments were impossible to ignore. He had no regrets about his decision. Railroads, telegraph, telephone, motorcars. Survival for Glenalder House and the MacDonnarts required change. He found it all thrilling.

The steam engine continued to hum along smoothly.

"What do the gauges read now?" Ross asked, peering at the panel once more.

He and the operator checked the readings again and discussed the acceptable operating ranges. Then, satisfied that the engine was running as it should, Ross swung to the top of the ladder to climb down. He was looking forward to showing Kerr the steam engine when he arrived from London. Little brother would be excited with the improvement, too.

From the top rung, he glanced down the hillside toward the drive leading to the house. Wedding guests had begun arriving the day before, and he was aware of his duty as host to greet new arrivals. But the steam engine's start-up had been too momentous to disregard. Still, his guests could not be ignored indefinitely.

Coming around the bend of the Glenalder House gravel drive, he caught sight of Ian MacCage's dilapidated wagon.

Ross grimaced. Instantly his good mood evaporated in a wave of irritation. The irritation rapidly swelled into anger—anger only a Camville ally could bring.

"What the bloody hell?" he muttered under his breath at the sight of MacCage urging his mismatched team of gray and bay geldings along the drive.

He was down the ladder in a flash. Retrieving his coat from the millworker, he strode down the path toward the house.

There hadn't been a Camville in the Highlands for almost fifty years. Nevertheless, for as many decades as Ross could remember, MacCage had seemed to feel it his duty to keep up the Camville end of the feud with his demands and expectations of rights no longer granted to any Highlander. The old scamp had never had a sense of his place. And it was just like him to present himself as a rightfully invited guest when he knew full well that he and his lot, including that woman sitting next to him, weren't welcome at the celebration.

A switch in the path offered another view of the drive. Ross stopped. His gaze went to the woman in gray, graceful and elegant seated next to MacCage. Clearly a lady. Where in the bloody hell did that scrappy old man find a woman like that to escort? Her presence would make telling MacCage he was unwelcome damned awkward, which was exactly what the old man intended, no doubt.

For a moment Ross considered letting his butler, Stratton, deal with MacCage. Turning away unwanted and inappropriate guests was part of a butler's responsibilities. Stratton knew how to deal with such things. No, Ross decided. The old coot might as well hear from The MacDonnart that none of his nonsense would be tolerated while the house was full of wedding guests.

Ross shrugged into his coat and marched purposefully down the hillside path toward the house.

The front doorbell rang just as he reached the back garden door of Glenalder House. He let himself in, and as he passed Stratton in the entry hall, he gestured toward the library. He would receive Mac-Cage in there. Clan chiefs no longer sat on thronelike chairs and presided over their clansmen in a great hall. Ross had seen to it that Glenalder's library served him just as well. The wood-paneled walls were lined with leather-bound and gilt-titled books, the chairs of leather, the wooden floor covered with a rich red Oriental carpet, the lamps of shiny brass. Everything spoke of wealth, power, and education.

Stratton, who had served as butler for the past ten years, acknowledged Ross's gesture with a nod, and without pause, continued on his way toward the front door.

This would be done quickly, cleanly, Ross decided, and then he would find Alice and take her out to see the new plantings in the riverside garden as soon as old MacCage was gone.

Impatiently Ross tugged at his cravat to straighten it and seated himself in his large leather chair behind the massive desk to wait. He listened to the voices in the entry hall. MacCage's booming voice. Stratton's precise, impeccably polite words.

Then the oddly deep husky song of a woman's voice caught his ear and held it. A youthful voice, not childish, but hardly that of a crone. Who was she?

Ross shifted in his chair. What was MacCage up to now?

Stratton knocked on the door before he entered. "My lord, Mr. Ian MacCage and Dr. Leonora Camville to see you," he announced, without betraying a single emotion.

"Camville?" Ross rose slowly. A true Camville here at Glenalder House? His heart pounded a little quicker at the prospect of the enemy on his doorstep. But surely this was some sort of jest. The last of the Camvilles and their chief had emigrated years ago, just before Ross's grandfather had become the MacDonnart clan chief. Camville?

"Yes, my lord, Dr. Leonora Camville, from America," Stratton repeated in his perfectly modulated voice.

"Of course, from America," Ross said as his mind raced. But a Camville, nonetheless. They were wily thieves. His father had taught him that and his fa-

ther before him and the MacDonnart before him.
Ross was well educated, well traveled, and thoroughly nurtured on the Camville-MacDonnart feud
stories. He heard them from his grandfather and his
father and visited the sites of some of the tales with
his brother Kerr. There was no reason to think that
dispossessed Camvilles were any more honest than
their ancestors. He would hear the woman out. Make
it clear that she was not welcome at Glenalder House
and send her on her way. "Show them in, Stratton."

Dr. Camville was taller than he'd expected. She
moved gracefully toward him with an authoritative
step that immediately told him, that despite her
youth, she was accustomed to taking charge. Old Ian
followed her, his cap properly removed and a
wooden brass-trimmed hatbox tucked under his
arm. To Ross's mild surprise, the proud old man
ducked his head in a submissive fashion that he'd
never displayed before.

The woman strode directly to Ross's desk.

"Ross MacDonnart, The MacDonnart?" she in-
quired in that startling, husky voice. She gazed at
him with a forthright but curious expression. None
of the coy eyelash fluttering the ladies frequently offered him. She presented only a polite smile.

Ian scurried to her side. "No, lass, I mean, ma'am,
ah, Doctor," the old man stammered. "This 'tisn't
proper. Let me announce ye."

"Stratton announced you," Ross told the old man,
though he couldn't take his gaze from Dr. Camville's
face.

She wore no earrings. Her chestnut hair was
neatly tucked beneath a small-quality gray felt hat
decorated with a gray ribbon. Only a gold lapel
watch adorned her gray traveling suit, which was of
the same quality and plainness as her hat. Though
no braid trim or lace accented its cut, her suit failed

to disguise her figure. She had the kind of shape a man noticed, whether wrapped in silk or homespun.

Ross involuntarily sucked in an appreciative breath.

She gazed back at him with calm dark gray eyes set in an oval face with winged brows. Her nose was straight and her somber mouth had a tantalizingly full lower lip. She was no delicate miss. Her presence and demeanor defied all the accepted rules of Victorian feminine deportment, yet Ross found her strangely appealing.

She turned slightly toward Ian who was staring at Ross expectantly.

"Then, if you must, introduce us, MacCage," Ross hastened to say.

Victory gleamed in the old man's faded blue eyes. Ian put the box down on the desk. "MacDonnart, this is Leonora Camville, daughter of Kenneth, son of Donald who was the son of Ewen Camville, the last Camville chief on Scottish soil."

Ross frowned. He needed no explanation of the import of Ian's recitation. He knew the Camville's genealogy almost as well as he knew his own. He understood exactly who stood in front of him.

"You are the Maid of Camville," he said, his heart thudding faster now, as it always did when he was faced with a Camville-MacDonnart feud. At least he thought the feud was why his heart was tripping over itself. But, sweet heaven, she was lovely. He steeled himself against reacting to his softer emotions. This was no time for weakness. He was facing the MacDonnart's age-old enemy.

A flutter in Leonora's belly at the sight of Ross MacDonnart sitting behind his desk warned her that returning the bridal cup was going to be more complicated than she'd imagined.

She'd never expected the task to be an easy one. Over the past two months since Uncle Grant's death, she had mentally prepared herself for coming face-to-face with the twenty-fifth MacDonnart chief. In spite of all her reading and enquiries, she'd been unable to rid herself of the sword-swinging, kilt-wearing warrior image that had first come to her. She knew it was a foolish picture to hold of modern Scotland.

Ian did not help her rid herself of the image when he informed her that MacDonnart had read for the law. In court, the man had proven himself an unbeatable adversary and was known to expect to win and always did.

That winning determination was etched on the man's face she saw across the desk. She could see the desire for victory in the grim set of his mouth and the burning blue intensity of his eyes. She saw a man powerful in his intentions and his resolve. That first chill she'd had when she envisioned the MacDonnart warrior and his claymore pursuing the Camville renewed itself, slithering down her spine despite the sunshine outside.

The important thing she wished Ian had not omitted was the chief's good looks.

Ross MacDonnart was a handsome man with dark hair, a strong clean-shaven jaw and chin, and a wide intelligent brow. He wore no armor. No kilt. No sword. But it was not that difficult to picture him with them.

Today, his well-cut dark blue linen jacket matched his trousers and checked waistcoat. His blue tie was slightly askew. Had he been up to some physical task before they called, she wondered. She liked to think so. It made him more human.

Calming her uncertainties as best she could, she approached the desk and offered her hand for a handshake. "How do you do?"

A moment of silence hung in the air. Ian MacCage cleared his throat. Leonora glanced at the old man who was holding his breath and staring at her proffered hand as if she'd committed a terrible *faux pas*.

She turned back to Ross MacDonnart whose delay did not surprise her. Men often hesitated when she offered her hand to them in a businesslike fashion. Anything beyond tipping their hat to a lady was unnatural to most men.

His gaze never flickered as he rose slowly, took her hand, and shook it. A firm brief shake, his palm cool and dry, his fingers long and strong, smooth, not callused, but not soft.

"How do you do, Doctor, is it?" he said without relaxing the grimness of his mouth. "I'm Ross MacDonnart, chief of clan MacDonnart and otherwise known as Lord Glenalder. How may I be of service?"

His voice was frosty. Ian had warned her that if they sent word ahead that they were coming, they probably would have never be received. She believed the old man now.

"We've come to return something," Ian said.

The MacDonnart cast the old man a quelling look. Indeed, those blue eyes could burn. Ian instantly stepped back and fell silent.

The exchange annoyed Leonora. "Mr. MacCage has been very helpful to me since I arrived in Scotland and presented myself to him without warning. I'm grateful to him. I'd hope I'd find some small portion of the same hospitality at Glenalder House."

"That depends on the reason for your call," The MacDonnart said, clearly not in the least concerned about his hospitality or the lack thereof. "We are preparing for a wedding at the end of the week."

"Yes, Ian told me of the coming nuptials," she said, determined not to be put off by the man. What could one expect from a MacDonnart anyway, even a handsome one? "We've no intention of imposing.

However, I think you'll agree, the timing is ironically fortuitous, because we've come to return something appropriate for the occasion."

"And that would be?" he asked, one brow raised in skepticism.

"Ian, please open the box." Her irritation with The MacDonnart's arrogance was growing.

Without saying a word, the old man unlatched the box, dug out the Camville plaid bundle, and handed it to her.

"My father died five years ago," she explained as she carefully began to peel away the wool. "Two months ago my uncle on his deathbed showed this to me for the first time. I was astonished. Until then, I had never known that the Camvilles were in possession of such a valuable artifact. My uncle asked me to return it to its rightful owner."

She allowed the last of the dark green plaid to fall away, revealing the ornate silver cup. "Here it is."

Afternoon sunlight streaming through the library window struck the hand-worked silver and set it to gleaming. Awed silence filled the room. The cup glowed rich, stately, and graceful on its elegant twined stem. None of them could take their gaze from it.

Once again she was surprised by how warm the metal was to her touch, familiar, almost friendly.

"The MacDonnart bridal cup," MacDonnart said in a near whisper. The cold tightness of his mouth slipped into less guarded intensity. He was as surprised and astonished to see it as she had been. Her annoyance with him faded a bit.

"Aye, laddie, that's exactly what it 'tis," Ian said. When no one chastised him for speaking, he went on. "And thankful ye should be to this lass for bringing herself all the way across the ocean just to hand deliver it to ye. And in time for yer nuptials, too."

* * *

Slowly, Ross lowered himself into his desk chair, his gaze fastened on the gleaming chalice. He had heard the stories of it from his father who had heard them from his father, but he'd never expected to see it in his lifetime. Now here it was before him, in perfect condition for his wedding. If he were a superstitious man, he'd think it an auspicious omen.

"Set it here," he said.

Without a word of objection, the Maid of Camville leaned forward to do as he asked. She set the cup on the polished wood, careful not to touch his hands spread on either side of the desk. As she stepped back, he was vaguely aware of the clean lemony scent of her.

"All my life I've heard the story of it, but I was uncertain as to whether it was real." He peered closer at the cup, studying the lines and the decorations as it glimmered like a magical thing.

"Here's the MacDonnart crest," the Maid pointed out.

He nodded, still too awed by the cup to trust expressing his emotions in words.

"There's little doubt that it is the bridal cup of legend," the Camville Maid said in that unique voice of hers. "And notice how little tarnish there is," she added. "It's miraculous, for silver of that age."

"Do you know the story of it?" he asked at last.

"Some of it," she said, a soft wariness in her husky voice.

"The bridal cup was a gift from St. Margaret meant for all the MacDonnart chiefs to share with their brides. Nearly a dozen grooms offered that chalice to their brides as MacDonnart clansmen cheered in celebration of the union of hearts and bodies. It served as the promise of a new generation. Then a canny Camville scoundrel stole the chalice before the twelfth clan chief could wed his bride."

The red rush of feuding anger surged through

Ross again. He glared across the desk at The Maid. How could she gaze back at him so calmly, so guile-less? "Have you no understanding of the insult of that? And to add insult to the injury, you bloody Camvilles took the cup with you when you left Scotland."

"I'm afraid that's so." She continued to hold his gaze without denial or apology. "And now I'm returning it."

Ross's eyes narrowed. Wily, the Camvilles. Wily, always, his father had told him. Did she think she could hide behind that look of innocence?

He rose from his chair slowly, in control and careful not to betray the full force of his fury. He would not give a Camville the satisfaction of seeing it. "So, just what is it that you want?"

The scowl on his face was enough to send Leonora retreating a step—but only one step. So this was the MacDonnart's character. Ice to fire. She preferred his earlier frostiness. But she could meet his fierce-ness, too, if she must.

"As I said, I want only to return the cup." She used her best calm-the-patient voice. There was no mistaking the man's outrage—raw and fresh as if he were the very chief from whom the cup had been stolen. The chief who had been insulted. "That's what Uncle Grant and my father and I want. To end the feud."

"End the feud?" The MacDonnart repeated as if she'd suggested the ridiculous, the unheard of, the impossible. "Feuds don't just end."

"And why not?" she asked. The words fell easily from her lips. As a woman doctor, she'd challenged more than one sacred cow. This feud was no holier than any other anachronism she'd faced. "I don't condone what was done centuries ago. So I am returning what was taken. I apologize for the insult on behalf of the Camvilles, and I declare an end to the feud."

"As simple as that," he demanded, obviously dissatisfied.

"If not as simple as that, then what else is necessary?" she asked, spreading her hands before her imploringly. "Is there some tradition here that I am unaware of?"

The MacDonnart studied her for a moment before shaking his head. He turned away and walked to the cold fireplace. With his back to them, he stood with his head bowed as if in deep thought.

She glanced at Ian. He shrugged.

"So we will leave the cup with you," she said, to the man's back. Had she been so foolish as to expect gratitude? From a MacDonnart? "And I wish you happiness in your marriage."

So, it was done. She turned to leave. Ian hurried ahead of her to get the door.

"Wait." The MacDonnart turned from the fireplace. "You're right, of course."

Ian turned and squared his shoulders. "Aye, she is, and you could say thank-you to the lass."

The MacDonnart ignored the old man. "Where are you staying?"

"The village innkeeper found beds for us for the night," Leonora said, puzzled by the question. "Tomorrow I take the train back."

"No, that won't do," The MacDonnart said, striding towards her. "An event as momentous as the end of a feud deserves to be honored. You must stay for the wedding."

"I'm pleased that you think of the end of the feud in that way, but it's really unnecessary for you to invite us to stay," Leonora said, pleased but uncertain about his change of heart. "If I offended you with the remark about hospitality, I'm sorry."

"But it is necessary for you to stay," he insisted,

taking her arm and leading her back into the center of the library. "MacCage is right. The least I can do is express my gratitude. We have a week of festivities planned. Picnics, dances, and dinners. Stay and see the bridal cup shared according to tradition. There's nothing like a Scottish wedding."

"Unless it's a Scots funeral," Ian said.

The MacDonnart glared at him once more and then turned to her again. A charming smile lit his face for the first time. The expression softened the harsh planes of his face and took the icy fire out of his eyes.

She liked the change in him. The fluttering renewed in her belly.

"You must meet my fiancée, Alice," he said, his voice filled with earnestness this time. "And if you would, present the bridal cup to us at the rehearsal dinner. It would be the perfect gesture at the perfect time."

"Here now, I donna know about that." Ian's expression clouded as he turned to Leonora. "Lass, I donna think we should—"

"A rehearsal dinner presentation is an interesting prospect, sir, uh, Lord Glenalder—" Leonora stammered. "I'm sorry, what should I call you?"

"Call me Ross," he said, stepping closer, suddenly the most gracious of hosts. "You'll stay then."

"We can stay at the village inn, lass." Ian tugged at her sleeve. "Ye donna need to do more for the MacDonnarts."

"I hadn't anticipated such a public announcement." She wanted to be gracious; she wanted no misunderstanding about her intentions in returning the cup. "However, it makes sense to be clear about the conclusion of the feud."

"I consider it a gesture of goodwill," he said, still smiling that captivating smile. "It is settled then."

The MacDonnart strode to the bell rope and pulled it. "You'll be my guest."

"I donna like it, lass," the old man muttered with a disapproving wag of his head. "But 'tis for ye to say."

"Then I say we accept your kind invitation, Ross," Leonora said. What harm could there be in attending a real Scottish wedding? "I'll make the presentation of the bridal cup to you and your bride and see it used as it should be."

"Excellent," Ross said, still smiling, but for the first time she noted a darkness in his expression that she hadn't seen before. Was that a shadow in those blue eyes? A harshness in the upward curve of his lips?

"I shall be forever grateful to you, Leonora Camville," he said as he summoned the butler.

Two

"I suppose every great house has a gallery like this," Ross said, speaking more modestly than he felt. He led Leonora Camville into the long black-and-white marbled corridor. Soft morning sunshine glimmered through the tall windows overlooking the white garden.

Breakfast was over. Though the house was already full of wedding guests, he had managed to take her aside, alone, which pleased him in a way he hardly understood. But he wanted to have her to himself, for this tour, at least. A visit to the gallery seldom failed to impress his guests.

"It's a lovely place, but I really wouldn't know about other great houses." With a small smile, she glanced from him to the dark wood-paneled walls crowded with oil portraits opposite the windows. "I came to Glenalder straight from disembarking at Southampton. This is the first lord's house I've visited."

"Right, I should have known," Ross said, determined to match her good manners with his own. "Often the great houses have a place where the family portraits are hung—a gallery, a grand staircase, a library. This is Glenalder's gallery. Here we have all the MacDonnart chiefs back to fourteen hundred and fourteen hundred and fifty-two."

Her eyes grew wide. "That's almost five hundred years."

He nodded. She walked past him, her gaze darting from portrait to portrait, her skirts rustling as she moved. He stepped back to allow her to examine what she would. Today she wore a plum-colored gown almost as plain as her traveling suit. But the color added richness to her thick chestnut hair and brought a decidedly feminine blush to her cheeks. The tiny lace edging around the neckline accented the vulnerable line from her bare earlobe down her graceful neck.

Where was the man in her life? he wondered. She could not have gone overlooked, not with a figure like that. The choice to be unmarried must have been her own.

He caught her scent as she passed him, the light clean aroma of lemon as he'd already noted. It was fascinating how different she was from the other women he knew—even the other Americans he'd met. Open and forthright but contained, possessing a casual graciousness. An easy regalness. Who would have thought to find all that in a Camville?

Of course, he'd already introduced her to his fi-ancée, Alice, at supper. Alice had liked her. The Maid had proven herself a congenial dinner guest, adept at small talk and adaptive to the situation— only slightly startled by the bagpiper playing as he paraded around the dining room three times before the meal was served in true MacDonnart fashion.

He'd realized when she started at the first blare of the pipes that no one had warned her about the tradition. But she'd recovered promptly and smiled at the piper.

She had strolled ahead of him along the gallery and was lingering in front of a small rendering of a piratelike bearded man.

"That's the earliest portrait we have," he said,

moving to stand behind her, surprised to find himself hoping to catch her scent again.

"No offense," she began with a soft chuckle, "but he looks to have been a bit of a pirate."

"He may have been," Ross admitted, amused by her honest observation. "After all, where does enterprise end and piracy begin? The clan goes back further than him, to Dalriada. Fearless raiders, all."

She paused. "Dalriada?"

"The first Scottish settlers," he explained, wondering how much clan history she knew. "Of course, as you can see there are some other family portraits mingled in with those of the chiefs."

"Children wrapped in tartans," she observed with a fond smile as she lingered in front of the youngsters' picture. "And dogs. And is this Glenalder in the background?"

"Yes, before the addition," Ross said, pleased that she had recognized the old section—the original fortified structure—as it had stood two centuries before. "The main part of the house that we occupy now is only about a hundred and fifty years old. We've done our best to keep it modern."

"Modern, hmm, yes," she said, smiling as if enjoying some private joke. She turned to look at the east wing of the house just beyond the white garden. "I like Glenalder very much as it is. Moss on the slates and lichen on the trees. It's like the place is steeped in forever."

He smiled now, unsurprised that even an American-born Camville could appreciate the MacDonnarts' age-old seat. "I can tell you that steeped-in-forever appearance isn't easy to maintain."

"I suppose it's not," she said, her smile fading. "Everything worthwhile brings its burdens, its responsibilities."

He eyed her silently as she strolled on toward another picture. What were her cares, her burdens? What kind of doctor was she? he wondered. Did she mourn when she lost a patient?

She stopped before a life-size portrait.

"This is my father and his father before him," Ross said, following her. "These are the MacDonnarts you might like to know about. This is Adair, the chief who sided with Montrose and led the clan against the Camvilles and others during the English Civil War in the 1640s."

"Yes?" She studied the man in the portrait indifferently.

Ross led her to another portrait. "This is Torran."

"Not another defeater of Camvilles?"

"No, not this time," Ross said, unable to resist smiling at the slight irritation in her voice. "This MacDonnart led the clan in support of Bonnie Prince Charlie in seventeen hundred and forty-six. The Camvilles were there, too, like us supporting the Stuarts against the English at Culloden."

"Where we were all defeated," she finished for him. She stepped closer to study the man in the portrait. "I do know that much history."

He nodded, wondering what had made him point out the one time the MacDonnarts and Camvilles had been allies. His intention in bringing her to the gallery had been to impress her with the MacDonnart heritage.

"It must be very satisfying to be able to look back on your family, on your ancestry like this," she said, moving to study Ross's father again. "You know exactly where you came from, what happened before your time."

"There you are," Alice called brightly from the gallery door where Ross and Leonora had entered earlier. "You dawdle here while the coaches are waiting for us."

"We'll be right along," Ross said, mildly annoyed

with the interruption. "I was just introducing Leonora to the other MacDonnarts."

"Ross can tell you all of their names," Alice said, ruffled skirts sweeping along and blonde curls bouncing as she walked down the gallery to join them. When she reached Ross, he took her hand and, out of habit, gave her a quick kiss on the cheek.

"This portrait is his father." Alice pointed to the appropriate painting.

"Yes," Leonora said, tilting her head as she studied the life-size portrait. "I noted the resemblance. Very handsome. Proud. Stern. Determined." She was silent for a moment and then turned to look directly at Ross. "He looks like a daunting foe. And I think he might have been, perhaps, a little unforgiving."

"Ross's father unforgiving?" Alice laughed and gave a shake of her head. "Oh, no. I knew him well. We visited often when I was a little girl. Isn't that so, Ross? He was never unforgiving and neither is Ross."

She latched onto his arm and smiled up at him. Ross suddenly felt uncomfortable under Alice's trusting regard and the cool scrutiny of The Maid. He'd never thought of himself as forgiving or unforgiving, but he had always made an effort to be fair.

"I won't bore you with a recitation of all my ancestors' names, Leonora." He put his hand over Alice's to mollify her.

"Darling." Alice urged him toward the gallery door. "It's time we climbed aboard the coaches and set off for the village. Come, along, Leonora. The village fair awaits us."

"Of course." Leonora smiled politely. "Thank you for introducing me to the MacDonnarts."

"My pleasure." He looked into those serene eyes and was surprised to find himself regretting that it was Alice's hand on his arm and not hers.

Still smiling, Leonora turned back for one last

glance at the MacDonnart gallery; then she followed him and Alice. He allowed Alice to lead them as she chattered on about the details of the fair. He smiled to himself, satisfied that he'd accomplished what he'd set out to do.

Leonora Camville was properly impressed with the MacDonnart heritage.

Ian was waiting for her near one of the three carriages lined up in front of Glenalder. She smiled at the sight of him. He looked vaguely uncomfortable surrounded by MacDonnart wedding guests.

Her walking boots crunched on the gravel drive as she approached. It was a glorious morning. The sky was clear, the sunshine bright, and the air filled with birdsong. Perfect for the day's trip to the nearby village fair.

"Is The MacDonnart treating you right, lass?" Ian demanded under his breath as soon as she reached his side. The day before, they had been separated soon after the interview in the library with Ross. At the time Ian had seemed to think it natural to be directed to the servants' quarters while she was escorted by Stratton to a spacious room overlooking the front drive. She'd not seen Ian again until dinnertime. Then he'd been seated at the far end or the table from the host—obviously below the salt—while she'd been included near the head. In the social commotion, they'd been unable to compare notes.

"Is he being respectful?" Ian asked.

"Of course, The MacDonnart is being respectful," Leonora said, amused by his suspicions but reluctant to admit she was being treated like royalty.

After she'd been shown to her room, a young maid had appeared and unpacked her few things. Then the servant had insisted on styling her hair and helping her dress for dinner. Leonora was accustomed to the aid of a housekeeper, but a personal maid was luxury. "Why wouldn't he be respectful? The MacDonnart is a perfectly civilized man who is proud of his family and pleased to be a good host at his wedding."

"Civilized?" Ian scoffed as he surveyed the other wedding guests. "Aye, so he would have ye think. But I'm satisfied if ye are that he be treating ye as well as the others."

Men in top hats and ladies in leg-of-mutton-sleeve gowns were climbing into the carriages. She saw two couples she had not met the night before. New arrivals? More family? The house, huge as it was, already seemed to be bursting at the seams with overnight guests, and the wedding was still four days away.

Glancing at the lead coach, she saw Ross help Alice into the handsome barouche. Her mother, Lady Preston, had already made herself comfortable in the vehicle. The top was fastened down so the passengers could enjoy the fine weather and passers-by could admire the happy couple.

Alice was talking excitedly. Ross moved to sit with his back to the driver's box and nodded politely as he listened to her. Alice fluttered her tiny white hands. She was exactly the kind of dainty female who conformed to the Victorian model of womanhood. For the first time in years, Leonora regretted that she did not fit the mold.

Alice had a pale heart-shaped face with wide brown eyes, a small pug nose, and a perfect little bow-shaped mouth. She clearly was already settling herself into the role of The MacDonnart's hostess. She was going to make a beautiful bride. An odd thought niggled Leonora. "Do you think he loves her?"

"What, lass?" Ian opened the coach door for her and stared, clearly mystified by her question.

"Do you think Ross MacDonnart loves Alice Preston?" she asked. It wasn't any of her business, but she wanted to know.

"How would I know?" Ian's gaze followed hers toward the happy couple. "Never the mind. It doesna signify. The MacDonnart is doing his duty. No chief marries for love. He marries for the good of the clan. The Prestons are a neighboring clan. 'Tis tradition for them and the MacDonnarts to marry. Ross, his brother, Kerr, and Alice grew up together. The wedding day was practically set the day Alice was born."

"An arranged marriage in this day and age?" Though the thought shocked Leonora, it gratified her to think that Ross didn't necessarily love Alice. Obviously he was a man who knew his duty and would do it. Yet, she did not like to believe that he would sacrifice his heart for duty alone. "This is a new age. The chief's leadership is not official. Not legally recognized."

"The MacDonnart knows his duty." Ian waved reality aside. "A chief marries a woman who brings strength to the clan, a respected name, good blood, a strong body for childbearin', and a courageous heart. She has to be a woman who can wipe the tears from a bairn's eyes and then rally the warriors to battle if the chief canna do it himself."

She had to smile at Ian—and herself. If she'd heard his words on a Boston street corner with streetcars rumbling by, she would have laughed. But here, with the Highlands looming just beyond ancient Glenalder's towers and the wolfhounds romping across the lawn, Ian's observation about duty and what made a good chief's wife made perfect sense.

Ian's eyes narrowed as he leaned against the open coach door. "And what do you think of the match, lass? Do you think he loves her?"

"I think he treats her as if she were his little sister." She glanced at Alice and allowed her professional eye to make an assessment. "I think the bride looks healthy enough to bear lively children if that is a necessary qualification. But Alice is too young to know her mind."

"Well, be that as it may, in my estimation, The MacDonnart has made a poor choice of a bride." Ian leaned close. "She's too docile, too fashionable, and too English. But now, that be his mistake, not ours."

Leonora gazed at Alice in the barouche again. Had Ross made a poor choice? Or had he chosen to do his duty? More important, had he chosen right for his heart? As she watched, Alice gazed adoringly across at Ross. Ross smiled in return.

Annoyed with her useless speculation, Leonora gave herself a mental shake. What Ross felt for his bride-to-be was none of her affair. He'd given her a guided tour of the Glenalder gallery to impress her. Nothing more.

And she had been impressed. MacDonnart after MacDonnart. Dalriada. Bonnie Prince Charlie and Culloden.

"Here you go, lass," Ian said, waving toward the empty carriage. "You ride in here, and I'll be above on the box."

She hesitated, her hand on the door, but her foot on the ground—her mind still filled with MacDonnart faces. "Ian? Are there no portraits of the Camvilles?"

" 'Course there are portraits of Camvilles." He blustered with indignation that she should even think otherwise.

"Where? Uncle Grant told me Castle Camville was destroyed years ago, before the family left Scotland."

"Nevertheless, the Camvilles have their ancestors, too, lass." Pride flashed in the old man's eyes. "Never doubt it. They're not all in one place, the great Camvilles. But I can show ye one or two. Get in the carriage."

Leonora climbed in and other guests piled in after her. During the short drive to the village, friendly chatter in the carriage never ceased. She made a point to join in. The wedding guests were pleased and curious to meet the American guest. More than one had raised a brow when she told them her last name.

As soon as the coaches stopped, the company descended on the village green in the mood for a fine celebration. Delicious smells of cut greenery and food cooking over open fires filled the air. Laughter drifted on the breeze, and she could hear a piper tuning up his instrument.

Ian appeared and plucked at her arm. "Come along. I'll show you Camvilles, lass."

They crossed a stone bridge that spanned a stream bubbling through the center of the village. With only a few words, Ian led her to a modest square stone church or kirk, as he called it. The tall heavy wooden door creaked as Ian pushed it open and ushered her into the cool dark depths of the sturdy unpretentious place of worship. While her eyes adjusted to the dimness, the sweet scent of incense and the moldy smell of dampness reached her.

"The Camvilles worshiped here until they left for America." Ian removed his hat and then led the way to the side aisle. "After their home seat was ruined and their chapel lost. 'Twere always generous to the kirk, they were."

Just like Papa and Uncle Grant, Leonora thought. Always donating something to their Boston church.

"And the MacDonnarts?" Leonora asked.

"They attend the redbrick church on the other side of the village." Ian led her to an alcove where a candle burned, offering the only light besides the jewel-colored rays that fell through the stained-glass windows. On the wall hung a large portrait of a handsome man in a red uniform. Across his chest was draped a plaid.

"The Camville plaid," she whispered.

"Meet Ardal Camville, Ewen's father," Ian said, the pride in his voice unmistakable. He stood back as if he were making a personal introduction. "Meet one of yer ancestors, lass."

"My great-grandfather," she calculated.

"And a fine man he was," Ian said. "A much decorated officer and a strong chief. Saw action in India."

Ian's pride was contagious. It crept into her soul. The resemblance of the man in the portrait to her father was eerie—and reassuring. She was a part of something much larger than herself, something real and good. Men and women. Family and spirit.

"While he was away, his wife served as chief in his stead," Ian said, a glint of defiance in his eyes. There was no mistaking it, even in the darkness. "Held the Camville men together and made sure the barins were fed. Donna ye believe them stories about the Camvilles being outlaws, lass. When they leave the Highlands, when the Camvilles reach out from under the MacDonnarts' power, they have always become men of influence and substance. Men to be reckoned with."

With a flutter of excitement, she turned to glance around the church. "Are there others?"

"No, not paintings, but here." He led the way toward the altar. When he stopped in the aisle, Leonora almost bumped into him. He was gazing down at a brass panel in the floor.

"There's a Camville and his wife here, but I donna know how far back they were laid to rest in this place. The dates are worn off with the years."

"Beneath the floor of the church?"

"In those days, 'twas a place of honor," Ian said. "There be portraits of Camvilles in other places. A library in Glasgow at the university, I think. There be one or two in Parliament in Edinburgh. Hold ye head high, lass. I donna know what the Camvilles have done in America, but they left their mark here in their homeland and a mark to be proud of, it is."

The church door creaked, startling her. She and Ian turned as a shaft of light pierced the gloom.

"Leonora?"

She recognized Ross's voice and his hatless silhouette immediately. Her heart warmed. Why had he followed them when he had so many guests and Alice to see to? Whatever his reason, she was glad that he had.

But at her side, she felt Ian bristle. She wondered if the old man had seen the same shadows in Ross's eyes that she'd seen the day before in the library.

Three

The sunlight vanished as the kirk door swung closed. Ross stood in the dark vestibule waiting for his eyes to adjust. He was certain he'd seen old Mac-Cage lead Leonora off in this direction. He did not like the old man keeping her to himself when she was a MacDonnart guest. Who knew what prideful Camville nonsense the old coot would fill her head with. Besides that, Ross could not rid himself of the desire to have her close so he could hear her husky voice and savor her throaty laugh.

"We're here," she called softly. Once again that rich voice stirred something indefinable inside him. He turned toward the sound. After a moment he could see shadows of them, Ian and Leonora, in the Camville alcove. He started toward them.

"The dancing is about to begin on the green," he said, when he reached them. "Alice and I thought you would like to see some true Highland footwork."

Ian harrumphed.

"That's kind of you," Leonora said, smiling. "Ian was just showing me the portrait of Ardal Camville."

"So I see." Ross smiled to make his words light, but Ian did not return the polite expression. "What stories are you telling our esteemed guest from America?"

"What's it to ye, MacDonnart?" MacCage's voice was little more than a growl.

Ross ignored the old man and turned his smile on Leonora.

"This was my idea," she said, studying Ardal. "Your tour of the MacDonnart gallery inspired me to ask about my ancestors."

"So I brought her here to introduce her to one." Ian glared at him.

Ross knew that the old scamp suspected that he wanted more from Leonora than just the public return of the bridal cup.

"I'm glad you thought of it," he lied, eyeing Ardal's portrait. Nearly a century ago, the old chief had donned his uniform and left for India while his warrior wife nearly stole the MacDonnarts blind of their cattle. It was a tale he had never forgotten. But Leonora did not need to hear it. It would only make her ask questions that he did not want to answer. "I'd forgotten about this fine old work of a man who was a hero, a worthy son of Scotland, even if he was not a MacDonnart."

"So now I know where I come from, too." Leonora laughed, obviously pleased. "Thank you, Ian, for bringing me here."

Her remark grated over Ross's pride. He wished he had had the good sense to show her Ardal's portrait and steal the advantage from MacCage.

"And there be more such Camvilles," Ian added, his shoulders square, his tone cold. "Heroes, all."

"I'm sure there are." Ross reached for Leonora's arm, eager to get her out of the kirk. "It's too fair a day to spend in a dark church. The dance contest is about to begin."

"Good, I want to see the dancing," Leonora said, allowing him to lead her from the Camville alcove.

Relieved that her curiosity was satisfied, Ross squeezed her hand and shoved the heavy door open. He led her into the sunlight, away from the past.

When the sun struck his face, he realized that the

feud was the last thing he wanted to think of today. He just wanted to play host and enjoy The Maid of the Camville's company.

A wooden stage had been built on the village green. Before the stage set a long table with chairs arranged behind it. Leonora saw Alice seated there, conversing with the vicar.

"Here we are." Ross led her to the table in front of the stage. "Alice, the vicar, the mayor, and I have been invited to be judges of the dancing. We thought perhaps you'd like to join us."

Suddenly aware of the solidness of his arm beneath her hand and her pleasure in the feel of it, she released him. The heat of a blush flooded into her cheeks. He did not seem to notice. She prayed no one else had either. She grasped her handbag with both hands and was alternately embarrassed and annoyed with herself for being so pleased that he'd sought her out in the church. He was her host—and another woman's fiancé, for heaven's sake. Why was she behaving like a schoolgirl with a crush? She must really get control of her reaction to him.

"Yes, I'd like to join you, thank you," she said.

"I promise you'll see some of the finest Highland dancing there is to see," Alice said. "The dancers come from afar to perform at the Glenalder fair."

Off to the side several pipers were tuning up and a score of youngsters in Highland dress were rehearsing steps and tending to their shoes. The wedding guests were strolling across the green between the shops and booths, while others were seating themselves on the benches prepared for the stage audience.

"Truly from afar?" Leonora made herself smile at Alice. "How exciting."

Soon she was seated at the table, Ross between her

and Alice. Ian, who had followed them from the church, stuck his hands into his pockets and wandered off in the direction of the horses.

The village mayor, a somber narrow-faced man with heavy dark brows and a shock of gray hair, presided over the activities. He moved things along with a straight-faced wit that had Leonora and all the audience laughing.

The dancing was loud and lively, the children smiling even as they remained intent on outperforming the previous group of dancers. Ross discussed the merits of each group with her before he wrote down his score. He leaned close, dividing his attention between her and Alice, to help her discern the quality of the footwork or the position of the dancers' hands.

Leonora soon found herself watching for the points he judged as vital to a superior performance. The man was clearly a perfectionist but that never kept him from praising the contestants. She enjoyed herself in his company, and she loved watching the apple-cheeked children.

When the contest was over, the pipers continued to play their lilting tunes as Alice, the vicar, and Ross put their heads together to tally the scores. Then Ross escorted Alice up the steps of the stage. As the mayor announced each winner, they presented a small loving cup to the group's leader.

"And do they not make a fine couple?" the vicar asked, applauding as Alice and Ross congratulated a bashful child. The vicar was a pink round-faced man with thinning silvery hair, thick white whiskers, and a benign smile.

"Yes, indeed," Leonora agreed as she, too, applauded for the winner. There was no denying they made an attractive couple, Ross and Alice. Alice stood, smiling, petite and fashionable with her lace-trimmed parasol and wearing a high-collar, snug-waisted walking costume. Ross loomed at her side, tall, bareheaded but distinguished and in authority, though obviously allowing the mayor to take charge.

Was this a chief's duty then? Being chief was more than making clan decisions. It was also about setting an example of generosity and concern for people. About upholding traditions and giving relatives and followers a sense of self and a role to emulate? Ross and Alice, the laird and his lady doing their duty.

How lucky Alice was. A cold twinge of envy skittered through Leonora's belly, catching her by surprise. Surely she'd outgrown such a childish emotion. She hadn't felt jealous since she'd been a schoolgirl and watched Janet hook her arm possessively through that of Jamie Hamilton, the banker's son. Leonora had known then that she would never marry. She'd made her choice to become a doctor, and she knew that marriage and medicine would never mix. Even a schoolteacher had to give up her calling when she married. A woman doctor could hardly expect to enjoy a family, too.

Here she was feeling jealous because . . . Why? Because Uncle Grant's death had made her doubt whether she was as good a doctor as she aspired to be? Because Alice and Ross looked as though they would be happy together? Because she knew her future would never hold such contentment for her?

She stirred in her chair, unhappy with herself, with her feelings. *Be glad that you've come to Scotland now,* she told herself. The timing was perfect. By some great good fortune she'd arrived just in time to return the cup to a couple who deserved to share it. *Be glad.*

But she wasn't. The icy green niggling in her belly persisted. She wasn't glad at all.

Alice and Ross stepped down from the stage hand-in-hand.

"Now it is time for the real dancing to begin."

The vicar rose from his chair and waved to his wife whom he'd introduced to Leonora earlier. The lady was an invalid in a wheelchair and sat on the village green surrounded by her friends. "My missus doesn't dance any more," the vicar said. "But we'd be pleased if you'd be my partner for the grand march."

Leonora had to smile at such generosity. "It would be my pleasure, sir."

She took his plump hand and joined the promenade on the green, determined to enjoy the festivities and forget her mean-spirited emotions.

Alice and Ross led the march, obviously a local Scots custom, as the vicar said they would. With couples lined up behind them, they paraded across the green to the grand strains of the pipers. When the march was done, the first dance began, Alice and Ross leading all of the couples in a reel. Then the dancing was open to any who cared to join in. And join in they did with exuberance.

To Leonora's surprise, the vicar proved a tireless and spontaneous dancer. He did not care in the least that she was ignorant of the steps and could only follow the examples she saw. Everyone laughed and helped her through the complicated figures. She danced, dance after dance.

The fresh air and activity cleared her head and swept back the edges of the grief that had overshadowed her mood since Uncle Grant's death. With a smile, she followed the vicar's example and gave herself to the joy of the dance.

Suddenly, a firm hand grasped her wrist. The heat of him coursed through her. She knew instantly that it was Ross. She glanced around to see him smiling at her, that captivating smile—without a hint of the darkness in his eyes, no harsh curve to his mouth.

"No, it goes like this," Ross said, demonstrating the fancy footwork for her once more. His movements were easy, free, and matched the music perfectly.

When she looked into his face, he was smiling, with her, not at her. "I haven't been doing this all my life," she said, suddenly self-conscious.

His smile faded. "Then what have you been doing all your life?" he asked as they stood motionless in the midst of the other couples.

"Very polite waltzes," she said, ignoring the obvious larger meaning of his question. Her Boston upbringing seemed tame and inhibited.

"Sometimes a polka," she added with a shrug.

"So be it," he said, leading her off across the green in the polka step, which suited the music well enough. She took energy from the heat of his fingers at her hip, his thumb pressing against her rib. Around and around they went. She savored the feel of his touch.

Tossing her head back, she laughed—truly laughed—for the first time in months. For the first time since Uncle Grant had died. The last weight of her grief vanished.

"Now, you have it," Ross said, laughing with her and speeding up their rhythm at the same time. "Even America can't take the love of dancing out of a Scot."

Leonora laughed with him again, though she knew it was no laughing matter. There was nothing logical about how she felt, certainly nothing any medical book could describe beyond the physical symptoms. The fluttering heart, the sweaty palms, the heat of a blush in her cheeks.

She'd experienced some of the symptoms before during her one futile affair of the heart with Stephen. But he had never made her feel this way—giddy and warm enough to melt. Even after they'd made love, it wasn't like this.

She had believed she loved Stephen and that he

loved her. As a fellow medical student, she was certain he would understand her desire to be a doctor—and have a family. In the end, of course, he hadn't understood at all.

But this pleasure—what was happening to her? Surely she wasn't falling in love with Ross, The MacDonnart, the Camvilles' foe—a man engaged to be married in four days? It could not happen.

The pipers stopped playing. Ross reluctantly released Leonora. But he could not bear the loss of the physical connection. He did not understand why her touch was so important and refused even to acknowledge the question. He just grasped her hand instead. Several tendrils of her hair had come loose, curling into unruly ringlets. He resisted the urge to tug on one. A blush pinkened her cheeks, stirring urges in him that were even harder to resist than holding her hand.

"Come on; let's find some refreshment," he said, to distract himself from thoughts he should not be having.

She nodded. He led her to the punch table in front of the village tavern.

"Ross MacDonnart," Alice said suddenly appearing at his side. "Don't you press that foul drink on our guest."

Ross glanced over his shoulder at her, surprised by her interest in Leonora. "Our guest needs some refreshment."

"Whiskey punch?" Alice turned to Leonora and in a conspiratorial whisper loud enough for him to hear said, "He is normally a very thoughtful host."

Leonora took the cup he offered and smiled up at him. "Ross is an excellent host."

Had Helen of Troy smiled at Paris like that? he wondered. No wonder the Trojans had kidnapped her and set the great armies of the ancient world to war. "There you are, Alice. Our guest endorses my hospitality."

"I did not mean to cast aspersions on anyone's hospitality, darling, only on the punch." Alice's lips pursed, then she laughed. "By the by, when does Kerr join us?"

"Kerr is scheduled to arrive tomorrow evening," Ross said. He knew how Alice felt. The wedding party would not be complete until his younger brother arrived. Kerr would bring the perfect touch of lightheartedness to the festivities.

"Wonderful, you'll love meeting Kerr, Leonora," Alice said, touching Ross's arm. "But honestly, the punch is a dreadful drink. Don't imbibe just to be polite. The next thing Ross will offer you is haggis."

"I know about haggis," Leonora said. "My Aunt Fiona made it every New Year's and whiskey punch, too. Haggis is not my favorite, but I confess to a certain fondness for a nip of fine Scotch whiskey for restorative purposes, of course."

"To restorative purposes." Ross offered a toast. Alice would never touch whiskey, but he suspected that this American Camville was made of sterner stuff. To his satisfaction, Leonora sipped her punch without blinking.

"Well, it seems you can stand your own ground, Leonora," Alice said with a laugh. "Excuse me, darlings, I see my mother waving. The dear loves the crafts she can find in the shops here."

"If she wants something, tell the merchant to put it on my account," Ross said.

Alice bounced up on her toes to kiss him on the cheek. "You are too good to us, my lord." She giggled and was off, scurrying across the green toward her mother, nodding greetings to acquaintances as she went.

"She will be a lovely bride," Leonora said, then drained her punch cup.

"Um, yes," Ross agreed, not really wanting to think about Alice or the wedding. He took Leonora's arm and led her away from the punch table.

"So you've sampled Scotch whiskey and haggis. Then your family didn't deny their Scot heritage completely."

"On the contrary," Leonora said. "There were tales, but Papa didn't like to speak of the feud, and he refused to allow anyone else to speak of it in his presence."

"No revered family portraits hung on the walls?" he asked.

"Only a few family things survive," she said. "A spinning wheel. A Bible. An old doctor's bag. There were doctors in the family before my father. But no swords or drums. No dirks or shields. My father was not a warlike man, nor was Uncle Grant. I didn't know about the bridal cup until Uncle Grant died two months ago."

Ross glanced in the direction of the horses where he'd last seen MacCage. Sure enough, the old man was still there, hands in his pockets, talking to one of the traders.

"Did Ian take you to see the Camville seat?" he asked.

"No, he offered to," Leonora said. "But I didn't see any purpose in it then. After seeing Glenalder, I've regretted my turning him down."

"Then I'll take you," Ross said, surprising himself with the offer.

"I don't want to impose," she protested. "You have the wedding guests and all. And Alice."

"No, it's the least I can do," he said, suddenly realizing how much he wanted to be there to see her face when she first laid eyes on the ruins of Castle Camville. "Alice will understand. It's right that you

should know about your family. It's not far from
here. We will go tomorrow. In the meantime, what
do you know about caber tossing?"

"Very little." She cast him that Helen of Troy
smile again. "Will you tell me about it?"

For that smile, he'd tell her anything. So he began
to describe the Highland game.

Four

When Leonora had decided to make this journey to return the bridal cup, investigating her Scottish heritage seemed to have little to do with her purpose. But now with Ian's prompting, and Ross's, too, knowing more about the Camvilles had become almost as imperative as fulfilling her promise to Uncle Grant. Was Castle Camville a grand place like Glenalder set among the trees and lawns? she wondered. Or was Castle Camville something different—a mountaintop fortress, a moorside manse?

The morning after the village fair, however, she learned from the footman at the breakfast table that the men had gone off either shooting or fishing. The ladies, who did not join the gentlemen, were sequestered with Alice for dress fittings. Neither activity seemed the place for her. Ross had apparently forgotten about his promise to take her to Castle Camville. And it was no wonder.

She had been involved in two high-society weddings in Boston, her best friend's from grammar school and Janet's. She thought she knew all about the whirlwind of showers, formal dinners, and balls necessary with nuptials between two influential families. But the Preston-MacDonnart wedding made the others seem like simple affairs.

Daily, the guest list at Glenalder House increased, and each evening the dining room table grew longer and more crowded. Everyday, activities were embarked upon for the amusement of the gentlemen and the ladies: drives, highland hikes, pony trekking, shooting, picnics, lawn games. And every evening, cards, parlor games, and dancing.

When Leonora had remarked on the flurry of festivities, Ian frowned and shrugged. " 'Tis the usual."

The man simply refused to enjoy himself under The MacDonnart roof. Leonora declined to take a similar view. She was enjoying herself and intended to continue to do so. Ross MacDonnart was an excellent host. There was no doubt in her mind that the return of the bridal cup would be a crowning event of the wedding celebration, just as Ross had suggested.

She lingered over the breakfast table, disappointed, sipping her tea and reminding herself that Ross had many guests and his bride-to-be to see to. It was hardly proper for a betrothed man to single out an unmarried lady to entertain. She would find Ian. He would take her to Castle Camville, she decided. A footman offered her more tea, but she waved him away just as Stratton, the butler, walked in.

"Mis—Dr. Camville, there you are," he said, obviously relieved to have found her. "His lordship is waiting for you in the front drive. He said to apologize. He would have come for you himself, but he is driving today. I hope you do not mind, I took the liberty of bringing your wrap," Stratton said, holding up her jacket.

So Ross had remembered her after all, she thought with a guilty, bittersweet pang of pleasure. She slipped into her jacket and hurried out of the breakfast room.

She found him in the drive, seated in a two-wheeled, one-horse gig holding the reins of a sturdy little garron.

"Alice agreed that I should show our American

guest her family's old home," he said, offering her a
hand as she climbed into the gig. "I would have
been along sooner. But I wanted to see that the gentlemen were settled in their shooting for the day.
Then I had to see how the new steam engine is operating."

"Steam engine to power what?" she asked, out of
curiosity.

"The lumber mill," he said. "An expanding venture of mine."

"I see," she said, settling on the seat next to him.
Who would have expected a clan chief to be tinker-
ing with a steam engine? "And how is the steam
engine doing?"

"Very well," he said, a genuinely pleased smile on
his lips. "But enough of business. Now we'll show
you the real Highlands."

They were soon headed out of the valley and up
into the mountains. He was wearing a tweed shooting jacket with leather elbow patches that made him
look every bit the country gentleman. But as usual,
he was arrogantly, recklessly hatless. The morning
breeze ruffled his dark hair.

He grinned at her—a disarming expression—as
he urged the well-groomed, inelegant but sure-
footed pony up a stony trail beside the wild stream.
As they went, the trail narrowed to little more than
a path, barely wide enough for the gig.

They followed the ridge of the hills upward, beyond the pines and alders of the valley. Then they
crested the ridge and Glenalder was left behind.
Ross pointed out the sights, identified the birds,
spied the shy animals, and named the soaring
rounded mountains for her. The highest white-
capped mountains pressed their shoulders against
the expansive blue sky and draped their rocky skirts
into the valleys.

He knew his land, and the words he spoke were

filled with affection for the rocks, the trees, and the wildlife. She gazed up at the sky and the land absorbing his appreciation. She was a world away from the clamor of Boston's narrow streets, and she loved it. Inside her, she felt some memory of this place, this homeland, begin to stir from its slumber.

They crested another ridge and drove into a grove of trees again, but not before Leonora glimpsed a long finger of blue water stretched along the fold of the valley. The pure beauty of it made her suck in a breath of the cold sharp air. It was all so beautiful, inspiring, and oddly familiar.

"There it is," Ross said, holding the reins in one hand and leaning close to point out something in the distance to the north.

"Where? What is it?" She tried to sight down his arm to see what he was pointing out, but the spicy scent of him filled her head. Momentarily she was distracted by his nearness. Her belly went weightless. She wanted to smell more of him.

He turned his face to her slightly. His cheek was so near hers she could see how smooth shaven he was, and those thick dark lashes . . . and his lips . . . What was it like to kiss him? He might be cold and frosty in his determination, but in his knowledge for his land and his ancestors there was warmth—even passion.

"Where?" she asked, forcing herself to look away in the direction where he pointed.

"Castle Camville sits on a peninsula in Lochrowan," he murmured without moving away. His breath tingled on her cheek.

She knew he wasn't looking at the castle either. Abruptly she pulled away. "I see it," she lied. For the first time she wondered about the wisdom of coming on this trip without Ian or Alice.

"Good, it won't take us long to get there now," he said, slapping the reins on the pony's back.

Leonora watched for the castle as they drove on. A little farther down the path between the trees, she glimpsed the towering arches of a ruin at the water's edge—gray and green, lichen-layered stone against the rough blue of the loch.

"It's been in ruins for a long time," she said, torn between dismay at the sight of the rubble and delight in the pure romanticism of the remnants. If Glenalder was a castle crowned with conical towers out of a Grimm's fairy tale, Castle Camville was a medieval fortress out of a Sir Walter Scott yarn.

"Yes, almost a hundred and fifty years," Ross said. "Since Culloden."

Neither of them spoke again as the pony picked its way down the winding path toward the shore. Clouds gathered, white and airy at first, then graying, darkening, to lower over the loch by the time they reached the ruin. A cold wind came up, icy enough to cut through the fabric of her jacket but not strong enough to blow away the mist that settled across the water. The far shore was barely visible when she climbed out of the gig. In her eagerness to explore the ruins, she forgot to wait for Ross.

So this is it, she thought as she stood at the foot of the bridge. Castle Camville, not a grand house, not a mountaintop retreat, but the clan seat and the proud sentinel of Lochrowan.

Leonora was out of the gig before Ross could tie the reins to the whip. He jumped out to follow her as quickly as he could.

He hardly ever visited Castle Camville. As boys, he and Kerr had explored the ruins and played conquering warriors there. Now, looted for its stone, the place was little more than a symbol of MacDonnart victory, if that. It was not a place MacDonnarts cared about beyond the knowledge that the clan that had once ruled from the rocky peninsula was long gone, vanquished to a land beyond the sea.

"Wait," he called, starting across the bridge after her. She was already ten yards ahead of him. She was going to break her neck if he didn't stop her. "If you insist on going out on the peninsula, at least let me lead the way. Who knows how treacherous these stones are now."

She turned to him, laughing, clearly pleased with the adventure. "They've been here a few centuries. I hardly think they'll give way now."

"Yes, well, let's not take a chance." Ross caught up with her and moved ahead, eyeing the stability of the half of the bridge that remained. Without saying more, he reached back for her hand and began to navigate the way. "All we need is for something to happen to you," he said. "Then those American Camvilles will pack up and come home to even the score."

She laughed again. "The Camvilles of Boston, and there are many of us, doctors, lawyers, bankers, engineers. We are very pleased with our lives in America. Uncle Grant invested in steel mills. My sister's husband is in railroads. I don't think they will be coming back, except to sightsee." Then she lifted her chin and went on. "And we've done other things, too. My father helped build a hospital and fund a medical school. If I may boast, I helped secure the funding for a women's clinic."

"Impressive accomplishments," he said. Camville success was no surprise. They had always been capable enough.

He and Leonora had reached the castle side of the bridge. He released her hand when she tugged eagerly to hurry on toward the gate. He followed her beneath the arch and into the ruin.

"This was quite a fortification." She gazed up at what remained of the castle curtain wall. She held out her hands and turned around. "And this would have been what?"

He surveyed the open space. "The bailey, I think."

"And that?" She pointed toward a wall on the loch side of the peninsula where enough of the structure remained to indicate five peaked Gothic-style windows.

"The great hall most likely," he said, wondering why he felt obliged to satisfy her curiosity. "I really don't know much about castles."

"And the chapel?"

"Probably on an upper floor." He looked upward as she did. Nothing remained to give a hint of a place of worship.

"The English blew it up out of spite after Culloden," he said.

"Why didn't the English blow up Glenalder?" She turned to him, a curious challenge in her eyes.

"They would have if it had not been for the fast talking and generous gifts from The MacDonnart of the time, Innis."

"And the Camvilles were too proud or too poor to do the same thing?" she asked.

"Some of both, I suspect." He moved closer to her. "It was the beginning of the end for them."

"Or maybe it was the end of the old and the beginning of the new," she said, plainly unwilling to accept the notion of defeat.

"However you want to look at it." He shrugged. Let her delude herself for the moment if she wanted. She was the one who had shown up on his doorstep begging to return the bridal cup. "The fact is Lochrowan and Castle Camville have been MacDonnart holdings for over fifty years."

She took a deep breath and closed her eyes.

A light mist began to fall, studding her chestnut hair with a thousand glittering dewdrop jewels. She looked like a princess, a bejeweled warrior princess.

When she opened her eyes again, she frowned and moved away toward the stone arch. Her mood had changed. He could feel the difference, see it in the way she moved. Slower. Each step more deliberate.

"The truth is the MacDonnarts set out to usurp Camville holdings centuries ago for only God knows what reasons," she said with a small, tight, angry smile.

The accusation stung. Frowning, Ross struggled with the anger only the Camville feud could draw out of him. "The truth is the Camvilles were cattle thieves."

Leonora faced him silently, her gaze level, her chin tipped at a resolute angle. "Well, they certainly haven't been for the past fifty years. That's over now, right?"

"Is that what you believe?" Ross caught her arm and gently swung her around to face him. Boldly, he cupped her chin in his hand, unable to take his gaze from her ripe lower lip, glistening from the mist. To his surprise and pleasure, she did not pull away from him. "You think centuries of bad blood can be ignored, can be wiped away and forgotten because you've decided to return a cup?" he demanded.

"Why not? Forgiven if not forgotten," she said toe-to-toe with him, prideful and unyielding.

"You think there should be no price to pay for the past?"

"What pri—"

Her mist-jeweled hair and her pride were too much for him. His mouth descended on hers. The truth was, the Camvilles had been defeated. He was not about to allow them to quit the field, without surrender.

He expected her to protest, but a low groan escaped her, deep and appealing. His anger faltered.

Her lips were warm, firm, and accepting—more than accepting. She kissed him back.

Confused, he released her, only long enough to gaze down into her face. Her eyes were closed and her mouth still raised to his, her hands warm and open pressed against his chest.

He framed her face with his hands.

"Everything has a price," he whispered, his lips nearly brushing against hers, his voice harsh with desire.

A furrow formed between her winged brows. She shook her head imperceptibly. "Hasn't it been paid?" She added huskily, "The Camvilles are gone and Lochrowan is yours. What more do you want?"

So much more. He bit back the words. "You" he wanted to say. Instead, he hungrily lowered his mouth to hers again.

Her arms slipped around his waist. Her lips parted for him. He swept her mouth with his tongue still determined to rid her of Camville pride. But he found none. He only tasted burning sweetness, moist, disarming, seductive, achingly rich acceptance. He wanted more of it.

He pressed her backward against the wall, his body aching to take possession, to pleasure her, to hear that sweet moan of hers again and again and again. His lips savored hers. Leonora returned his kisses as ravenously as he bestowed them. Her hands threaded into his hair, holding him as ferociously as he held her.

An icy cold finger ran down his spine. He started, but he did not release her. A cold sobering shower pelted down on them, drenching his head, and trickling down his back.

"What are we doing?" she whispered when he looked into her face again. The furrow returned. She touched his cheek, his jaw. He turned his head slightly to catch her fingertips with his lips. In spite of her words of denial, she did not push him away. "I mean, there is Alice," she added.

He did not move, caught in a sweet painful web of desire. He stared into her face, at her smooth skin, flushed from his kisses.

"Right, Alice." Abruptly, his whole being lurched, his head, his heart, his soul. He knew something had changed

His bearings lost, he stepped away from Leonora and raked his fingers through his wet hair. He felt as though he had just been ejected from heaven onto a cold rocky reality. She stared back at him, concern on her face. "That was unforgivable," he said.

"No, I provoked you," she stammered, hastily sliding along the wall away from him, creating a distance he regretted. "We shouldn't have come here alone, Ross. Even with Alice's approval."

He stepped toward her but stopped. He wanted to deny what she said. But his anger returned, not the feud anger, however, something vague and irritatingly fuzzy. Something more frustrating than their aborted kiss.

The rain grew heavier and began to soak their clothes. Dealing with the weather seemed safer and more imperative than dealing with his feelings.

"Let's get you out of here." He grasped her arm and led her out of the Castle Camville along the crumbling bridge.

Five

Leonora hastened to help Ross raise the top on the gig against the downpour. There was little time to dream over a kiss. But by the time they had it set into place, the rain had returned to a light drizzle. Even though their clothes were already wet and becoming chilly against their skin, the protection overhead felt good. As the gig pulled away, she glanced back at Castle Camville for one last look.

The stone arches had been swallowed by the fog. They'd vanished as if they'd never existed. As if the castle had never been the site of the most exciting, extraordinary kiss she'd ever experienced. Almost merciless at first. Fierce, demanding. But then it had changed, fracturing like a kaleidoscope into other patterns of emotion. Passionate. Tender. Sweetly possessive.

Her insides quivered at the memory of it.

When she glanced at Ross, his features were stony. He was angry. Neither spoke.

The dampness crept into Leonora's bones. The situation was impossible, of course. He was The Mac-Donnart. Tradition had him engaged to wed another. She should never have allowed her attraction to show, to compromise his position. She should never have allowed something as personal as the kiss to pass between them.

When Glenalder came into view, the place was a

flurry of activity with wagons and riders pulling into the stable yard. Apparently the men, also cold and damp from the rain, were returning from their shoot. She was thankful for the confusion. Their awkward return would hardly be noticed in the turmoil.

She decided to offer Ross the only olive branch she could. "Perhaps it would be best if I left tomorrow."

"No." His reaction was immediate, strong. He turned to her. "No, you must stay. If the bridal cup is to be returned and the feud to come to a proper end, it is only right that a Camville witness the return and use of the cup."

"Ross, after what happened at—"

"What happened at the castle was my fault," he said, his gaze never wavering. "It was uncivilized and ungentlemanly. I deserve whatever you think of me, but don't leave."

Her emotions warred between anger with herself for giving in to the urge to kiss him and the frustration of keeping up appearances. Even more perplexing was the confusion she sensed in him.

"How would it look if the Camville who returned the bridal cup walked out on the festivities?" he added.

"Awkward," she agreed. Then there was her own reluctance to leave him, a reluctance she could only explain as her own foolish softheartedness.

"I'll stay if you wish it," she said.

He gave her a curt nod of satisfaction, and then he urged the pony onward down the slope to home. As she suspected, amidst the confusion of the returning hunters, their arrival was almost unnoticed.

Still, the apprehensive mood that settled over her was impossible to shake. After a hot bath, a rest, a change of clothes, and a good meal, her emotions were only slightly calmer. But she had sorted through them enough to know that she had serious feelings for Ross. Not a silly schoolgirl crush. She cared for him. The question remained, how did he feel about her—or, perhaps more accurately, how did he feel about Alice?

That evening she stood by the fire alone, contemplating the question while warming herself. Other guests sipped after-dinner drinks and the bagpipes blared in the foyer. Twilight lingered outside on the Highlands. The nightly chill had settled over the valley and Glenalder House.

As much as she wanted to believe that Ross didn't love Alice, wasn't it possible she was deluding herself? Alice was young, barely twenty-one, and in the bloom of womanhood. Leonora was ready for the old-maid shelf. Alice had been brought up and educated to be the lady of the manor that she would be as Ross's wife. Leonora was a doctor and a women's rights sympathizer. Hardly glowing credentials for the wife of a Scottish earl.

Unexpectedly, Ian sidled up to her as if he would suffer some dreaded penalty if he were seen talking to her.

"So he took ye to see Castle Camville, now did he?" Ian asked, glancing furtively around the room.

"He did," she said, amused by the old man's circumspect manner. "And I was impressed."

"Aye, a grand place it was," Ian said. "Those were grand days when the Camvilles ruled from the shores of Lochrowan. I'm glad ye saw it, lass."

"I'm glad, too," she said, her words genuine, and understanding growing of how people like Ian could speak of a distant past as if it were part of their own memories.

"Here, I think you should have this." Ian pressed something disklike into Leonora's hand.

"Ian, what are you doing?" she asked, almost laughing at the way he behaved as if they were conspirators in the enemy camp. She looked down at what he had placed in her hand. "What's this?"

" 'Tis a Camville brooch, lass," Ian said. "Ye should have one to wear with the plaid."

"You mean the plaid the bridal cup was wrapped in?"

"Aye, you'll want to wear that when the time comes," he said. "Ye'll want everyone to know exactly who ye are. Hold yer head high."

"But where did you get this?"

" 'Tis been in my family from long ago," Ian said. "A gift for services to the clan. The MacCages were more than just tenants, donna ye know. But ye have need of the brooch now, seeing as ye donna have one of yer own."

She studied the mythical creature wrought among intricate silver Celtic knots on the brooch. She'd seen the crest before. But beyond the respect that family things deserved, it had meant little to her.

Unceremoniously, the library doors swung open. The men who'd lingered over the dining room table to smoke entered the room. She glanced up to see that Ross and another gentleman were walking side-by-side, discussing a future hydropower electric project to be built in the mountains.

At the sight of Ross in full Highland formal dress, Leonora's breath hitched. The kilt and fur sporran hinted at narrow hips and strong thighs. The velvet jacket and ruffled shirt emphasized broad shoulders and a strong jaw. The look was impressive—elegant and powerful.

And the costume hinted strongly at what he would have looked like two centuries earlier. The kilt would have been nearly the same. But in place of the velvet and ruffles would have been brass-studded leather and fleece layered over homespun—less elegant, fiercer, more mighty.

She forced herself to take a normal breath. What

a contradiction the man was. The chief, the lord, and the Victorian gentleman. Duty and leadership. Tradition and technology, Leonora thought. Past, present, and future.

With a soft cry of pleasure, Alice waltzed across the floor to Ross, kissing him on the cheek and hooking her arm through his. Leonora watched his features soften as he gazed into his fiancée's face. If he did not love Alice, he certainly felt something for her.

He never gazed at her like that, Leonora thought with a pang of disappointment.

And he wasn't supposed to, she scolded herself. He was engaged to Alice. She would do well to avoid the temptation to be alone with him again, for her own sake if not his.

"Wear the brooch, lass, and be proud," Ian said, eyeing Ross as if he were Lucifer himself. Then the old man leaned closer to her and whispered, "Yer forefathers fought the English at Culloden. And later they defended the bloody English in India. And at Waterloo. Be proud, lass. Donna be taken by The MacDonnart's worldly ways and good looks. Donna fall for everything he tells ye."

The next morning dawned clear. The rain and fog of the previous day had vanished, and the sky was perfect for the scheduled riverside picnic.

In Glenalder drive, Ross peered over Alice's shoulder into the basket that had just been loaded onto the back of the last wagon headed for the picnic site. He was pleased to see Cook's best sweet cakes and finest crusty loaves of bread wrapped in spotless white linen.

"I must remember to send my compliments to Cook," Alice said, turning to smile up at him. "She has done well, in spite of the large number of guests to be fed."

With affection that made Ross feel like a lout after his kiss with Leonora, Alice threw her arms around his neck and bussed him on the cheek. The wedding guests finding their way to the other wagons for the picnic chuckled and murmured approvingly.

Ross smiled tolerantly. Alice's youthful warmth and spontaneity were part of her charm, but there were times when he simply did not have the patience to deal with it. She was such a sweet innocent thing. He looked forward to the time when her exuberance would mellow, and she would leave him to carry out his duties while she carried out hers as his wife.

"This is going to be the perfect picnic," she said. "You'll see. People will be talking about the earl of Glenalder's wedding for years to come."

With a giggle of delight, Alice turned to instruct the footman who was loading a stoneware container of lemonade, a must for the ladies.

Ross stepped back to inspect the line of wagons preparing for the trip. They appeared to be in good order, yellow wheel spokes gleamed, spotless brass harness fittings jingled, and the horses' coats shone like black and chestnut satin in the morning sun. He expected nothing less from his stable.

One of the guests smiled and waved at him. He returned the greeting. Then he saw Leonora and Ian climb aboard the vehicle behind the lead one.

Today, she was wearing a soft sprigged cotton gown that clung to her hips, revealed the fullness of her breasts, and accented the narrowness of her waist. His mouth went dry. He knew the feel of that waist moving beneath fabric. His loins warmed with the memory of her lips beneath his, warm and eager, drawing him into her warmth and strength.

His appraisal caught her attention. She smiled at

him uncertainly and then ducked her head. They had not spoken since the day before.

He was unable to resist returning the smile. She was much too pretty to be a doctor. Doctors were old men with woolly jowls and potbellies, weren't they?

He turned away, sudden dark apprehension roiling in his gut. His reaction to her at Castle Camville had kept him awake all night. He'd begun to wonder if he should reconsider his plan to have her present the bridal cup to him at the rehearsal dinner. By dawn he'd convinced himself that his problem lay in the unfortunate fact that Leonora was a Camville *and* a damned attractive woman. Why should the one fact make him change his plans? He had his duty to the clan to perform.

A quick movement to his right caught Ross's eye.

"What's this frown, brother?" Kerr, his younger brother and groomsman, laughed and landed a solid thump on Ross's shoulder. "You're about to marry the prettiest girl in all Scotland."

Ross winced but laughed and punched playfully back at Kerr. "I expected you to arrive last night."

Kerr shrugged. "Delayed by a bridge out near Berwick. Where's the bride? Where's little Alice?"

"Kerr, darling," Alice cried, throwing herself into her future brother-in-law's arms. "I thought you would never get here. The party is simply incomplete without you."

"Let me have a look at you," Kerr demanded, holding Alice away and motioning for her to turn around and display her pink lawn gown and straw hat for him. "Oh, I was wrong. Did I say the prettiest girl in Scotland?"

He leaned toward Ross and said in a stage whisper, "Your bride is the prettiest girl in England, too. But don't tell her I said so. It goes to her head, you know."

Ross laughed along with Alice and Kerr. It was

good to be together again, the three of them, like
old times. Kerr could always make Alice laugh.

"Now that I'm here, let's go to the island and play
pirates," Kerr said, thumping Ross a bit more gently
on the back this time.

"Right," Ross said, signaling the wagon drivers to
make ready for departure.

He and Kerr had played pirates often as boys. But
at the age of twenty-six, Kerr was now a London
banker with a growing reputation as a solid but
shrewd investor, if not a bit of a pirate still. But Ross
knew that for all his lightheartedness and fraternal
rivalry, Kerr could be counted on to be loyal.

Earlier that morning Ross had ridden out to the
river to oversee the placement of the tables among
the alders on the island. The site had never been
used for anything more than their own playground.
When Alice had suggested it, he'd been surprised by
her choice, but he'd agreed to the idea. It was an
out-of-the-way place where they'd often played as
children. Setting up the tables had been quite an
undertaking, requiring the hiring of several extra
men for the job, but there was nothing a MacDonnart groom would deny his wife-to-be.

He was certain Alice was right. People would talk
about this Glenalder island picnic and the wedding
for years.

The river was quiet here, forming a clear rocky-
bottomed pool. In the middle of the large peaceful
pool was anchored the wooded island that Alice had
dubbed Treasure Island. When the wagons pulled
up, the picnic tables, complete with white tablecloths
and vases of garden flowers, awaited them.

Kerr immediately took to the duties as groomsman and secondary host. He ushered guests into the
boats and took one of the poles from the acting fer-
rymen and put his shoulder into the job himself.
With great dash and piratelike merriment that kept

Alice in a fit of giggles, he ferried several boatloads of guests to Treasure Island, laughing and talking all the way.

When Ross looked back as he helped Alice and her mother from a boat, he saw Kerr talking intimately with Leonora. She laughed.

Ross sucked in a breath of irritation.

So Kerr had spotted her already. Little brother never missed an introduction to a pretty face. Tall, graceful, and poised in that casual American way, Leonora was difficult to miss in any crowd. Ross wondered how much Kerr knew about her. He had yet to tell him the good news about the bridal cup. He wanted the presentation at the rehearsal dinner to be a surprise for the wedding guests. Only he, Alice, Stratton, MacCage, and Leonora knew of the arrangements.

"Kerr is such an incorrigible devil," Alice said, her gaze following Ross's. She gave a laugh of admiration, and then she sighed. "It is so good to have all three of us together again. How long has it been?"

Ross made a begrudging sound of agreement. "You're right. Too long."

He took her hand and smiled at her. After Lord Preston's death, Alice and her mother had spent several summers with the MacDonnarts at Glenalder. At first, having a girl to include in their summer explorations and games had been a trial and an insight for Ross and Kerr. A girl slowed them down and chafed at his sense of responsibility. But a girl also gave them new ways of looking at things. She had kept them from forgetting all the manners they'd been taught at school. Ross had had the advantage of getting to know the girl he was promised to.

"Let's go find our pirate castle later, shall we?" he said, smiling at Alice.

She brightened and nodded. "Let's do."

The piper filled his bagpipes with air, and lively

music floated out across the water. Guests found their way to the tables, and servants began serving food.

Dining was followed by games of lawn tennis. A cricket ball and bat appeared, and even a croquet game had been set up on the rough meadow. None of the balls rolled straight through the tall grass. Some of the guests played cricket seriously, and Ross joined them. A hardy few returned to the boats to drift serenely across the water. Kerr had grabbed Alice's mother and set to dancing with the lady. The guests loved it.

"Let's explore now," Alice whispered into Ross's ear after he'd won his cricket match. "Our guests are occupied. Now you must turn your attention to your bride."

"Indeed, I must," Ross said, unable to resist returning her endearing smile. She did deserve more attention than he had given her. Pretty words. A few kisses. A caress.

He took her hand and led her away from the group, into the woods, the long way around the island.

"Let's build a folly here," Alice said, as she followed him along a narrow overgrown path. "It could be like a Roman ruin. Wouldn't that be romantic?"

"That is a possibility," Ross said, though he had little desire to change anything about Treasure Island. He liked the wilderness of it.

"To think you and Kerr swam in that dreadfully cold water," she said when they stepped out of the woods on the far side of the island. Here the river rushed past, the icy water gleaming in the sun.

"It did not seem so cold at the time," Ross said, pushing aside a leafy tree branch for her. *How different things seemed when you're young,* he thought. Like Treasure Island—once it had been a place to explore and to be free. Now it was a place for him to either protect or make the best use of for the clan.

"Whew, I forgot how big the island is," Alice said. "Is it far to the castle? I should have worn my pith helmet and veil like a proper lady explorer. The midges are dreadful."

"It's not far now," Ross said, following the turn in the nearly overgrown path. He had to agree, a walk in the woods was hardly romantic with insects swarming in your face.

As he rounded a tree, he caught sight of the outcropping he and Kerr had defended as their pirate castle. When he looked up, someone was already sitting atop the tower—the highest rock.

"Why look who's here," Alice said, pulling the brim of her straw hat low to shade her eyes from the sun as she looked upward. "Dr. Camville."

Six

Ross glanced up at Leonora with a pang of guilt. She and he had not spoken face to face since the previous morning when they had returned Lochrowan. He had not intentionally avoided her because of the kiss, but he suspected she had avoided him. He deserved no less.

"Hello," Leonora said, politely smiling down at them from the outcropping that he and Kerr as boys had named the castle. She swung her feet over the edge of the rock edge, her hem barely revealing trim ankles in white high-button shoes.

"Avast, ye mateys," Kerr roared, appearing at the top next to her. "I've the Maid of Camville as an ally in my fortress. Be ye friend or foe?"

"How'd you get here?" Ross demanded, aware of being more annoyed with seeing Leonora in Kerr's company than with having his tryst with Alice interrupted.

"We came across the short way, brother," Kerr said with a laugh.

"So, this is the MacDonnart pirate castle," Leonora said, a glint of challenge in her eyes. "And I thought the Camvilles were the only outlaws in this part of Scotland."

"But the MacDonnarts weren't real pirates," Alice explained to Leonora. "It was only a boy's game."

"Yes, I know." Leonora smiled gently at Alice's ingenuous defense of the MacDonnart clan.

"The Maid told me about the bridal cup, brother," Kerr called down from the rocky summit. "You always were a bloody lucky bloke, Ross. You'll go down in clan history as getting the prettiest girl and the return of the bridal cup."

"I hope you don't mind that I told him," Leonora said, frowning. "He is your brother."

Ross shook his head and wondered what else she'd told Kerr. "I was going to tell him myself this evening."

"Isn't it exciting, Kerr?" Alice clapped her hands. "The MacDonnart bridal cup will be used for the first time in centuries at our wedding."

Kerr's smile faded as he gazed down in earnest at Alice. "It's a beautiful thing, and to have it at your wedding is no less an honor than you deserve, Alice."

"Have you seen it?" Alice asked. "I've never seen it. Ross has it locked away."

Leonora frowned at Ross. "You've never shown Alice the cup?" Indignation and disbelief filled her voice, making him feel vaguely guilty.

"Stratton and I tucked it away for safekeeping," he explained.

"Well, I haven't seen it either, Alice." Kerr began to climb down from the rock. "But I read a description of it once in some ancient documents."

"Will you tell me about it?" Alice asked. As soon as Kerr dropped to the ground, she latched onto his arm. "Ross just calls it a silver goblet."

"It is of solid silver," Kerr began, as he started back toward the picnic site. He stopped and looked back over his shoulder at Ross. "And—do you mind, brother? Someone should describe this cup to your bride-to-be if you won't."

"Yes, tell her about it, Kerr," Leonora said, before Ross could reply.

Feeling strangely like a petty scoundrel who had neglected his bride, Ross shrugged. "Of course. Go ahead. I'll bring Leonora."

"No need for you to worry about me." She was already making her way down the rocks, surprisingly at home on the stone surface. "Uncle Grant always said I was too much of a tomboy for my own good. I can see why the three of you loved it here. It's a perfect castle. A perfect place to be a pirate."

With appreciation, Ross watched her bottom as she climbed down. The sight was enough to make a saint's hands itch. Finally, he gave way to lust and seized her by the waist, swinging her down off the outcropping. Her body was warm and yielding. He could feel the heat even through the layers of cotton. When her feet touched the ground, she tried to step away. But he held her close, their bodies never touching, yet the scent of her stirred him.

All the memories of yesterday's kiss struck full force. He longed to capture her mouth again and feel the warmth of her, inside and out. He had to know. "I pray you did not tell Kerr about the kiss, too."

"No, I did not." She turned her head, lowering her gaze so that her dark lashes lay against her fair skin. "I would not embarrass Alice. She is a sweet deserving girl, who will try to make you a good wife, and Kerr will make a handsome groomsman. He is right. You are a lucky man."

He released her. Alice and luck were not what he wanted to talk about.

He wanted to know, had she felt nothing yesterday? Had nothing changed for her? Because something had shifted in him, something deep and profound that had not revealed itself to him yet. "Look at me, Leonora."

She did. For the first time he saw his own bewilderment mirrored in her eyes. Her confusion gave him hope—for what, he was uncertain—but she turned away from him.

"Is there nothing between us?" he asked, surprised at the hoarseness of emotion in his own voice. He needed an explanation for the urge he felt to possess her. His heart was in his throat as he waited for her to answer. What would he say if she said yes? How could he go on with the rehearsal dinner and the wedding plans if she looked into his eyes and begged him to kiss her again? He pulled her around to face him once more.

When she looked up into his face, her bewilderment was gone. She would do no begging.

"There is nothing more between us than should be, my lord," she said, holding his gaze. "You have agreed to a marriage out of duty to your clan. It is not my place to interfere."

"What is wrong with an arranged marriage?" Ross asked, offended that she equated his marriage to Alice with mere duty, as if he had no will of his own. "My parents' marriage was such a union, yet they were happy all their years together. Love grows with time."

"I hope you will be as fortunate," she said, her eyes clear and honest. She meant what she said. Then she frowned a bit. "Otherwise, if something ails you where I'm concerned, I prescribe a dose of cod liver oil with a whiskey chaser."

She pulled free of him and started down the path behind Alice and Kerr, her skirts switching with haste. After a moment's hesitation, Ross followed her.

Whiskey, yes. He could use a good swig of that, but cod liver oil? That seemed a bloody steep payment for a stolen kiss.

* * *

When they reached the picnic tables, the guests were gathered on the shore watching something out on the water.

Leonora and Ross joined them. She was glad that there was something going on to take their attention away from each other. They'd not spoken during the brief walk back to the picnic site. There was nothing to say.

"What's happening?" she asked Ian at the water's edge. On the water several of the boats were circling with the polers, Kerr among them, and a couple of other young men were waving their poles at each other.

"Young Kerr has started a battle at sea," the old man said. "The lad has always been given to such antics."

Ross left her side to move on down the bank, his gaze on Kerr's boat. Alice was in it, laughing as she clutched the sides of the wallowing flat-bottomed skiff.

The young men called good-natured insults at each other. The insulted one swung his pole at the offender, the blows generally missing, some glancing off a shoulder or back. The guests laughed, but Alice's mother, went to Ross, obviously out of concern.

He called a warning to Kerr. But the young man brushed it off and threw out a ribald challenge to Ross to join the foray.

Leonora watched apprehensively as the insults grew a little less good-natured. Poles swung. One of the young men lost his balance, fell in, and swam for shore.

Alice cried out in alarm for his safety. But he appeared to be a strong swimmer and was soon wading ashore. The water was too cold for bathing, even for wading. Out of habit, Leonora started toward him, calling to the servants to bring blankets and whatever throws they had to wrap him in.

But the mishap never slowed Kerr. He was bent on revenge for his fellow and swung a return blow at the attacker. The effort made his boat bob dangerously, water slopping over the sides. Alice cried out.

Leonora only caught glimpses of what was happening as she grabbed the defeated sailor who just staggered ashore. She had to get his wet clothes off him and get him wrapped in something warm and dry. Cold water sapped the body's strength faster than people realized.

Frightened now, Alice started to rise from her seat. As Leonora watched, Alice saw Kerr swing back around, intent on his foe. She managed to duck the accidental blow from the pole. But the move made her lose her balance. She tried to regain her stance. Her arms pinwheeled in the air for an eternal moment, but the boat was too unsteady. Kerr saw what was happening and reached for her, but he was too far away. Hands flailing, Alice teetered for another second. Then she fell backward into the icy-cold water.

The guests gasped. Alice's mother screamed.

Leonora stifled her cry of dismay. She glanced at Ross who had already stripped off his coat. He dived into the water without hesitation. Kerr did the same.

This time Leonora began to issue orders in earnest. There was no time to think about doing otherwise, to question whether she was a good doctor or a bad one, to think that the woman in the water was the beloved of a man she herself loved. Her skills would be needed.

Full of authority, she turned to the gaping servants. Even Stratton seemed stunned and at a loss.

In a steady voice, she demanded that all the towels, the tablecloths, and warming cloths for the food be brought to the water's edge. When the butler hesitated, she grasped his sleeve.

"Shawls, jackets, wraps of any kind, take them from the guests," she instructed. "Bring the horse blankets if there are any in the carriages. Send someone back to the house and tell the staff to be prepared.

"Do this now, Stratton," she said. "Alice and the men will need our help. There will be no time for delay."

He gave her a dazed nod, but when he turned to the gawking servants, he clapped his hands. That sent them scurrying in pursuit of what she wanted.

All the time as she worked, she reminded herself of Kerr telling her how he and Ross had swam with their ponies in these waters. Ross was a good swimmer, a strong swimmer. She had to believe that.

She returned to the first defeated sailor to check his pulse. It was slower than she liked, but strong. However, he'd begun to shiver. A serious symptom.

"Back to the house now," she ordered.

"I'm all right," he said. "Just a bit damp."

"Out of those wet clothes and into a dry nightshirt," Leonora ordered. "Go to bed. Order hot soup from the kitchen and a warming pan for your bed. Doctor's orders. Go now."

"Actually that does sound bloody good," the young man admitted, allowing the footman to lead him away.

Then she turned to Ian.

"Have they got her?" she asked, only glimpsing out over the water, searching for the sight of Ross. "Did she go under?"

"No, they haven't found her," the old man said, also watching the boats that had converged on the spot where Alice had fallen in. "Sank like a stone, she did."

"Her skirts pulled her right down," Leonora thought aloud.

Several men had stripped off their jackets and joined the watery search.

"The lass couldna swim. How far could she have gone?" Ian asked.

"There's a current," another young man said. "You can feel it grab the pole. Down deep, but it's there."

"How long has it been?" Leonora asked more of herself than the men. She looked at her lapel watch. Three minutes, maybe. Not too long yet, but long enough.

She looked out over the water again just in time to see Ross break the surface and take a breath. Kerr surfaced beside him, gasping. They exchanged a few breathless words, gulped air, and then disappeared again.

"Dear God," she prayed unashamed of her selfish prayer. "Don't do this to Ross. Don't take someone from him he cares about. It's too painful."

It was another long stretch of minutes before she saw Ross surface again, this time shouting for the boats. Relief rushed through her. Kerr shot to the surface near him, Alice's body in his arms. The current had pulled her downriver. The men in the boats paddled downstream to reach them. Lifeless, she was soon lifted into a boat and ferried to shore.

All Leonora could make out as Ian poled her and the dry blankets from the island to shore was the profile of Ross bent over Alice in the boat. Water dripped from his hair. Stark planes of grief set on his face. Her heart ached for him.

When he came ashore with Alice, Leonora was there and had already ordered a makeshift pallet laid out. Ross lowered her gently to the dry bed. Ian appeared with more blankets. The onlookers spread them over Alice.

Leonora knelt on the other side of the girl. Alice was unconscious, her lips blue, and her skin had an underlying blue cast. She did not appear to be breathing.

Leonora touched the girl's throat for a pulse. Her heart sank. Nothing detectable. She cursed silently, longing for her doctor's bag.

"Is she gone?" Ross half-choked, his voice full of emotion and his eyes dark with vulnerability. His bleakness almost brought tears to Leonora's eyes. But she held them back. A doctor could ill afford to become emotionally involved when action was called for.

"Not necessarily," she said, though it was her policy to be wary of giving hope where there was little. "First, I want you to get yourself wrapped in something warm and dry. The last thing Alice needs now is a groom with pneumonia."

Ross's only response was to snatch a blanket from Ian.

"What can we do?" Alice's mother pleaded, her face pale but composed. She was not panicked. She was a mother fighting for her child's life.

"Help me roll her over," Leonora said, already taking the girl by the shoulders. "We need to get as much water out of her as we can, and we need to get these wet clothes off of her."

Alice's mother complied immediately. Ross helped.

"Ross"—Leonora touched his arm—"see that we have a wagon ready to take us back to the house."

"Right away." With a curt nod he left to do as she asked.

Leonora began what she had to do to get the girl breathing again. It could be done; she'd read about it. Science was learning. Drowning needn't be the automatic death sentence that it once was. Better understanding of the condition led to ways to defeat it. She had won the battle against illnesses and infections before. She would do it again—against drowning. She would.

She channeled all her life force toward Alice and used everything she knew, every instinct she had. She cleared out the girl's mouth and breathed into it hard, over and over, carefully pacing the breaths.

Nothing. Alice's mother began to weep.

Leonora ignored the woman, not out of heartlessness but determination. She could not allow herself to despair. She worked steadily and focused on the task. She'd seen this work with babies. Did the air help the patient, or did it stimulate some reflex? She did not know. But she would make Alice live.

Leonora tried again.

Suddenly, Alice sucked in a shallow shuddering breath. Leonora paused, waited, listened.

The crowd gathered around them, held its breath. Alice's mother went still, her weeping silenced by hope.

Alice heaved and began to choke. Leonora hastened to roll the girl on her side again. Water erupted from Alice's mouth.

"Alice?" Ross called, shoving his way back through the onlookers to his bride's side. Kerr was at his elbow this time.

Alice took another breath. Then she groaned.

A wary thrill of victory coursed through Leonora. She grabbed Alice's wrist to get a pulse. The girl's skin was still too cool. But life throbbed, weak and slow, so slow, but it was there.

She looked across at Ross who was watching her. She couldn't keep the victorious smile from her face. "Yes," she said, knowing that was all he wanted to hear, to know.

"This is only the first step," she said, warning herself and Ross that the fight was not necessarily over.

"Her body temperature is too low. We must get her back to the house and warmed up."

"You mean, if the water did not take her, the cold could?" Kerr asked, his voice full of disbelief and regret.

"That's what I mean," Leonora said, her confidence growing in the possibility of Alice's recovery, but her good sense cautious. "We are not out of the proverbial woods yet."

"You heard the doctor." Ross stood and gave orders for the wagon to be brought around. "Let's get moving."

Seven

In the hours that followed Alice's near-drowning, Ross realized that he had underestimated Dr. Leonora Camville. She was a fighter. Her war and her weapons were not the traditional ones of a soldier. The first thing she'd ordered when they arrived at the house was her black bag. She immediately set to work with her stethoscope around her neck. Her battlefield was not that of an army's. Nevertheless, she fought with a ferocity that any clan chief had to admire. That afternoon on the riverbank and later at Alice's bedside, Leonora did battle.

Every order she uttered was carried out immediately, without question. He saw to it. Victory was theirs. As Leonora worked, he watched the color seep back into Alice's face. Her lips became pink once more and the blue tint of her skin faded. If there were no roses in her cheeks, at least the deathly paleness was gone. She woke only briefly, long enough to say Kerr's name and his, and then she slipped back.

With her stethoscope, Leonora bent over Alice.

"Her lungs are clear," she reassured him, Kerr, and Alice's mother who had gathered around the bed. "She's sleeping."

"Are you sure she is asleep?" Kerr questioned. Ross and Kerr had donned dry clothes. Kerr looked tired, but Ross did not feel especially worn-out. The only reason he hadn't thrashed Kerr for his role in this near-tragedy was that he looked as if he could never forgive himself. After all, Kerr loved Alice, too.

Reverently, Kerr touched Alice's hand. "It's not a coma? She is so still and she feels so cool."

"It's not a coma," Leonora said, her voice full of that curious mixture of assurance and caution that only a doctor could make credible. "Her need for sleep is to be expected. If her recovery proceeds well, her body temperature will slowly rise to normal. In the meantime, she needs rest and warmth. By morning, we'll know if she's taken a serious chill. I'll be here with her to monitor the progress during the night."

"Of course, I will be here, too," Alice's mother said, drawing a chair up to the bedside.

"I am not leaving." Kerr glanced from Ross to Leonora.

"Nor will I," Ross said, moving toward the bell. "I'll have supper sent up, and we'll make ourselves comfortable for the vigil. Stratton can manage the guests for now."

A long night it was. After supper, Leonora went to check on the other divers who had helped rescue Alice. They all seemed to be well but were willing to accept the doctor's orders to get a good night's rest. There would be no dancing that night at Glenalder.

Kerr was the first to drift off to sleep in Alice's room. Leonora had extinguished all the lights except a small oil lamp burning on a corner table. Only it and the fire in the hearth remained to light the room with a dim soft glow.

As soon as Kerr slumped in his chair, Leonora went to him. Ross watched her unbutton his brother's collar and listen to his heart with her stethoscope. She touched Kerr's forehead, her eyes narrowing ever so slightly as she made some assessment.

"Is he all right?" Ross asked, starting to rise from his chair. He had been so worried about Alice and so annoyed with Kerr that he had not thought about his brother suffering ill effects from the rescue.

"He's fine," Leonora said. "He needs rest, too. He just will not admit it."

Reassured, Ross settled back in his chair. Only then did he realize that she was gazing at him intently, meaningfully.

"I'm all right."

She came toward him. "You were exposed to the cold for as long as your brother was. Longer. Now that I have you cornered, unbutton your shirt."

"I'm all right," Ross protested again. "If there was anything wrong, we'd know by now."

"Let's be sure, shall we?" She shook her head at him and held up her stethoscope as if it were a weapon.

Ross glanced toward Alice and her mother who was seated at Alice's bedside. The lady had also fallen asleep, her head resting on her daughter's pillow.

"They're all right," Leonora said, drawing a footstool up to his chair. "You're my last patient. I shall not rest until I'm satisfied with your condition also."

Realizing that cooperation might be the better part of valor, Ross unbuttoned the first two buttons of his shirt. "In the spirit of putting your concern to rest—"

"Shh." Leonora placed the stethoscope against his skin. The bell was warm from being held in her hand. "Don't talk while I'm listening."

Ross fell silent.

As she bent close, he studied her hair, noting the red glint that burnished its shine. Tendrils had slipped from the simple knot at the back of her neck. Mud streaked the hem of her skirt. She lowered her eyelids as she listened.

He vaguely remembered her brushing dried mud off herself earlier after they had settled Alice in bed. Other than that, she hadn't taken a moment for herself except to drink black coffee that she'd ordered from the kitchen.

But it wasn't her selflessness that stirred him. It was her scent that brought the memory of the kiss at Castle Camville flooding back. He closed his eyes, aware of the warmth of her knuckles brushing against the skin of his chest as she listened to his heart.

He closed his eyes against the rush of desire and hoped his heartbeat did not reveal his condition, did not tell her how the memory of her mouth moving over his aroused him. How he still remembered her slenderness in his arms. Her fingers in his hair. Her heat pressed against him.

His eyes snapped open. Lord, how he wanted to kiss her again.

He wanted to know the parting of her lips beneath his once more, not in surrender, but in seductive response.

The more he remembered of her reaction to him, the clearer his realization became. She had had a lover in her past. And why not? She was a woman of nearly his age. He had been no monk. There had been the London mistress he had left when he gained the Glenalder title.

His gaze went to her mouth, which was tight and pursed as she listened to his beating heart.

Leonora frowned, took the stethoscope bell away, and stared at him. "Your lungs are clear, but your heart rate is rather elevated."

He could only stare at her. Of course, she'd had a lover. What man wouldn't want her, warm, strong, a heart so big she wanted to heal everyone who came within range of her stethoscope.

"Is something wrong?" she asked, her frown undiminished.

Reaching for her elbows, he lifted her onto his lap. He hated the other man, whoever he had been. It was on the tip of his tongue to demand who the fool was, where he was, but that would wait. Ross wanted her. He wanted Leonora for himself. Desire pumped through him. If she were his, he'd make love to her until he'd seared the other man from her memory.

She put her hand on his mouth. "Ross! What are you—"

Urgently, he pulled her hand aside, brushing her fingertips with his lips, and then he kissed her. She resisted. At first. Then her arms slipped around his neck and her body settled against his, her breasts pressed against his bare chest. The kiss deepened. She made a low sound that made him attempt to gather her closer.

Abruptly she pulled away, placing her hands on either side of his face. "I was so afraid for you today. When you kept diving down to find Alice in that cold water."

"There was nothing to fear. You were the strong one," he said, meaning every word. "I'm glad you were here. I do not know what we would have done without you."

He covered her mouth again. He had no right to do this. First, there was Alice. Second, Leonora had done a great service for his family. That deserved respect. Thirdly, he was a MacDonnart—The MacDonnart—and she was a Camville, the Camville who had come to return the bridal cup.

But how could such a wrong thing feel so astonishingly good?

Suddenly, Leonora struggled against him again. "No, no. That's enough."

She was strong enough to succeed in freeing herself from his embrace. In doing so, she unceremoniously slid from his lap and thumped back onto the footstool.

"That's enough, sir." Wide-eyed, she glared at him. "We are allowing the events of the day to get the better of our good sense."

She was right, of course. He wrestled with his good sense in silence. Lord, how he wanted her. But, she was not a woman you asked to be your mistress, even if he was the kind of man to be unfaithful. She was a Camville chief.

She rose from the stool, taking her stethoscope from around her neck, and moved to the table where her black bag was. Only then did Ross see the dark smudges of exhaustion under her eyes.

"You need to get some rest, too," he said, ignoring doubts about his plans. He was suddenly aware of his bare chest. He hastened to button his shirt, to shut off his feelings, to deny his desire. "Alice is going to be all right, isn't she?"

Leonora turned around and gave him a long measuring look. "I believe so. But it's early yet. We'll see how she feels in the morning. If it's the wedding plans that you are thinking of, it is possible that with rest you can carry on with them."

"Excellent, and you'll stay, of course?" he asked, his relief at the prospect of Alice's recovery almost over shadowed by the fear of Leonora leaving. "I mean there is no one waiting for you?"

"No," she said. "I promised Uncle Grant I would return the cup, and so I shall."

"Good." His relief was complete. The important thing was that Alice was on the mend. Kerr was none the worse for his escapade, though he deserved to suffer.

He could count on Leonora—and Lord knows he was beginning to wonder if he deserved to.

* * *

"I can tell you it was a strange feeling, miss," the maid said, as she helped Leonora dress for the rehearsal dinner two days later. She had just draped the Camville plaid over Leonora's shoulder, down and then up again, draping the end over her shoulder once more. Leonora observed the process in the mirror.

"And what was so strange?" she asked, gazing at her reflection and wondering where the brooch should be fastened.

"Why, the pressing of the Camville plaid on a Mac-Donnart ironing board right there under Stratton's eyes," the maid said. "Made him frown, I can tell you. But it did not bother me, as strange as it was. It's all over, isn't it? The feud and things. That stuff is for the old days, for the old folks, not for the new times."

Leonora nodded. "It's over. That's what this is all about, for anyone who thinks such things still exist or ever should have in the first place."

She liked the look of the dark green Camville plaid on herself, lying against the lace of her best shirtwaist. The green wool threaded with blue, yellow, and red flattered her fair coloring and gray eyes.

"Here's your brooch, miss," the maid said. "It goes right there on your shoulder. Perfect. It's just perfect."

Leonora pinned the brooch in place. The silver gleamed in the lamplight, fierce and proud. Pride flooded through her, pride in a clan that had had the strength to survive in a changing world, that had had the courage to face the new world when the old one had no place for them. Hardy souls who had kept their families together and faced the hardships. Not deserters. Not cowards. Courageous, hardworking men and women who loved and laughed and knew how to work and how to celebrate. She was a part of that. She wondered if Uncle Grant knew she would discover the Camville spirit when she came to Scotland.

Perfect—that's how she felt, whole, complete, not so much because she knew she looked good, but because she knew who she was.

Alice's recovery was a bonus. After a day's rest, the girl was absolutely hale and hearty. Part of the recovery was due to Alice's own strong constitution, but Leonora also knew that part of it was due to her own skill as a physician. She hadn't cured anyone of pneumonia or found the cure for tuberculosis, but she had made a difference. Wasn't that what being a doctor was about? Somehow she suspected Uncle Grant would have told her as much. She knew her father would have.

Just that morning Alice was well enough to scold Kerr for his foolishness as she hugged him for saving her, thanked Leonora for her lifesaving treatment, and latched onto Ross as if she thought he was going to escape her. The girl refused to entertain any suggestion that the wedding plans be delayed. The rehearsal had been held as scheduled that afternoon in the redbrick village church.

Leonora had avoided it. No need for her to be there to watch Ross take one more step toward fulfilling his duty.

She frowned at herself in the mirror. Thoughts of Ross and the wedding—especially since that night in Alice's room—occurred all too frequently and were much too disturbing.

Her frown deepened as she assessed her reflection. Ross was not hers to dream of, to long for, she reminded herself. He belonged to Alice. And that was as it should be.

She'd always known that having a man for a partner in life was not for her. She was a doctor and Alice's recovery should serve to remind her of that.

She'd chosen a road other than wifehood and marriage. And Ross had chosen the path of duty.

She found Ian waiting for her at the door to the dining room. His hair had been slicked back, and he was freshly shaven. Leonora could still smell the soap. He wore the same wool coat he'd worn to every dinner at Glenalder though it looked as if it had been recently brushed. Under his arm was the rowan box with the bridal cup retrieved from the silver closet.

"And now, donna ye look like a Camville, lass," Ian said, appraising her as she joined him in the hallway. "Look at that, the plaid and the brooch on yer shoulder. Ye do the clan proud."

"I am proud to be a Camville," Leonora said, smiling truthfully. "How did the rehearsal go?"

"The word is it went well," Ian said.

He fell silent as several guests passed them. This evening the ladies were dressed in their glittering ballroom best and the men wore formal Highland dress.

"There be a lot of excitement about the dinner tonight," Ian said. "Are ye sure this is what ye wanna do, lass? Ye wanna return the bridal cup? Are ye sure ye ken what yer doing?"

"I know," Leonora said, thinking more of Ross than the bridal cup. As if on cue, the earl of Glenalder appeared coming down the stairs. He, too, was in full Highland dress.

Alice and her mother came down the stairs at Ross's side, both ladies dressed in jewel-colored rustling taffeta and lace. Kerr followed, also wearing formal Highland garb.

Ross nodded a quiet greeting to Leonora and Ian, no smile, just a sober searching look as he approached her. His gaze obviously took in her Camville plaid sash and the crested silver brooch on her shoulder. When their gazes met, what she saw jolted her. The shadow was back. Even more than a shadow this time, something steely glinted in his dark eyes, as if by wearing the plaid she'd issued a challenge.

"We are so excited about tonight," Alice chattered, her blonde curls bobbing with animation. "I can hardly wait to see it. It is so good of you to do this, Leonora. The bridal cup will make our wedding the talk of Scotland for years. We'll be telling our grandchildren about it, isn't that right, Ross?"

He only nodded. "Kerr, would you escort the ladies into the dining room? I need to have a few words with Leonora before we start."

When Alice and Lady Preston had disappeared with Kerr, Ross turned to her. "I've arranged for you and Ian to sit at the head of the table with Alice and me."

"I understand."

"You know everyone by now," Ross continued, without meeting her gaze. "But I'll introduce you and the occasion. Then you can say a few words and pass the cup to me."

"And it will be official," Leonora finished for him, offering a smile. "The feud will be at an end."

"Yes." He glanced at her, his expression grim and wary. Then he and Ian exchanged a tense look that it was impossible for her to interpret.

Ian leaned close and murmured. " 'Tisn't too late, lass. Ye can still change yer mind. We can walk out of here right now."

Astonished, she stared at him. *What is Ian concerned about?* she wondered, her own apprehension growing. They were making history tonight. They were going to make peace. What could be wrong with that?

Eight

The rehearsal dinner went smoothly. Course after course came to the table, perfectly prepared and presented, hot and tasty. The bagpiper played his tunes, parading around the table three times. The guests were in a fine mood, talking and laughing when the blare of the music permitted.

Leonora had found each evening that the music made conversation difficult. Sometimes that was a good thing, depending on whom you were seated next to. This evening, sitting next to Ross, she decided that it was just as well that they could not talk before the presentation.

This was not the moment for a personal exchange between them. She was no more anxious than she would be if she was presenting a paper to the medical society, but she did want to strike the right tone. She picked at her food and considered what she wanted to say.

When the sweet plates had been taken away, Ross glanced at her. She nodded that she was ready. He rose to gain the attention of his guests. Kerr, who was seated on Lady Preston's side, obligingly clinked his crystal goblet with his spoon. The dinner guests fell silent.

Ross opened his remarks with some humorous comments about the activities of the day. There had been a serious croquet game on the east lawn, which

Ross had won, and some of the gentlemen had enjoyed a round of golf. An especially accomplished player had lost to a rank beginner. The guests laughed.

Then his genial smile disappeared, and Leonora knew her moment was at hand.

"As many of you know," Ross began, "we have a visitor among us from America, a Camville who has returned to Scotland. Not just a Camville, but The Maid of the Camvilles."

Around the table, heads nodded and faces turned toward Leonora, expressions sober, expectant. Where were the smiles of goodwill she had expected from people she had spent the last few days enjoying various entertainments with?

Her gut went still and tight. At her side Ian shifted uneasily, but he avoided her gaze when she glanced at him. Something was wrong.

Ross continued. "And as many of you know, long before the Clan Camville departed for the New World, a feud raged between them and the MacDonnarts."

Heads around the table nodded.

Leonora stirred in her chair and wished he wouldn't dwell on the past.

"No one seems to remember what started the feud, but the ultimate insult came in the darkness of night when a lone Camville stole away the pride of the MacDonnarts, the silver bridal cup. According to legend, it was given for services performed for St. Margaret. In the years that followed, many unforgivable crimes were committed. In the fullness of time, some things can be forgotten if not forgiven. But the theft of the cup has remained a sore point. Now, the Camvilles have returned from America to admit defeat and surrender the cup to its rightful owners, the MacDonnarts."

Ian leaped to his feet. "Here, now, 'tis not defeat."

Defeat? Surrender? Leonora repeated silently. She stared at Ross in astonishment. All the polite sentiments that she'd been composing in her head about hospitality disappeared, vanquished by Ross's words.

Understanding dawned. Victory was why he had wanted her to stay so desperately. Not out of hospitality. But for this moment of MacDonnart triumph.

A sinking sense of betrayal seeped into her heart. *How can he say that? Returning the cup has nothing to do with defeat.*

She glared at him. His face was somber as he stepped back so she could rise.

She stood, her hands spread on the table before her. She held her chin high. Thank heavens she'd worn the Camville plaid and brooch even though the other ladies were dressed in their ballroom best. She was proud to stand among the MacDonnarts wearing the evidence of her heritage. *Defeat. Surrender. Is that what he thinks this is about?*

Without taking her gaze from Ross's face, she motioned to Ian to give her the cup. Swiftly, Ian opened the box and handed the silver goblet to her.

The guests at the table gasped at the sight of the gleaming double-stemmed silver goblet.

Ross held her gaze without a flicker of apology. Then his gaze went to the cup.

That's when the full measure of the impossibility of her love for him struck her—and she almost sobbed aloud.

It wasn't just the hopelessness of him being engaged to another while he was a MacDonnart and she was a Camville. It was the differences in their goals. However passionate their attraction to each other might be, he would always have his duty to win for the MacDonnarts. She would have hers to heal.

She swallowed her aching disappointment and ignored her hollow heart.

Holding the cup up for all to see, she studied the

faces around the table. All eyes beheld the cup. Each face glowed with the pleasure of seeing the symbol of their heritage; just as her face had glowed when she'd been introduced to Ardal Camville in the village kirk portrait.

"It pleases me very much to come here to return this cup to the MacDonnarts, especially at this time," Leonora began. She purposely avoided Ross's presence and forced herself to smile at Alice. Ross's stubbornness was not the poor girl's fault. "What could be more fitting than to hand it to my host for him to use at his wedding."

Excited murmurs circulated around the table.

"However, I dare to contradict my host." She shot Ross a forbidding look before he could reach for the cup. "I came here to return this bridal cup not out of defeat or of surrender. When clan members decided to leave Scotland it was to fight the battle that needed to be fought, the battle for survival. The Camvilles have not been defeated. The Camvilles have not surrendered. We are alive and prosperous in America. The defeat, the surrender was not of Camvilles or of the MacDonnarts. It was of the old ways. The world has moved on. Feuding has been left behind. That is why I am returning this cup. I come as a healer. Not in defeat. Not in surrender. But to heal what should be healed. An archaic, useless division between countrymen, between men and women with the same proud heritage."

Toward the middle of the table, the vicar leaped to his feet and shouted, "Hear! Hear!"

Without a murmur of agreement or dissent, the rest of the assemblage stared at her. Sober faces now. Tight-lipped mouths. Round eyes.

At last, Leonora turned and offered the cup to Ross. "With best wishes for a prosperous MacDonnart future."

He hesitated before reaching for it. Only when

she stepped toward him did he take it without a word of thanks.

"I think a tune from the piper would be appropriate now," she murmured to him as he accepted the cup.

His expression was unreadable. Polite applause broke out around the table as he held the cup up for all to see. Then he nodded a signal to the musician who immediately set his pipes to humming and started marching around the table.

Guests rose to congratulate Ross and Alice. A few stopped Leonora on her way out of the dining room to thank her. She smiled and accepted their gratitude as best she could. She only wanted to leave as soon as possible.

Truth was, she should have left that first day she arrived at Glenalder. When he'd looked at her with narrowed, shadowed eyes and demanded, "What do you want?" He hadn't understood then why she'd come, and he didn't understand now. She should have put the cup in Ross's hands and walked out the door without a look back. It would have saved her a lot of heartache.

"Ye set 'em straight, lass," Ian said, scurrying along at her side as she strode into the hallway. "The feud is dead. And proud I am to be a Camville. Set 'em straight, yer did."

He stopped when she reached the stairs. "Where are ye going?"

"I'm going to pack," she said. In the ballroom she could hear the stringed quartet tuning up and the chatter of folks already gathering around the punch table where the whiskey punch was being mixed. She had no heart for a celebration and certainly not for a wedding. "Would you be so kind as to ask Stratton for a carriage to the village? I'll take the train out in the morning."

"You're not going anywhere this time of night."

Ross appeared at her side. His mouth was grim and his eyes dark with annoyance. No doubt, he'd disliked being shone up at his own dinner table.

"I'll do as I please, my lord," she said, sorry to hear her words sound so childish.

"We need to talk." Ross reached for her hand resting on the mahogany banister.

She snatched her hand away. "I have nothing more to say."

"In the library," Ross said, as if he had not heard her. He took her elbow with a firm grip and guided her across the hallway.

She resisted but did not struggle. Reluctant to cause more of a scene than she'd just created in the dining room, she allowed him to usher her into the library.

With a frown, Ian followed them. "Here, now—" He sidled in the door behind her.

Ross's eyes narrowed. "This is between Leonora and me."

Glancing at Ian, she nodded. She did not need anyone at her side to tell Ross what she thought.

At the sight of both of their faces, Ian backed out of the room and latched the door closed.

"I misjudged—" Ross began.

"How could you—" she blurted at the same time, beyond tears or sobs.

They stopped and stared at each other with only the popping of the fire to break the silence.

Ross studied the woman standing before him and knew he'd never faced her like before and probably never would again. She held her head high and carried the Camville plaid with all the pride and bravado of the ablest clan chiefs.

"You were right to contradict me," he said. "I misjudged—"

"Misjudged, my eye!" Her voice was lower and even huskier when she was angry. "I told you why I was here from the beginning. I never claimed defeat or victory. How dare you claim victory! I was even foolish enough to think that we'd—that we were friends."

"I did not intend to mislead you," he lied, the vivid memory of their kiss evoking feelings beyond friendship. That day at Castle Camville, they had touched each other not as Camville and MacDonnart but as man and woman, as souls seeking warmth, strength, and life. One knowing the other's pain, the other's pleasure, the other's fears and confusion. That day, something had shifted inside him. And he was beginning to understand that it had to do with how he felt about her.

"Nonsense, that's exactly what you intended," she corrected with all the righteousness she deserved to feel. For an instant a glimmer of pain shone in her eyes.

The sight of her hurt flayed his heart.

"You knew I didn't understand what you wanted," she continued. "You were the kindest of hosts. All the time knowing—then you betrayed me and in front of all those people!"

He longed to deny her accusation, but he could not. She was right. He had known all along that she did not fully understand the emotions surrounding the feud. She had every right to feel betrayed. She had every right to spurn his offer of hospitality.

"I've done what I came to do, and I'm ready to go home." Leonora folded her arms across her breasts, and the pain in her eyes glittered into cool fury. "Would you be so kind as to order the carriage?"

"You've carried out your duty admirably," he said, stalling. His insides warred against the thought of her leaving, even now that she had returned the cup. Even now as she heaped her anger on him. How could he make her stay? Why did he want her to? "Alice and I owe you our gratitude. You are welcome to stay and watch the bridal cup used for the first time in centuries."

"How can you think I want to stay and watch that?" she blurted, her response sharp, abrupt, full of indignant disbelief. "I am happy for you and Alice. Believe me, I am. Alice is a sweet young woman who will make you a good wife. But I have no obligation to stay. I've done my duty and tomorrow you will do yours. Isn't this what you wanted?"

"I thought so," Ross said, honestly. Her disdain stung. She spoke the truth. She had done her duty and he would do his. Nevertheless, he wanted to roar no, a thundering *no* to her request to leave. Unreasonable as he knew it was, he wanted to act like a chief of old. But he had not that right, not that power. With effort, he clutched his hands into fists to keep himself from locking her in her room.

Instead of roaring, he asked in a civil voice he hardly recognized, "Then, you wish to leave tonight?"

She took a deep breath. "I think it would be best. I'll catch the first train from the village in the morning."

"Yes, of course." He nearly choked on the words. "I'll ask Stratton to do whatever your departure requires."

"Thank you," she said, obvious relief in her voice, relief that sent another flash of pain through him. Just like that, she would pack up and walk out of Glenalder. Out of his life.

He had made a terrible mistake at the rehearsal dinner—in forcing a concession from a woman as proud of her heritage as he was of his. A woman who understood duty as well as he did. A woman who had the courage to face the new century and all its marvels just as he did.

She started for the door, and he knew that, due to

his own bloody stupidity, he'd never see her again. He was lost.

She stopped when she reach the doorway. "Under the circumstances, I think it best if you say my farewells to Kerr, Alice, and her mother."

"I shall," Ross said, forcing himself to stay where he was, not to rush across the room and beg her to stay.

Then she was gone.

He lingered for a moment. Hell's bells. He raked his fingers through his hair, paced the floor, and cursed the day he had first heard of the bridal cup.

"Ross, darling, there you are." Alice bustled into the room all smiles, ribbons and curls, and lacy sapphire blue ball gown. Her pretty cheeks were flushed with excitement. "Was that Leonora I saw leaving? Does she really have to go? Such a shame. Come, darling, the dancing is about to begin."

"Yes, I hear the music," he replied, not really thinking about what he was saying.

Alice leaned against him, her dainty hands pressed against the lapels of his velvet jacket. She offered him a coy smile even though he made no move to touch her. "Does her leaving disappoint you so? She and the old man are welcome, are they not?"

"I told her as much," Ross said, his head full of the unpleasant image of Leonora traveling alone in the dark.

"Well, then it was her choice," Alice said, touching his arm tentatively. "There's nothing you can do about that. Our guests await us. Let's dance." She tugged him toward the library door and the music. "Tonight is our last night as a betrothed couple."

Her smile was sweet, youthful, entreating.

The last night—tomorrow they would be married. The thought gave him pause. He resisted her tugging at first. But Alice was right. They had an obligation to their guests. "I need to talk to Stratton first," he said. "I'll join you in a moment."

When Alice was gone and Stratton arrived, Ross gave orders for the carriage to be brought and for the butler to give Ian MacCage enough money to enable the man to accompany Leonora to Southampton. It might be a modern world where women went about on their own, but no single lady who was a MacDonnarts' guest was going to journey across England without the safety of an escort—even if it was MacCage.

Having mollified himself that Leonora might be leaving, but she would be safe, at least, Ross walked into the ballroom intending to dance with Alice.

She was waltzing in Kerr's arms. The sight darkened his mood.

Without hesitation Ross tapped his brother on the shoulder and swung his fiancée into his arms. When Alice saw his grim face, she laughed nervously but immediately paced her steps to his.

As they whirled across the floor, he noted that the bridal cup sat in a place of honor on the fireplace mantel. It loomed there, shining and graceful with a presence all its own. He was glad, satisfied. Everything was as it should be for the wedding.

When the waltz was finished, he offered to get punch for Alice. He passed the entry hall in time to see Stratton close the door on the departing carriage. The clatter of the horses' hooves on the gravel drive set his heart beating rapidly—from the exertion of the dance, of course.

Stratton saw him, came to the ballroom door, and spoke quietly. "It is done, my lord, just as you wished. Dr. Camville is on her way home. Ian MacCage agreed to escort her. I think he was glad of the request."

Ross gave a curt nod of understanding, but the knowledge left him cold and empty. The oddest sense of foreboding sank over him—foreboding and loss. He glanced around the ballroom at the bridal cup. When he saw it—when he envisioned sharing that silver goblet with his bride—he knew Stratton was wrong.

It was not done.

Nine

"I just want to make sure that yer state room is taken care of, proper and all," Ian said, bustling ahead of Leonora along the ship deck six days later. "And that yer luggage has arrived."

They wove their way through the excited crowd of passengers. The New York–bound ship was booked full, so full Leonora had feared she would not get passage on it. But waiting at the ticket agent office had paid off. A last-minute cancellation had opened. She'd just had time to wire Janet about her arrival date before she returned to the inn for her bags.

Then Ian had insisted on seeing her on board. She suspected he'd never been aboard an ocean liner before. She could hardly blame him for his curiosity, though. She had been just as curious a few weeks before when she'd boarded one for the first time.

"Here 'tis," he said reading the numbers posted on the hallway walls. "It must be right down this passage somewhere."

She followed him. He'd been a good companion all along the way, seeing to her luggage and arguing over fares when it was called for and when she didn't know any better. She didn't know how he'd afforded to stay with her. He always refused anything she offered him for his help. He always managed to get himself on the same train or bus or to find a modest room at the same inn.

"I found it," he crowed. She heard the key jingle as he unlocked the room.

Exhaustion was beginning to settle over her. The long days ahead at sea were just what she needed. She could rest and sort through her feelings. By the time the ship docked in New York, she would be ready to travel on to Boston and go back to the clinic. She would start again as a doctor. Because she knew she could. Alice's recovery had given her confidence. And she'd learned much from her brief visit with Dr. Elizabeth Blackwell, America's first woman doctor who now lived in England. Her confidence in her medical future was considerably bolstered. A gentle thrill of excitement with the prospect of healing others again surged through her.

But it could not completely wash away the sense of loss she felt over Ross. She had met the one man who she could love beyond all else, and he was committed to his family duty to wed a Preston. She would never have been able to love him had he been any other kind of man.

She had returned the cup and then found an impossible love. She would learn to live with the ache in her heart—every day.

"This door wasna locked," Ian complained as he turned the handle and the door opened with ease.

They both saw it immediately, the rowan wood box sitting on the small table beneath the porthole. Atop the box stood the gleaming silver bridal cup.

Ian sucked in a noisy breath.

Leonora's heart went still. What was the cup doing there?

Ian crept into the room as if he expected an ambush. She followed him, her gaze fastened on the cup she knew she'd left behind at Glenalder.

From the doorway on their right came a familiar voice. "So there you are."

She and Ian whirled around to face Ross.

"I was watching for you near the gangplank, but I must have missed you in this crowd," he said, speaking quietly as if they had had plans to rendezvous.

"What are ye doing here?" Ian blurted.

Ross ignored him and spoke directly to her. "I don't think we finished talking the other night at Glenalder," he said, his gaze searching her face.

She was glad to see him again, but she refused to allow her feelings to show.

"I had a devil of a time locating you. Nearly burned up the telegraph lines between the village, London, and Southampton. Called in a few favors. I hadn't anticipated that you would take a couple of days in London to see Dr. Blackwell. But I'm glad you did. Gave me time to locate your booking."

"Where's Alice?" Leonora asked, wondering if the new bride was going to walk in at any moment. "She's all right, isn't she?"

"She's with Kerr," Ross said with an amazing lack of concern. "She and Kerr are on their way to Italy on their honeymoon. Lady Preston is with them."

"Alice and Kerr? Honeymoon?" Leonora could only stare at Ross in disbelief.

"So ye came to yer senses and called the wedding off," Ian said, grinning gleefully. "And ye decided to return the cup to the Camvilles."

"What happened?" she asked, nearly speechless with astonishment.

Before Ross could reply, the sound of the ship's whistle split the air, warning visitors to begin disembarking.

Ian looked expectantly from Ross to Leonora and back again. "That's my signal to leave, I'll wager."

Ross nodded.

Ian turned to her with a look of resignation. "It

has been a pleasure to meet ye, lass. To know ye. Yer a worthy Maid of the Camvilles. Give my regards to those American Camvilles of yers."

"Thank you, Ian. For all your help." She took his hand and kissed his wrinkled cheek. "I'll write you."

"Do that lass." The old man pursed his lips as he walked past Ross. "Be quick, my lord. The whistle blows only three times. On the third, the ship is leaving the dock."

"So I've been told," Ross said.

When Ian was gone, Leonora met Ross's gaze directly for the first time. "What happened?" she repeated.

"Simple." He glanced at the bridal cup. "I looked at that cup sitting there on Glenalder's mantel and knew I should not share it with Alice."

She bit her lower lip against hope and fear.

"It seems that Kerr and Alice have had feelings for each other for years and I was too blind to see it." He paused. When she said nothing, he eyed her and asked, "Aren't you going to ask me whom I should be sharing it with?"

"The choice is yours," she said, her emotions raw, churning in an unbelievable turmoil. "When I handed you that cup at the dinner table, the impossibility of us anything special ever existing between us became very clear. We shall always be separated by our names. By a feud no one seems to want to die."

"But you also said that these are new times." He reached around her and picked up the cup.

"Are you going to throw my words back in my fact?" she asked, her turmoil turning into irritation.

"And why not?" he said, admiring the cup. "I learned a lesson from you that night. This cup is a symbol of the past, a symbol of heritage. Heritage is an anchor in a changing world, not an encumbrance. I knew that. I learned it long ago with my head. The knowledge made me successful in business. But I hadn't learned it in my heart until I met you. Until that night when you made it clear to me in front of all those MacDonnarts. Can you forgive me?"

"Forgive?" she stammered, almost shouting. Was the man daft? "For the humiliation you put me through? In a century or two maybe."

"Careful." He gave her a mock frown. "That kind of feeling keeps feuds alive."

The second whistle blew before she could reply. She realized time was too short to linger on the past.

"Forgive me, Leonora," Ross said, taking advantage of her speechless exasperation. Slipping an arm around her, he continued. "Share this cup with me. I love you. I suspect from the way you kissed me that night in Alice's room that you might harbor some gentle feelings toward me."

Heavens, he was declaring his love. Her anger evaporated. She allowed him to pull her closer. The solidness, the male scent of tobacco and shaving soap, engulfed her.

The floor beneath them shuddered gently as somewhere in the bowels of the ship, the boiler fires were stoked and the steam pressure built.

"Ross, I'm not sure the depth of my feelings is what's important," she said, trying to keep a level head. "I'm an American and a woman doctor. There are things about my life I am *not* going to give up and that you are hardly prepared for."

"But, do you love me, dearest?" he murmured, his lips against her temple.

She hesitated, her body tingling with the warmth of his embrace. The immensity of the differences between them still yawned before her.

"I know you love me," he said, his lips threatening her ear this time. "Maybe you didn't love me the first time we kissed. But there was love in that kiss we shared in Alice's room. You cared whether I drowned or not."

"Yes, I love you," she admitted, speaking aloud what she'd known in her heart since that day at the castle. "But, you and I, it's impossible."

"I knew it," he said, his whisper full of victory. "I know it will not be easy. There are clan members on both sides of the Atlantic who will not take to this kindly. Do you think old MacCage will ever take a liking to me? But we can make it work. Dearest, fool that I am, I do know that happiness does not offer itself often. A wise man seizes it when it does—whatever the price."

Before she could counter, a knock sounded on the door. She almost whimpered in disappointment when he released her to go to the door.

It was a steward with a bucket of iced champagne. Ross tipped him, brought the bucket in, and sat it down next to the bridal cup.

"Where were we?" he asked as he prepared to open the bottle.

"You were seizing happiness," she said, able to think more clearly now that she stood alone. "As if happiness is something to possess not earn, to be taken as a prize. Not shared but held up to others and gloated over."

"You're right." He stopped working on the bottle and turned to her with an earnest expression. "I won't gloat, this time. I will surrender, if you like. I am defeated. You win."

"Ross, I told you this is not about winning or losing or about victory or defeat."

Suddenly he took her in his arms again. She pressed her hands against his shirtfront, thrilled but wary. She could feel his heart beating, rapid but steady.

"Then show me what it is about," he said, his face so close to hers she could feel the warmth of his breath against her cheek. "Kiss me," he said, "Then tell me what it is about, this thing between you and me."

His mouth lowered to hers, nibbling at first, enticing her to join him in the tender feast, lips against lips.

She closed her eyes and moaned, savoring the pleasure of his arms around her. Slipping her arms around him, she turned her cheek, giving him no choice but to feather more kisses along her jawline.

"Are you going to make surrender difficult, lass?" he murmured against her cheek, his mouth clever and teasing. He pulled at her coat.

"It is not without its price," she said, parting from him enough to allow him to remove her wrap, but he did not let her drift away.

"Whatever the cost," he said, tugging now at the pins in her hair and massaging her scalp in an erotic way. "I'll pay."

When her tresses fell free, he threaded his fingers through them and pulled her face to his again. He took her mouth this time—gave her no choice of turning a cheek.

This wasn't the hard ruthless kiss he'd first demanded from her that day at Castle Camville. This was seduction itself. Tender, wondrous, sweet. The incredible taste of warm firm lips working their way across hers. The tease of a tongue, the testing, the searching. She could not resist his surrender. She opened to him.

He moaned, a low sound full of satisfaction and possession. He explored her mouth slowly.

A shiver of excitement stole through Leonora, snatching away the last of her wariness.

He released her only long enough for his hands to find the buttons at the back of her gown. She gasped for breath.

"I need to taste your skin," he whispered against

her temple once more. "To touch your body. To surrender inside you."

"Yes" was the only word that came to her mind. Her whole body tingled with the prospect. "Yes," she whispered again as his hand fumbled with her buttons and she fumbled with his.

Becoming naked had never seemed to happen so fast, and she had never realized how fascinating a man's body was until she allowed him to pull her down onto the narrow berth. Long lean lines, sinewy contours, and hardness. Still his touch was tender.

The ship's whistle blasted again.

Leonora sucked in a shocked breath and struggled to sit up. "That's the last whistle."

Ross pulled her down. He kissed her lips lightly as he spread a hand over her bare hip, his arousal pressing against her thigh. "It seems we have two choices."

"And those are?" she asked, breathless and her body humming with need for him.

"We can dress quickly, go ashore, and check into a hotel where we will share our first toast from the bridal cup," he said, nibbling at her ear as his hand slipped upward to cup her breast. "Then return to Glenalder for the wedding. Or we can sail on the ship. I'm sure the captain would oblige us with a wedding ceremony."

"Wedding ceremony?" She closed her eyes, her body soft and pliant under his hands, his mouth. "Ross, we hardly know each other."

"That is the challenge of it," he said, taking her chin and turning her face to his. "A lifetime to know each other. I have no desire to attempt that arduous task with anyone else. Say you'll allow the ship's captain to marry us at sea. I wouldn't mind seeing America, visiting new kinsmen. When we return to Glenalder, you can practice medicine, just like Dr. Blackwell does. We can even build a clinic, if you like. But I surely don't feel like getting dressed while I'm in this condition."

He put her hand on his arousal. It was smooth and firm. Ready.

Leonora chuckled softly. "Nor do I. But—"

"Say yes again, just like you did before," he said. "Such a sweet sound."

As he settled against her side, his mouth found her throat, her breast. He drew lazy circles with his tongue until his mouth captured her aching areolas. The sensation was a pure thrill in her belly. His tongue was so clever and his hands persuasive, relentless, touching, searching, caressing. She wanted nothing more than to accept him.

"Yes," she whispered, stroking him. "Yes, I love you."

He covered her. She arched against him, helping him make his surrender long and deep.

Beneath them, the engines shuddered with power and the ship eased away from the dock.

Incredible pleasure spun through Leonora, from him buried inside her, through her body and to her heart, to her fingertips as they raked across his back. Her cry of pleasure was drowned out by the ship's whistle.

Ross tensed in her arms, his body hard and urgent against hers. Then he groaned against her neck.

After a moment he eased to her side, pulling her against him. "I love you," he whispered. "Whatever is to come, we will face together. We share it all. Traditions and challenges."

"Old and new," she agreed, thinking of the traditions her father and uncle had kept from her. "Not knowing my heritage left me ill-equipped for my future."

Without saying anything, Ross climbed from the berth. Naked as a newborn, he popped the cork from the champagne bottle and poured the bubbling wine into the silver bridal cup.

Leonora sat up so he could sit beside her.

He held the cup up. "Share it with me. Share it with me now, my bride, and through the years. And when the time comes, we will pass this to our children."

"Yes." Leonora smiled. With her hand on one of the stems and Ross's on the other, together they drank from the ancient bridal cup.

Promises To Keep

Patricia Waddell

*To Ann, a good friend and my
unofficial editor.
Here's to handsome cowboys
and feisty ladies.*

One

Central Texas
Spring 1867

Luke Maddock watched from the sidewalk that fronted the saloon as the stage pulled into town. A large trunk swayed on top of the rickety coach. He wondered if Jolene Chapman's wedding dress was neatly packed inside the dusty luggage.

Luke was tempted to tell the driver not to waste his time unstrapping the hodgepodge of luggage that belonged to Russell McClain's newly arrived bride-to-be, but he didn't. The young lady from Memphis, Tennessee, deserved more than a tip of a man's hat and a go-back-to-where-you-came-from welcome.

She deserved the June wedding that would never take place.

Shaking the wrinkles from her traveling dress, Jolene tried to hide her nervousness as she stepped away from the confining stagecoach and its uncomfortable seats. She searched the street with optimistic eyes, hoping for a glimpse of the childhood friend who was destined to become her husband, but Russell was nowhere to be seen.

"Miss Chapman?"

The stranger who sauntered off the sidewalk and

addressed her had brooding dark eyes and a lazy Texas drawl, but Jolene sensed that his hesitation wasn't normal. There was a surety about the man that didn't match the reluctance in his dark eyes.

"Yes. I'm Jolene Chapman. Did Russell send you?"

Luke wished like hell that he could say no. He wished he could walk away from the young woman with sapphire eyes and burnished copper hair and forget that he'd ever known a man by the name of Russell McClain.

But he couldn't.

"My name's Maddock," he said, touching the brim of his hat. "Luke Maddock."

"Did Russell send you to meet me, Mr. Maddock?"

"You could say that," he replied, staring down at her. She wasn't very tall, but she was nicely rounded in all the right places. The enticing color of her hair and eyes held his attention a moment longer than politeness allowed. It was a damn shame to put a prime piece of woman back on the stage, but that's exactly what Luke hoped to do, come morning. Until then, he had a promise to keep.

"We need to talk," he said.

Jolene didn't have the slightest idea what she and Luke Maddock had to discuss. "My fiancé was supposed to meet the stage. Do you work for Russell?"

"I rented a room for you at the hotel," Luke told her, deliberately avoiding the question.

"What do we have to talk about, Mr. Maddock?" Jolene repeated impatiently. She'd just finished coming halfway across the country. All she wanted at that moment was a hot bath and ten hours of sleep, but she wasn't about to tell Luke Maddock that. He was a complete stranger.

She looked up at the man who was standing so close she could see a small scar on the underside of his chin. He was a dark silhouette against the afternoon sun. Under the brim of his hat, onyx eyes

watched her with a male curiosity that made her skin
tingle.

"Apparently, you know Russell. If he sent you to
fetch me, then say so. If not, then kindly get out of
my way so I can find him for myself."

Russell said she'd be feisty. But then, Russell had
done nothing but talk about his Tennessee sweetheart for the past two years.

Luke pointed toward the hotel. "We can talk inside."

Jolene couldn't believe her eyes as the stranger
turned and started walking toward a two-story whitewashed building.

"Mr. Maddock," she called out, hurrying to catch
up with him and get the explanation he'd so easily
avoided.

Luke kept walking. The sooner he got Jolene inside, the sooner he could have the drink he'd been
promising himself. He'd delayed having it, because
he hadn't wanted to meet Russell's bride-to-be with
whiskey on his breath. But after seeing her, Luke was
more determined than ever to march into the saloon
and drink the place dry.

If he had any sense, he'd forget the promise he'd
made to Russell and ride out of town. But he had
made a promise, and nothing this side of heaven or
hell was going to make Luke break it—which meant,
all he could do was get the words said and hope for
the best.

"Mr. Maddock!" Jolene reached out and grabbed
his arm to slow him down.

Luke came to an abrupt stop as her fingertips
brushed over the faded cotton of his shirt. He
couldn't remember the last time a woman had
touched him. He drank at the saloon, but he didn't
indulge in its other pleasure. But then, Jolene Chapman wasn't a saloon girl. She was a soft-spoken lady

from Tennessee who had traveled to Texas to become another man's wife.

"Please," she sighed wearily. "I'm too tired to run after you for answers. Why can't you just tell me where Russell is?"

"I'll tell you everything once we're off the street and inside the hotel. The sun isn't going to get any cooler, and you look like you're at the end of a short rope."

Luke's words were blunt, and definitely unflattering, but the concern in his voice softened their impact.

"Very well," Jolene relented. "But once I'm inside, I expect an explanation."

Luke knew exactly what Jolene expected. She'd come to Texas expecting to find the man she loved. What Luke didn't know was how she was going to react when she found out that Russell McClain was dead and buried.

Jolene waited while Luke asked the clerk for the key, then followed him upstairs to the second floor. Once they were inside a room with a double bed, a scarred dresser, and a rocking chair that faced the room's only window, Jolene turned to the man who had whisked her off the street. Sensing that if she backed down now, she'd be forever stepping out of Luke Maddock's way, Jolene kept her composure and met his gaze. "I'd like my explanation now."

With dark eyes that grew darker the longer they looked at her, Luke decided being a plainspoken man had its disadvantages. Jolene deserved comforting words, not cold hard facts that would take away everything she'd come to Texas to find.

Knowing there was no way around it, Luke said what had to be said. "Russell's dead."

"Dead!" The word came out in a rush of disbelief.

Luke let the news sink in, waiting for hysteria to follow. He'd never been any good with women, especially the kind who carried lace hankies and moved in a rustle of petticoats and satin. Ladies were rare in Texas and almost nonexistent in the rough country where he'd been born and raised. He'd fought Indians and droughts and rustlers, killing when he had to, surviving on his instincts and lessons learned the hard way. He didn't know any gentlemanly words or soothing phrases. When Russell had been killed by a gang of no-account, cattle-thievin' vermin, Luke had gotten good and drunk.

Then he'd got on with doing what had to be done.

He'd dug a grave, buried one of the best men he'd ever known, and made a solemn vow to himself and Russell's memory that one day he'd send the murderin' bastards to hell at the end of a rope.

"How?" Jolene asked in a shocked whisper.

"Rustlers," Luke told her. "Last month."

Last month she'd been crossing the Mississippi, praying that the mighty river would stay calm until the raft ferrying the wagons across the silty water arrived safety on the western bank. Russell had been dead, while she'd been daydreaming of a new life and promising herself that her childhood companion would never know that she didn't love him the way a woman should love the man she had promised to marry.

The ironic twist of fate that had brought her to Texas, only to find herself once again orphaned by violence, hit Jolene so hard she staggered backward and gripped the edge of the dresser. The war had spared their Tennessee farm, but it hadn't spared her family. Her father and three brothers had been killed, fighting for the South. When Russell's letter had arrived, telling her about his dreams for a future in Texas, Jolene had soaked up the words, needing them like flowers needed sunshine.

"We were herding up cattle to sell to the garrison at Fort Worth," Luke began. He didn't say that his partner had wanted to sell the steers so he could buy Jolene a wedding ring and a new cookstove for the rough-timbered ranch house. "The rustlers started a stampede. Russell was trying to turn the herd when he caught a bullet."

Jolene felt the damp heat of tears on her face as she thought of the handsome blond boy who'd taught her how to put a worm on a hook and then laughed when she'd tossed the fish back into the pond because it looked like a wet rainbow and she didn't have the heart to clean it for supper. That was what Jolene remembered most about Russell McClain: his ability to laugh.

He'd always worn his best smile for her.

Then the war had started and Russell had ridden off to join the fighting. Jolene had cried at his departure, fearing the unknown future that had suddenly become a harsh reality. But even war couldn't take away Russell's smile. The few letters she'd received from him had been full of his spirit, always seeing the best in people and circumstances, always promising to come home so he could take her fishing again.

Finally, he had come home. Older and wiser, but still smiling.

They'd gone fishing again, and he'd told her about his dreams for the future. A ranch in Texas. He hadn't asked her to marry him that day, but Jolene knew it was part of his plan. When the letter came, she read it over and over. Russell's way of seeing things had made Texas seem like a wild fairyland. He'd wired money to the bank in Memphis, enough for her to get to Texas, if she was willing to come and share his dream.

She'd come. Partly because she didn't have the courage to break Russell's heart, but mostly because she did love him. It wasn't a passionate feeling, but it was deep and true and loyal, like the love she'd had for her brothers.

The silent tears streaming down Jolene's face sent a gut-wrenching pain through Luke. He'd prepared himself for wild sobs, not slow tears shed one by one. He'd seen death often enough to know what grief looked like. A part of him wanted Jolene to rant and rave at the injustice that had robbed Russell of his life. Watching her sorrow displayed in tiny silver droplets made the pain Luke had carried around inside himself since his friend's death harder and harder to contain.

Another part of Luke wanted to pull Jolene into his arms and give her the comfort only another grieving person could offer. He'd loved the young man from Tennessee like a brother. "Russell was the best man I ever knew," he said, meaning very word.

"I'm glad he wasn't alone. He was afraid of the dark when he was little," Jolene managed a weak smile."

For a long moment the only sound was the clicking of a small clock on the dresser and Jolene's soft shaky breathing. Luke watched as more tears slid from beneath copper lashes. The delicate trembling in her hands as she reached for a handkerchief matched the slight tremor of her bottom lip as she tried to contain her grief.

"When we were children, Russell used to tease me about my hair. He said it made me look like an over-ripe pumpkin." Another smile, this one bittersweet. "I told him he was as skinny as an ax blade."

Luke didn't say anything because he didn't know what to say. He knew a lot of things about Jolene Chapman: facts and dates and how she liked straw-berries better than anything in the world. But he didn't know how a woman talked about the man she loved.

Not until now.

With misty eyes, gleaming with pain and devotion, Jolene rambled from one childhood memory to another. Luke let her talk, enjoying the soft southern tones of her voice. Then Jolene stopped talking and looked at him with eyes blue enough for a man to drown in.

"I'd like to see Russell's grave."

"You need some rest," Luke said. "We'll talk again later."

Jolene started to protest, then didn't. Russell was dead. Her beloved friend, the man she'd come to Texas to marry, was gone. So was the future she'd dreamed of building with him. She felt full of emotions and as empty as a dried-up well, all at the same time. The daydreams that had kept her alive had turned into a cold cruel nightmare.

Luke walked toward the door. He looked over his shoulder as Jolene moved away from the dresser, more shaken by the news of Russell McClain's death than she wanted to reveal to a stranger. Her face was pale. Tears gleamed in her bluebonnet eyes, and she was wobbling on her feet.

"Maybe you'd better sit down," he suggested.

"I'll be fine," she said weakly. "I appreciate your . . ."

Jolene felt the words drifting away as the world faded into a swirling haze.

Luke's curse was short and quick as he moved to catch Jolene before she crumpled to the floor like a rag doll. The feminine weight in his arms brought another curse, this one low and deep, like the desire that raced through his body the moment he had her in his arms.

He lowered her onto the feather mattress as gently as he'd put a baby in a cradle. With little else to entertain his eyes, he watched the gentle rise and fall of her breasts as her body began to relax. He couldn't help but wonder what it would be like to kiss her. To feel those pink lips opening under his, to taste the warm damp cavern of her mouth, to forget the grief that clung to him like a shadow since the day he'd buried Russell McClain.

But he couldn't forget.

She's mourning the man she loves, Luke reminded himself, taking a sizable step back from the bed. *No matter how tempting she is, she belongs to Russell. But Russell's dead. Jolene is alive and young and soft enough to make a man forget all his worries.*

Angered by the betraying thought, Luke turned and headed for the door and the bottle of whiskey waiting at the saloon. Russell had been his friend and partner. He should be horsewhipped for even thinking about Jolene in any context that didn't involve being a big brother and watching over her the way he'd promised.

But Luke wasn't feeling like a big brother. He felt like a man being ridden hard by lust and wanting the one woman he'd be a fool and a traitor to touch again. The partnership that had ended with Luke digging Russell's grave had meant more to him than just land and cattle, it had filled the void after the war. Crooked Spur Ranch was his home now. The first real home he'd had in years.

With his hand resting on the doorknob and his conscience beating him to death, Luke watched Jolene's lashes flutter as she recovered from her faint.

"Please, don't go," she said, realizing that Luke was about to leave her alone.

Luke's conscience wasn't the only one acting up. The moment Jolene opened her eyes she knew she'd been wrong to let Russell believe that she had loved him. Instead of being honest, she'd let him believe a lie. Although the lie hadn't been the cause of his death, she couldn't forgive herself for misleading him. She should have had the courage to write him, to explain that he held a very special place in her heart, but she hadn't. Instead, she'd accepted his proposal of marriage and convinced herself that she could spend the rest of her life hiding the truth from her best friend. It had been foolish and selfish. She knew that now, but it was too late.

"You need to rest," Luke said. "Get some sleep. I'll check in on you later."

He left before Jolene could stop him, heading down the hotel steps and out the front door. He didn't stop walking until he was in the saloon with a bottle of whiskey in front of him.

Luke tried to enjoy the hot sensation of the liquor running down his throat and burning into his stomach, but it was quickly replaced with the image of a girl with bluebonnet eyes and hair like a new copper penny. His mind raced with the erotic fantasy of what it would be like to do more than deposit Jolene Chapman onto a feather bed and walk away.

Damn!

Telling himself that Jolene was off-limits wasn't doing him a hell of a lot of good. One thought and his body tightened with the same urgency he always felt just before he drew his gun. But this time his blood was being heated by desire, not adrenaline.

There had been women in his life, but he'd always been smart enough to stay away from the good girls. The past few years it had gotten easier. Working dawn to dusk kept him too exhausted to think about women. He wasn't a lusty boy any longer. He was a grown man with enough sense to know that sitting in a saloon, sipping whiskey, and thinking about another man's woman was one of the dumbest things he could do. Russell might be dead and buried, but he wasn't forgotten. Not by Jolene, and certainly not by Luke.

He rebuked himself with a mumbled curse, then stood up and tossed a coin on the table to pay for the whiskey. Instead of wondering what Jolene Chapman would look like wearing nothing but a smile, he ought to be out searching for the bastards who'd killed his best friend.

First things first, Luke told himself. He'd promised Russell that he would take care of Jolene. He grimaced at the thought of what it was going to cost him to fulfill his promise.

How in the hell was he supposed to share a ranch with a woman he couldn't have, when all he could think about was having her?

Two

Jolene sat in the rocking chair, staring out the hotel window. Russell's proposal had meant more to her than a chance to put the war's painful memories behind her. It had held the promise of laughter and companionship and the hope of a family to replace the one the war had taken from her.

But once again death had turned the promise of so much into so little.

As difficult as it was to imagine Russell gone, it was even harder for Jolene to envision the smiling young man from Tennessee being partners with a man like Luke Maddock. Russell's heart had been full of the joy of life. Luke looked as though he hadn't laughed in years. His lean face had the quality of a statute, carved from stone. And his eyes. They were dark pools that revealed nothing about the man himself.

Russell was dead.

There was nothing Jolene could do but go on living.

The question was how and where?

Returning to Tennessee held no comfort for her, and Fenton had little to offer, judging by its limited businesses. She could teach school. The only other thing she knew how to do was cook and clean and sew, things any woman could do. There was nothing special about her qualifications, nothing that could earn her a living in a small town with fewer buildings than she had fingers and toes.

Wives were hard to come by west of the Mississippi; Jolene knew she could easily find a man to take care of her. The thought made her shiver inside and out. She had agreed to marry Russell, allowing him to think that she returned his love. Her motives had been selfish, but she had fully intended to do her level best to make him a good wife. Marrying another man for the sake of having a roof over her head and food on the table had no appeal whatsoever.

Postponing the cold hard fact that the money Russell had sent her would soon run out, Jolene got dressed and went downstairs to the hotel's dining room.

She found Luke sitting at a corner table. His hat was on the empty chair beside him and the room's dim light made his hair seem as dark as the devil's. Thoughts of her uncertain future were quickly replaced with thoughts of the tall lean man who had met her at the stage. Who was Luke Maddock? He seemed comfortable with his western surroundings. Had he been born in this wild country, or like so many men who had fought in the war, had he come West to find a dream?

Jolene felt something inside her stir to life. The mystery of fate and why Luke had been the one to meet her stage instead of Russell would always go unanswered. Russell had been a warm summer breeze, offering comfort. Luke was an unpredictable storm, threatening Jolene's senses in a way she didn't understand. Yet, she couldn't take her eyes off him as she moved across the room, not stopping until she was standing by the table.

"Good evenin'," Luke said, coming to his feet. "How are you feeling?"

"Better," Jolene admitted. "You were right. I needed to rest."

She sat while Luke walked to the door that led to the kitchen and told whoever was cooking that night to rustle up Miss Chapman a bowl of stew and some biscuits. When he returned to the table, there was a prolonged silence that made Jolene unsure she'd done the right thing by searching him out. Luke might have been Russell's partner, but he didn't owe her anything.

"Crooked Spur is a good day's ride to the north-west," Luke said, breaking the tense silence.

For a moment Jolene wasn't sure what had sparked the remark, then she remembered that she'd asked to see Russell's grave.

"Tell me about the ranch," she urged.

"Crooked Spur isn't as big as some of the spreads south of here, but it's one of the best," Luke said proudly. "It sits in the middle of the sweetest little valley you've ever seen. Good water and lots of grass. That what's it takes to raise cattle. Crooked Spur has both."

Jolene smiled. "You like ranching, don't you?"

"It's all I've ever wanted," Luke admitted honestly.

A stout woman, with a massive bosom and gray hair, delivered two bowls of stew and a plate of biscuits. Jolene picked up her spoon and began eating. Nothing more was said until her bowl was empty and she was nibbling on a biscuit smeared with fresh honey. She looked across the table at Luke and smiled. "Thank you. I'm not sure what I would have done if a stranger had had to tell me about Russell."

"I am a stranger," Luke reminded her.

"Not to Russell," she said. "He wouldn't share a ranch with a man he didn't like. You were his friend or you wouldn't have taken the time to meet the stage."

Before he let his mind wander too far from the

purpose at hand, Luke said what he hadn't finished saying earlier that day. "Russell didn't die right off. He talked about you."

Jolene's smiled faded. "Was he in a lot of pain?"

Luke shook his head. "I pumped him full of whiskey. He slid off to sleep like a baby."

"Thank you," she said, holding back the tears.

Luke reached for a cheroot, then hesitated. "I'd better smoke this outside."

Thinking he meant to leave her alone again, Jolene followed him until they were standing on the sidewalk outside the hotel. She noticed the gun strapped to his hip. He wore it too comfortably to call it anything but an old friend.

"Have the authorities found the men responsible for Russell's death?" she asked, as the saloon doors opened across the way. A cowboy staggered toward his horse, then rode out of town in a flourish that left the street clouded with dust.

"What authorities?" Luke scoffed. "This isn't Memphis, Miss Chapman. You can't find a constable on the street corner. It's Texas. Out here a man is his own law. And if it comes down to it, he's judge and jury. Nothing comes easy. It's a fight or die kind of place."

His cold hard tone made Jolene flinch. "Do you know who killed Russell?"

"His names doesn't make any difference," Luke replied with chilly precision. "He'll be dead as soon as I find him."

The certainty of his declaration told Jolene that Luke wasn't going to sit around and wait for the rustlers to come back and steal more cattle.

"How will you find him?"

Luke's half-smoked cheroot left his hand in an arc of red light that ended up glowing in the dirt. He moved out of the shadows and into the dim light filtering through the hotel window. "I'll find him.

Too much whiskey one night and he'll start braggin'
about him and his friends running off some cows
over toward Fenton. He'll start getting loud about
how he put two bullets in a man before the feller had
a chance to draw his gun. Cowards get real brave
when the liquor's flowin' and the whores are lis-
tenin'."

The night air took on a chill as Jolene realized
Luke Maddock meant every word he was saying. Unlike Russell, he didn't look for the good side of people. The matter-of-fact way he talked about death
said that he'd seen more than his share.

Luke wondered if Jolene was going to faint again.
Most women didn't like hearing such things. He
watched her, half hoping that he'd have an excuse to
hold her again. When she took a deep breath, then
drew her shawl more closely around her shoulders,
he figured she was going to be all right.

"Russell wanted you to have his half of the ranch,"
Luke announced.

Jolene stared up at him, unsure if she'd heard him
correctly.

"He made me write it down, all legal like," Luke
went on. "Russell's half of Crooked Spur Ranch belongs to you now."

Jolene was speechless.

Half a ranch!

Russell had loved her. Truly loved her. She'd
known it, of course, but not being able to return the
emotion had forced her to think of his affection in
the same terms as her own. She'd come to Texas
wanting a home, but Russell had sent for her wanting a wife. A wave of guilt rushed over her. Without
knowing it, she'd betrayed her best friend. Russell
had died with thoughts of her filling his head and
his heart.

What would Luke think of her if he knew the
truth? What would he think of a woman who had

lied about loving a man? The very man who had
been his friend and partner. The man whose death
he had vowed to avenge.

Jolene felt truly ashamed of herself.

She couldn't ask Russell to forgive her, but she
could keep the promise she'd made to him and to
herself. She could do her best to make sure she did
right by him. Doing right now meant that she'd do
her very best to honor his memory. Russell had left
her the only part of his heart that he could leave.
He'd bequeathed her half of his dream.

It was humbling.

It was also a prayer answered.

She wouldn't have to go back to Tennessee.

Jolene didn't know what to say as she looked up to
find Luke studying her with an intensity that made
her blood heat. Suddenly, she realized that the other
half of the ranch belonged to the gruff Texan. The
home she'd inherited was also Luke's home. The
thought was disturbing, but not as frightening as the
thought of having nothing to call her own.

"The stage can take you back to Galveston in the
morning," Luke said. "I'll send you half of the
money I get when we sell the herd. It won't be much
at first, but there'll be more money next year and the
year after that."

"Money?" Jolene asked, confused. "I don't care
about money."

Luke straightened to his full height. "Half the
ranch belongs to you now. That means half the steers
and half the money they bring when we sell them. It's
yours. You can go back to Tennessee and teach school
again. In a few years, you can do whatever you want.
You're young. You can get married—"

"I'm not going back to Tennessee," Jolene interrupted him. "If Russell left me half of the ranch, I
owe it to him to make my home there."

Only the few manners his mother had instilled in

him before she'd died kept Luke from cussing long and hard. "Do you know anything about ranching?"

"No," Jolene said, shrugging her shoulders. "But I can learn."

Luke sighed as he studied her determined face. "I'd do some more thinkin' on it before I jumped into something I wasn't ready for," he advised her. "Ranchin' is hard work. Damn hard work."

"Man's work," Jolene retorted.

"Don't get your feathers ruffled," Luke said. "All I'm saying is that—"

"I know what you're saying, Mr. Maddock," Jolene said curtly. "I know you were Russell's friend, and I also know that you feel obligated toward me. If you didn't, you wouldn't have met the stage today. I thank you for that, and I appreciate your concern. In time, I hope we can be friends."

The woman's loco!

It wasn't the work that worried Luke. There was plenty to do around the house. The six men he and Russell had hired as riders needed to be fed. There was always laundry to be washed and shirts to be mended.

Everyone at Crooked Spur knew about Jolene. Russell hadn't kept any secrets about sending for her. Although each and every one of the men had respected Russell, Luke wasn't sure how they'd handle having an unmarried woman around the place. Hell, he might as well be truthful with himself. He was more worried about how *he* was going to react if Jolene became a permanent resident than he was about the hired help.

Luke considered himself a decent man, compared to some he'd met, but he wasn't made of stone. And he'd have to be chiseled out of granite not to notice a warm-blooded woman like Jolene Chapman. How long could he keep his hands in his pockets if Jolene was within reach?

"I can be ready to leave first thing in the morning," Jolene informed him.

"Now, just wait one cotton-pickin' minute," Luke said. He towered over her like a mountain at the edge of a valley, but she didn't back away. "I didn't say nothin' about you comin' to the ranch."

"I want to see Russell's grave," Jolene said, ignoring his disgruntled tone. She was used to men thinking they always knew best. She'd grown up with three brothers and an overprotective father. "I know you think I need taking care of," she continued. "But I don't. Just because I'm a woman doesn't mean I can't take care of myself. I managed during the war. I'll manage now."

"This isn't Tennessee," Luke pointed out. "It's Texas. Out here a woman needs a man to look after things."

"You should have told Generals Lee and Grant that," Jolene remarked. "If they had settled their differences off the battlefield, I wouldn't have been forced to keep our farm running single-handedly. When I wasn't taking care of the animals, I was plowing enough ground to keep a garden planted. I chopped my own wood and hauled my own water." She gave him a scathing look. "I'm not a city girl, Mr. Maddock. I know what hard work is.

"I want to see Russell's grave," Jolene reiterated in a clear voice. "And I'm not going back to Tennessee."

"I'll take you to his grave," Luke relented, "but we've got some more talkin' to do before you unpack your things and take up housekeeping."

Jolene's hands went to her hips. She didn't care if the hotel clerk was leaning over the counter, listening to every word she said. It had been a long time since she'd lost her temper, but the events that had taken place since her arrival in Fenton had her emotions on a short leash. "Does half of Crooked Spur Ranch belong to me or not?"

Luke told himself that trying to talk sense to a woman who'd just found out that the man she loved was dead wasn't the smartest thing he'd ever done. He decided Jolene wasn't thinking clearly. "I'll take you to Russell's grave. That's all we're deciding now."

"No. That's not all," Jolene said, moving to stand directly in front of him.

She knew she must look ridiculous, stepping in front of a man twice her size as if she could stop him from stomping off. But she had to make Luke realize that she was serious. Discovering that Russell had left her his share of the ranch had changed everything. She'd come to Texas to make a new life, and that's exactly what she intended to do.

The cold look Luke gave her would have sent a grown man running for cover, but Jolene didn't budge. They were like two gunfighters, facing each other, appraising each other, waiting for the other to make the first move.

Jolene watched Luke's face, mesmerized by the dark color of his unblinking eyes and the strong angles of his nose and chin. She barely knew this man, but she sensed so many things about him. He was hardworking and honest. His friendship with Russell spoke to those qualities. Although it was apparent that he didn't like people getting too close, Jolene couldn't deny that she felt a certain camaraderie with him.

They had both cared deeply for Russell McClain.

Now, they both owned half of the same ranch.

Like it or not, their lives had become entwined. Jolene forced herself to stop at the analogy. If she let her imagination go any further, she'd start feeling guilty again.

"Try to understand," she said, breaking the taut

silence. "I owe it to Russell's memory. He wanted us to have a life together. Knowing we couldn't, he left me his half of the ranch."

The promise he'd made his partner loomed over Luke's head like an angry cloud.

He hadn't been lying when he'd told Jolene that Texas wasn't any place for a woman alone. Not a young pretty woman. Once the word got out that Miss Chapman of Memphis, Tennessee, was as pretty as a baby kitten, every cowboy within a hundred miles would be looking for an excuse to stop by Crooked Spur. Luke knew one of the reasons Russell had extracted the promise from him was because he realized that Jolene was going to need protection. Giving her half of the ranch had been his way of providing her a home. Knowing Luke owned the other half ensured her safety.

If Luke sent Jolene packing, he'd be breaking his word. If he let her stay, as sure as hell was hot, he was going to have trouble on his hands.

"I plan on leavin' at sunup," Luke said firmly. "Can you ride?"

"Yes."

"Be packed and ready to go then." Luke turned away. He was halfway to the saloon when Jolene stopped him by saying his name. He looked over his shoulder. Her hands had dropped away from her hips and the temper had vanished from her eyes.

"Thank you," she said, offering him a smile.

"Don't thank me yet," Luke said, settling his hat on his head. "Russell may have given you his half of the ranch, but that doesn't mean you're going to like it."

Her meekness faded. "Does that mean that you're not happy about having a woman partner?"

If wasn't having a woman as his partner that had Luke's blood running hot, it was having this particular woman. "I've got nothing against women, Miss Chapman. In the right place at the right time."

A sassy retort was on the tip of her tongue, but before Jolene could say it, Luke ended their conversation with a parting remark.

"Before we head out in the morning, there's one thing you and I had better get straight," he said. "I own the half of Crooked Spur that gives the orders. You own the half that takes them."

Three

Dawn was a gray-and-pink streaked sky painted over the darker horizon of the land. Jolene stepped out of the hotel and looked toward the livery stable. Across the street the doors of the saloon were closed. She studied the unpretentious building with its unwashed windows and sagging roof. Had Luke slept in one of the rooms above the noisy bar?

Had he slept alone?

Jolene shivered at the unladylike thought. The sun was still playing hide-and-seek with the dawn, and she was already thinking about the man who had tossed a verbal gauntlet at her feet.

She got her answer about Luke's sleeping quarters when she saw him walk out of the livery stable. His boots were dangling from his left hand. His shirt was unbuttoned and flapping closely as his sides. Dropping the boots beside the water trough, he pumped until water exploded from the metal nozzle, then leaned over and put his head under the silver stream. Once he'd completed his crude but effective ablution, he straightened up, wiped his face on the tail of his shirt and walked to the back of the livery stable. When he reappeared, he was tucking his shirt into his pants.

Jolene found herself wishing that the livery wasn't so far away. She wasn't close enough to discern if the shadow that covered Luke's chest was the result of the dim morning light or a manly pelt of hair.

What was wrong with her?

She'd been raised in a house with a father and three brothers. She'd seen a man's chest before. Plenty of times.

"Why am I letting him get under my skin?" Jolene asked herself as she set her small valise on the bench in front of the hotel. "He's no different from any other man. Giving orders and taking over like I wasn't born with the sense God gave a small goose."

Glumly, Jolene realized she was mumbling to herself. When her stomach growled, she decided she was going to have breakfast while Luke saddled their horses. Then, while he was eating, she'd arrange to have her trunks and other luggage stored until a wagon could be sent into town to retrieve them. Luke may have his doubts, but Jolene didn't.

She was here to stay. Russell had offered her part of her dream and she was going to hang onto it with both hands.

A short time later, Luke joined her in the hotel. Jolene sipped her second cup of coffee and tried to remember that the only thing she had in common with the tall Texan was half a ranch and the memory of Russell McClain. Whatever emotions stirred her imagination were better left alone. Untouched and undefined. Anything else and she knew that Luke's opinion of her would sink lower than a snake's head on a downhill slither. The last thing she wanted was a partner who thought her unworthy of his trust.

"Are you sure you want to do this?" Luke asked, thinking that Jolene may have changed her mind about visiting Russell's grave. If he was lucky, some common sense may have sunk into her head while she was sleeping.

"I've already made my decision," Jolene told him. "If Russell left me half the ranch, it was because he wanted me to stay in Texas. That means, I'm staying."

Luke stood up, glaring down at her as he reached inside his vest pocket for a coin to leave behind on the table. She got the distinct impression that if she wasn't packed and ready to climb into the saddle by the time he walked out the front door of the hotel, he'd leave town without her. Making sure he didn't get his wish, Jolene matched him step for step until they were outside. Without speaking a word, Luke reached for the valise in her right hand. Relinquishing it, Jolene watched him tie it behind the saddle of a bay gelding.

Luke was chewing on his thoughts as he mounted his own horse. He wondered how long it would take before the grief hit Jolene full force. The shock of finding out Russell was dead couldn't have worn off yet. When it did, he was going to have a lonely broken-hearted woman on his hands.

"Is all of Texas this empty?" she asked as they rode out of town.

"Not all of it," Luke said. "East Texas is piney woods and green meadows. The Panhandle is more sky than land. The plains are cut by long narrow gorges that look like mountains turned upside-down."

Jolene smiled at the analogy. The expression was another turn of the knife in Luke's already aching body. For some unknown reason, this woman had the uncanny ability to burrow under his skin. Every moment he spent with her felt life-threatening, as if she knew his most vulnerable point and was just waiting to take aim.

The next few hours were spent riding side-by-side, their horses walking lazily toward the valley they now both claimed as home.

Jolene continued scanning the landscape, enjoying the random appearance of a jackrabbit or the

sudden flurry of birds, disturbed whenever one of
the horses blew or snorted. Unlike Tennessee, where
the hills were draped in leafy elms and towering
oaks, Texas trees seemed to sprout out of nowhere.
Clusters of them dotted the grassy range, like people
gathering around a fire for warmth.

When they reached a creek that wasn't more than
three feet across, Luke reined in his horse. "Walk
around and stretch your legs," he said. "We've got
another four hours before we're on Crooked Spur
land."

"Four hours!" Jolene felt like she'd been riding
forever.

"I usually cover it in less time, but with you
along—"

"I'm sorry if I'm slowing you down," she retorted,
sliding free of her saddle.

Luke hadn't offered to help her mount that morning, so there was no use waiting for him to help her
dismount. The few words he'd spoken to her since
leaving Fenton could be counted on one hand. The
man could at least pretend to like her, Jolene
thought, as she walked around, making sure her face
didn't reveal her aches and pains.

Once she could smile again, she turned around to
find Luke kneeling by the narrow stream. Sweat
dampened his gray shirt, causing it to cling to the
broad muscles of his back and shoulders. Her gaze
drifted down to the waistband of his jeans, then
gradually lower, taking in the strength of his lean
thighs and the longs legs that ended in a pair of
scuffed black boots.

Jolene shifted her weight uncomfortably. Something she couldn't define made her feel suddenly
self-conscious of the fact that she was a woman alone
in the middle of nowhere with a strange man. When
Luke stood up, wiping the dust from his face and
neck with a wet bandanna, Jolene realized she'd

been staring at him. She turned around and looked for somewhere to sit while they ate the meager lunch of cold biscuits and bacon Luke had asked the hotel cook to pack for them.

Spying a flat rock that would serve as both table and chair, she started to unbuckle the saddlebag only to find Luke standing right behind her. He was so close she could smell the musky scent of sweat and man as her fingers fumbled with the strap and buckle. When she turned around, he was still hovering over her like a hawk over a henhouse. Hard-lined and lean of features, he reminded her of a predatory animal, wary but strong enough to fight whatever threatened him.

"Are you going to hold those biscuits all day or are you going to untie that towel so we can eat and be on our way?" he asked in a stiff voice.

"I'm sorry," Jolene replied. She spread the towel on the flat rock, selected a biscuit, then walked downstream. Far enough away to be by herself, but close enough to Luke to keep him from thinking she was avoiding him altogether.

After she ate, she walked to the edge of the narrow creek. She was bending down to get a drink of water when Luke's hand stopped her. The feel of his fingers gripping her arm sent a bolt of emotional lightning through Jolene's body. She jerked back as if she'd been struck by the real thing.

Luke noticed the telling sign, but he didn't react to it. She hadn't been expecting him to touch her. It was a normal reaction, nothing more. "I've got a cup in my saddlebag," he said, dropping his hand to his side. "No reason to get those pretty clothes dirty."

The forest green riding habit had been an indulgence before she'd left Memphis. The fitted jacket called attention to her figure but in an elegant way. Jolene knew the color suited her, and deep inside she was pleased to know that Luke liked it as well.

For a long moment, they just stood there, staring at each other in a silent battle of wills that neither realized was rooted in the same attraction. An intangible current of emotion passed between them, binding them more closely than the memory of the dead man who had brought them together. Jolene held her breath, while Luke's eyes softened to a deep warm brown. For one terrifying second, she thought he was going to kiss her.

Finally, Jolene averted her gaze, unable to look into the depths of Luke's eyes without wanting to know more about him than his devotion to a promise. The devastating effect the man was having on her sensibilities made her take a step back. The soft ground of the creek bank didn't support the heels of her riding boots and she flayed her arms for a moment, fighting for balance.

"Damn!" Luke reached out and grabbed her around the waist, to keep her from ending bottom down in the cold water.

Like it or not, Jolene was in his arms again.

"Relax," he grunted, as he felt her spine stiffen. The feel of her body pressed intimately against his made his heart kick like a mule.

"Thank you," Jolene said as her feet touched the ground and his arm slid from around her waist. She wanted to crawl under a rock and hide. She felt embarrassed and clumsy, and she wondered if she'd ever get used to the way Luke affected her senses. It reminded her of the one time she'd been bold enough to taste whiskey. The liquor had gone to her head like a flashfire. Luke had the same effect on her, but Jolene sensed that it wasn't going to go away with time.

The sound of horses, being rode hard and fast, broke the silence.

"Get ready to ride," Luke ordered in a curt voice. Jolene didn't ask him why he was being so belligerent. She didn't trust herself to speak. When Luke had kept her from falling into the creek, she'd wanted to wrap her arms around him and hang on for dear life. She'd wanted to ask him to kiss her, to take the loneliness away, a loneliness she hadn't known existed until yesterday.

Luke pulled a rifle from the leather scabbard on his saddle and checked the chambers. Then he reached for the six-gun at his hip. The smaller weapon underwent the same quick but thorough inspection before he mounted, placing himself and his horse between Jolene and the approaching riders.

An odd shimmering sense of danger filled Jolene's body as the men charged toward them. She looked at Luke. He was sitting atop his horse, totally relaxed, as if he were waiting on the front porch for Sunday visitors.

The creak of leather joined the sound of horses thundering toward them. The men were dressed in coarse jeans, faded shirts, and leather vests, similar to the clothing Luke was wearing. Their hats were pulled low over their eyes. When the dust settled, there were four men and four guns on the opposite side of the creek.

"Howdy, Luke," an unshaven, thick-chested man said as he inched his horse in front of the others. "Didn't expect to find anyone between here and Fenton."

"Sanders," Luke said in the slow lazy drawl that often fooled people into thinking he was slow about everything he did. "Ridin' those ponies pretty hard, aren't you?"

The man's jaw tightened. It was apparent he didn't like having his actions questioned. He turned his attention to Jolene, eyeing her with an open curiosity that made her skin feel dirty. "Is this McClain's woman?"

"This is Miss Chapman," Luke said, not taking his eyes off the four riders.

"Please to make your acquaintance, *Miss* Chapman," Sanders said, tipping the brim of his hat with a gloved hand. "McClain was well liked in these parts. My condolences."

In spite of his manners, which spoke to a southern upbringing, Jolene didn't believe a word the man was saying. There was something cold and distant in his voice, and his eyes looked like pale amber lanterns against the tanned texture of his face. There was no warmth in the man, nothing to make her think he gave a damn about anything or anyone but himself.

"Hear you lost some more cattle the other night," Sanders said to Luke.

"A few head. Wouldn't happen to know anything about them, would you?"

The man stiffened as Luke openly accused him of stealing the steers. His companions shifted in their saddles, bringing their hands closer to their guns.

Jolene looked at Luke.

He was still relaxed. One hand was holding the reins, the other was resting palm down on his thigh.

"The only thing I know is that you're grazing too close to the Leon," Sanders remarked with a sly grin that didn't come close to being a smile. "That's wide-open country. If you're losing cattle because you don't have enough riders, there's not much anyone can do about it."

"I wouldn't be so sure of that," Luke said. There was an icy promise in his words.

The tension between the two men was noticeable for several long seconds. Then Luke let a slow smile lift the corners of his mouth. He tipped his hat, then turned his horse north. Jolene followed suit, putting the lean Texan between herself and the four riders who were watching them with open hostility.

It was several minutes and a good two miles later before she urged her gelding in front of Luke's, blocking his path. The look he gave her said she'd better have a damn good reason for what she was doing.

"Why didn't you tell me that the rustlers are still at work?" she asked abruptly. "I have a right to know."

"It's nothing to worry about," Luke said, edging his horse around hers. "You've got enough troubles on your mind."

"I'm not helpless," she argued. "Was Sanders right? Do we need to hire more men?"

"An army couldn't patrol the whole valley," Luke replied. "A ranch isn't a general store, Miss Chapman. We don't keep all the goods under lock and key."

Knowing it was going to take a large dose of patience and an even larger amount of time to get Luke to open up and discuss things freely, Jolene assumed her place by his side. Their horses moved with an easy gait as they rode silently over the land, but the continued silence began to wear on her nerves.

"You think Sanders has something to do with the rustling, don't you?"

Luke looked at her, his face shadowed by the brim of his hat. "I don't trust him."

The simple declaration confirmed what Jolene had felt when Sanders had raked his eyes over her. Still, she asked. "Why?"

Luke shrugged. "No reason in particular, and a lot in general."

Jolene laughed, earning her a long cold stare from her partner.

"You remind me of Gerald," she said. "Getting him to talk was like pulling quills out of a porcupine."

"He was your oldest brother, wasn't he," Luke replied, remembering all the facts and figures Russell
had quoted about his childhood sweetheart and her
family.

"Yes," Jolene said sadly. "There was a time when I
didn't think I'd ever stop crying. First I got the news
about Papa, then Wayne, then Gerald." Tears glistened in her eyes. "Then Donnie. He was the youngest."

"And now Russell," Luke added in a low voice.

Jolene nodded. She wasn't sure how to breach the
subject of Russell's affection or his loss without opening herself to Luke's biting criticism and the doubts
he was certain to entertain once he realized she had
agreed to marry Russell without feeling a strong passionate love for him. How did a woman explain the
tender feelings that gave her a sense of security after
so many years of war? How could she tell Luke that
she had wanted to make Russell happy at the same
time she was deceiving him?

She couldn't.

Everything was too fresh, too raw. Russell hadn't
been dead that long and the revenge Luke seemed
determined to seek was still blazing in his eyes. She'd
seen it at the creek, when he'd looked at Sanders.

Jolene dared to push for the answers she so desperately needed. "I assume Mr. Sanders either owns
or works for a neighboring ranch."

"He rides for the Lazy M."

"And . . ." she urged.

Luke let out a frustrated sigh. "It's twice as big
with four times the cattle we're running."

"Then why steal more?"

"I didn't say the Lazy M was rustlin' cattle." He
glared at her.

Jolene glared back. "I may be fresh off a Tennessee farm, Mr. Maddock, but I'm not deaf or blind.

You think Sanders had something to do with stealing your cattle and murdering Russell."

There was no avoiding the subject, and Luke knew it. "Sanders has had a chip on his shoulder ever since he found out I fought in a blue uniform," he said bluntly. "He's been ridin' my temper, hoping to push me into a fight."

Jolene surprised Luke by accepting the news of his Union loyalty with little more than a raised eyebrow. "A gunfight or a fistfight?"

"Doesn't matter. He won't be satisfied until I knock that chip off his shoulder and shove it down his throat."

Jolene reined in her horse. "You think Sanders was with the rustlers that night, don't you? You think Russell was shot by mistake. You think Sanders was out to kill you."

Jolene's assumption matched Luke's suspicions word for word. Stopping his horse, he looked at her, uncertain if she could blame him for Russell's death any more than he already blamed himself. "I didn't see anyone that night," he said adamantly. "The shots came out of the dark."

"Suspicions aren't based on what we see," Jolene replied. "If they were, they wouldn't be suspicions. They'd be facts."

She had a lot of unanswered questions, so she decided to get them answered while Luke was in a talkative mood. "Tell me about the men at the ranch? Who named it Crooked Spur, you or Russell?"

Luke gave her a disgruntled glance, but it was wasted. Jolene wasn't going to give up until she knew all there was to know about Crooked Spur and the men who lived there. Underneath his irritated expression, Luke admired her grit.

They rode on, while Luke told her about Grizzly, the cantankerous foreman, and the other men.

"There's Jasper. He's old, but he's a good black-smith. Then there's Hank and Chet. They're broth-ers. Calhoun's still green behind the ears, but he can set a horse better than the rest. They're all good with cattle and guns. Gene hired on last year. He used to ride for one of the big Spanish ranches down south, until the war. He lost an arm."

"One of Russell's charity cases, right?"

Luke smiled. "Russ had a soft spot for folks on the down-and-out. I wasn't hot to hire Gene, but Russell insisted that we give him a fair shake. He was right. That man can do more work with one hand than most men can do with two."

It was a comfort to Jolene to know that Luke wasn't too stubborn to admit when he was wrong. Riding beside him, watching his dark eyes scan the landscape for anything that didn't belong to the wild beautiful country, listening to the soft rich tones of his Texas drawl, made the bittersweet taste of guilt and grief leave her for a while. Still, there was no ignoring the fact that she wouldn't be in Texas if Russell hadn't sent for her. She'd come west to marry the man from Tennessee, to be his wife and to have his children.

And soon, she'd be visiting his grave.

Four

Russell's description of Crooked Spur hadn't exaggerated its beauty. The house sat atop a grassy knoll. Long and rambling, it had a front porch that faced the setting sun and stately pecan trees that shaded the roof in summer and created a windbreak in winter. At the base of the hill, below the house, there was a large barn linked to several paddocks and numerous smaller structures. One of them was the bunkhouse.

Cattle dotted the landscape that ran in a long graceful basin toward the Leon River. Jolene's curious eyes surveyed her new home and the fragile balance that existed between man and wilderness. She studied the outline of the sloping terrain, awed by the possibilities the land presented. No wonder Russell had called it a dream come true.

As she and Luke approached the main compound of the ranch, a burly man with a thick beard and bushy eyebrows exited the bunkhouse. He was wearing loose-fitting twill trousers, a black shirt, and red suspenders. Jolene knew it had to be Grizzly, the foreman whose name fit his disposition.

"Thought I'd see you about now," he called out in a deep rough voice. "This here be the gal?"

Jolene reined in her mount and looked down at the barrel-shaped man with sparkling gray eyes. "I'm

Jolene Chapman. It's very nice to meet you, Mr. Grizzly."

The foreman laughed. "Just Grizz will do. We ain't fancy 'round here."

Jolene smiled, and Luke knew she'd just wrapped the gruff old-timer around her little finger.

"Things are goin' to change around here real quick like," Grizzly said, looking from Jolene to Luke, then back again. "Yep, real quick."

Luke wasn't in the mood to comment on the transformation the ranch would undergo once a pretty redhead from Tennessee moved into the house at the top of the hill. The old mountain man turned cowhand was looking at his new employer like she was made of pure gold. If Grizzly reacted that openly to Jolene's charms, Luke was going to have a hell of a time keeping the other men in line. Hank, Chet, and Gene weren't bad looking when they took the time to shave and put on a clean shirt. The last thing he needed was some randy cowboy courting his partner with posies and walk-in-the-moonlight invitations.

"Promise me, Luke. Promise that you're take care of Jolie. She's going to need you."

Luke had promised.

As he helped Jolene dismount, feigning indifference to the feel of his hands around her narrow waist, Luke wondered if the promise he'd made wasn't quickly turning into a curse.

While he was pondering the twist of fate that had given him a woman partner, Jolene was staring at the house she'd soon call home. Leaving Grizzly and Luke to discuss where the men were riding and what they'd be doing the next day, Jolene walked up the hill.

When she stepped onto the front porch, she was all smiles. There was a swing suspended from the beamed roof and two large rocking chairs. The main door to the house was cut from sturdy oak. She hesitated before pushing it open.

Thanking Russell for a dream come true, Jolene stepped inside. It was cool and dim as she walked slowly from one room to the next, seeing bits and pieces of the past in every corner. There was a daguerreotype of her on the mantel above the fireplace in the front room. The books Russell had worked so hard to afford were lined up neatly on a shelf. She touched the worn leather of the McClain family Bible as tears glistened in her eyes.

The rooms were sparsely furnished and dusty, but Jolene didn't see them the way they were. She saw them the way they could be, warm and inviting and filled with laughter. The way her beloved Russell had seen them.

She went into the kitchen and squealed with delight when she saw the pump. Russell had fashioned a cabinet around it, with a drying board for dishes and a deep wooden trough where she could set a wash basin.

Jolene was about to leave the kitchen and continue her tour when the back door opened and Luke stepped into the room. He sat her valise on the floor and hung his hat on the row of pegs by the door before looking her way. Jolene could see the question in his dark eyes. Did she know how much work Russell had put into the house? Did she like it?

"It's perfect," she said, breaking into a teary smile. She looked toward the pump. "I used to grumble something fierce about carrying water in the winter. Russell must have remembered."

"He remembered everything about you," Luke said.

A tense silence followed his words as the two people facing each other felt the invisible presence of the man who had brought them together, binding a man born in Texas to a young Tennessee woman as tightly as wedding vows bound a husband and wife.

"I'll put some coffee on," Jolene said, needing something to do before she threw herself into Luke's arms for a third time. They were partners, nothing more.

Seeing the tears glimmering in her blue eyes bit into Luke's conscience like the steel teeth of a bear trap. The thought of what the future could have been, of Russell and Jolene getting married in the front parlor, of having their love and laughter fill the empty house, tore at his guts. He didn't want to think about the bedroom at the end of the hall. The thought of Jolene lying in that bed with her coppery hair spread over the pillow and her jeweled eyes glowing up at the man she loved, turned his insides green with envy.

Guilt washed over Luke as he told himself that Russell had been his best friend. His partner. He had no right to look at Jolene without anything more than brotherly love. But somehow, his mind had joined the idea of Russell giving Jolene half the ranch with the idea that Russell had given Jolene to him. That must be why he felt so possessive of her. Why he couldn't stop thinking about taking Russell's place, not just in her life, but in her bed.

Luke stepped away from the door, hating himself for mentally betraying the man he'd recently buried.

The sound of his spurs brought Jolene around. She looked at the tall Texan, filling the doorway and smiled. Luke didn't smile back. There was a bleakness in his eyes, and once again they shared something silent but real. Something that reached deep inside Jolene's heart.

She looked around the room, seeing the details that most men would have overlooked in the construction of a home. Russell hadn't overlooked them. Everything about the house suited her, but then it had been built just for her. It would serve her right to be reminded day and night that Russell had loved her and that she'd betrayed that love by not being truthful with him. It was fitting punishment for the crime she'd committed.

Once she'd poured Luke a cup of coffee, Jolene excused herself to tour the rest of the house. She looked at each room, smiling at the memories that came to mind. The sound of riders and Luke's voice told her that the men had come in from the range.

What would they think of her?

The obvious, Jolene was sure. She was a woman grieving for the man she'd lost. The man they thought she had loved with all her heart. Guilt and a strange weight made up of fatigue and loss prevented Jolene from going outside to introduce herself. There would be time enough for that in the morning.

She shut the door of the room she was almost certain Russell had intended to be the nursery. It was empty now, except for a large chest that held extra blankets for winter. The only room left to inspect was directly across the hall. Jolene knew it was Luke's room. There was no need for her to explore its secrets. The only thing that should concern her was the Texan's ability to keep the ranch running smoothly and profitably.

She mumbled to herself as she returned to the kitchen. Luke was gone. Jolene knew he was giving her time to get adjusted to her new surroundings, but she didn't need time. She'd felt at home the moment she'd stepped over the threshold. What she needed was conversation. How was she going to be Luke's partner if he wouldn't talk to her? She wanted him to understand that she shared his grief. And his doubts about the future. She wanted someone to end the long years of having no one to tell her feelings to except a tired old house cat named

Curly Tail and a slouchy bluetick hound that had belonged to her father.

Jolene poured herself a cup of coffee and walked outside to the porch. Sitting down in the swing, she looked over the valley as moonlight bathed it in silvery shadows. Things were different in this strange wild country where men wore guns and used them whenever the need arose. The situation filled her with apprehension and anticipation. There was the excitement of being in Texas, of embarking on a new chapter in her life. There was the grief of Russell's death and the dreams that she had woven around the smiling young man from Tennessee. Dreams that were still inside her, waiting to be shared with someone.

With a hesitant admission that brought a sad smile to her face, Jolene realized that Luke Maddock had stepped into those dreams. It was probably sinful for her to think such a thing, but it felt too right to be wrong. Something about the gruff-talking Texan had touched her heart and no amount of logic or reason was going to erase the feeling.

Dawn was a transparent flow of light on the eastern horizon when Jolene met the men who rode for Crooked Spur. Grizzly was the first one to come stomping into the kitchen, hanging his hat on the peg by the door while he complimented Jolene on the aroma of her coffee. Luke followed a few minutes later. No one had commented on his decision to move his things into the bunkhouse. Jolene might be his partner, but she was also a young unmarried lady.

Jolene hadn't realized how lonely the house had seemed until Luke stepped into the kitchen. The night had brought a restful sleep, because she'd been exhausted, but seeing Luke walk into the room was like having her heart come to life. His dark eyes searched her out and Jolene found herself smiling, really smiling for the first time in years. Luke wasn't the only one to notice the transformation. She went from being pretty to being breathtakingly beautiful in the blink of an eye.

"We got washed up down at the bunkhouse," Grizzly said, pulling out a chair and making himself at home while the other men filed into the room.

The foreman introduced them, then reached for the platter of flapjacks Jolene had prepared to go with three pounds of bacon, two dozen eggs, and two trays of biscuits.

Jolene gave the men a bright smile as she carried the coffeepot to the table. "Don't be shy," she told them. "Working men need a good breakfast."

Jolene was too busy serving up second helpings of everything to notice the admiring glances she drew from the men.

Luke did the noticing for her.

By the time she sat down at the opposite end of the table from her partner, Luke was ready to hang a few admiring cowboys from the tree behind the house. Hiding his reaction, Luke began his usual routine of handing out orders while he filled his plate.

"Gene, you and Hank check out the southeast range. I saw Sanders and some of his boys riding in from that direction yesterday. Make sure no one's been up to any mischief."

"Yes, sir."

"What kind of mischief?" Jolene asked.

"Nothin' in particular," Luke replied matter-of-factly.

"Nothing in particular covers a lot of ground, Mr. Maddock," Jolene remarked, drawing everyone's eye, including Luke's. "I'd like an explanation. If

there's a threat to this ranch, from any quarter, I
have a right to know about it."

Several of the men shifted their feet under the
table. Grizzly cleared his throat. Luke poured himself a second cup of coffee.

Jolene waited.

A second before she was about to demand an explanation, Luke met her gaze. She knew he was remembering when he'd told her that he owned the
part of the ranch that gave the orders and she owned
the part that took them. But she wasn't going to be
delegated to the kitchen. As willing as she was to
cook and clean, she was still Luke's partner. He
needed to know she wasn't going to be a silent one.

"Sanders enjoys stirrin' up trouble the way a tor-
nado stirs up dust," Luke finally said.

"What did you do to him, except insult his sensibilities by wearing a blue uniform?" she asked, noticing the smile on Grizzly's bearded face.

"Luke smoked him good," Calhoun chimed in,
anxious to please the new lady of the house. "Slicker
than sin, too. Sanders didn't clear his holster before
he was lookin' down the barrel of Luke's Colt."

"Why?"

"Why what?" Luke countered much too smoothly
for Jolene to think he didn't understand the question.

She glanced around the table. The men were all
looking at her, and not one of them was about to
offer an answer to her question. Jolene rolled her
eyes toward the ceiling, then let out a frustrated sigh.
"Mr. Maddock," she said none too politely. "Why
did you draw on Sanders?"

"The reason isn't important." His tone said the
subject was closed.

As the men finished their meal, Jolene realized
she could only push Luke so far before he pushed
back. She might be the woman Russell had loved,

and part owner of the Crooked Spur, but Luke was the boss. Before she could find a ladylike way of protesting his curtness, he stood up and reached for his hat, calling an end to breakfast. Within minutes the rest of the men followed him out the door. Jolene was tempted to forget her manners and call him back, but her instincts told her she was going to have ample opportunity to disagree with the man again.

Her partner was moody, insufferable, arrogant, downright rude, and thoroughly exasperating.

He was also handsome, strong, honorable, and . . . Jolene forced herself to stop before she assigned Luke a role in her life that he might not want to play.

Five

The next few days saw a routine developing as Jolene cooked and cleaned and made her presence known by baking molasses cookies and pampering the men with apple pie. Luke walked into the kitchen at the end of the week to find bright yellow curtains and a blue-checkered tablecloth. Slowly but surely, the rambling ranch house was beginning to resemble the home Russell McClain had meant for it to be.

Jolene greeted Luke with a brief smile, then started pouring coffee.

As always, he noticed every move she made. This morning she was wearing a blue cotton dress with white lace around its squared collar. Her hair was pulled back and tied with a blue velvet ribbon that matched her eyes. His first glimpse of her in the morning always made him wish he'd been able to kiss her good night. It was an unsettling feeling that Luke couldn't seem to shake, no matter how many times he reminded himself that she'd come west to marry another man.

"If you have time, I'd like to see Russell's grave this morning," Jolene announced as she placed a white mug of steaming coffee in front of Luke.

The kitchen went as silent as a tomb. The men, praising her cooking moments before, turned their eyes to their breakfast plates, leaving Jolene and Luke to stare at each other.

For a long moment, nothing was said.

"I need to see Russell's grave," Jolene rephrased her original request.

"I buried him at the north end of the valley," Luke said. "I'll take you there."

Jolene nodded, then sat down. The meal continued, but the tension in the room was noticeable. It didn't make any difference. She had to finish what she'd started. The sooner she said her farewells to the boy from Tennessee, the sooner she could put the doldrums of grief behind her and get on with the future.

After breakfast, Jolene found Luke on the back porch, looking at the land the way she'd seen men look at the women they loved. The way Russell had once looked at her.

"I'm ready," she announced.

Luke nodded, then stepped off the porch. Nothing more was said while he saddled two horses and helped her mount. They rode north, taking a trail that led away from the valley. The land took on a more rugged appearance until they reached a sharp bend in the creek. Luke followed the narrow stream for another mile or so, then reined in his horse.

Jolene saw the grave. It was under a sprawling cottonwood tree. The branches were spread wide and hanging close to the ground, forming a natural grotto. A wooden cross marked the sight were Russell McClain had been lain to rest.

Jolene slipped from her saddle before Luke could help her. Her eyes misted with tears as she walked toward the solitary grave. Luke stayed with the horses, giving her privacy.

She knelt by the grave. "Oh, Russell," Jolene whispered softly. "I miss you so much."

Jolene's only answer was the soft song of wind through cottonwood branches.

"I did love you," she whispered reverently. "You were my best friend. Your smile was my fortress. The war seemed to last forever. Sometimes, I thought I'd go insane, waiting for the fighting to end. Waiting for someone to come back home. Then one of your letters would arrive, and I'd smile again, because you always had something wonderful to tell me. Something to lift my spirits and put hope back in my heart."

"How can I thank you for that." Tears streamed down her face as Luke kept his distance. "You gave me so much of your heart, and all I gave you in return was deception. Can you forgive me for that? I'll do everything I can to help Luke build this place into what you wanted it to be. I'll work day and night, I'll . . ."

Emotion overtook her, stealing Jolene's voice. Her shoulders shook with the force of her tears. She wanted to lift her face to the heavens and demand that God return her beloved friend, but she didn't have the strength. Instead, she lowered her head and let the tears wet the lap of her dress. She cried anew for the father and brothers the war had taken away. She cried for the loss of a good man, a man who had done nothing in his life but give joy to the people around him.

Jolene's deep heart-wrenching sobs made the man at the base of the hill grit his teeth. It wasn't Luke's place to comfort a woman when she wanted another man's arms. If he'd had any doubts about Jolene's love for Russell McClain, they were put to rest as she knelt by the young man's grave and wept until her breath came in short broken sobs and her body shook with the violence of her grief.

Luke felt the wall that separated him from Jolene more surely at that moment than he'd ever felt it before. The wall that Russell McClain had built around her heart. He didn't question the jealousy that seeped into his chest. It wouldn't do any good to lie to himself. A big part of him had always envied Russell's plans for a wife and family.

How many times had he come to this very spot and asked himself why God had chosen the young man from Tennessee to die that night? How many nights had he lain awake reliving the night Sanders had ridden against their camp and shot Russell?

Luke didn't have any misgivings when it came to Sanders's guilt or innocence. He'd bet his half of Crooked Spur that the range rider was the one who had shot Russell in cold blood. It was a truth Luke knew deep done inside his gut, the same way he knew that he wanted Russell's woman and that he'd go on wanting her for a long time to come.

"Russell. Oh, no. Russell!"

Jolene woke herself up screaming. She was cold and there was a throbbing pain in her chest, as if her heart was pounding itself to death.

"Jolene?"

Luke was in the doorway. He was naked, except for hastily donned pants that weren't fully buttoned.

Jolene cleared the dream from her mind as she stared at his bare chest. Wide at the shoulders, Luke's body tapered to a hard flat stomach. The thick mat of hair that covered his upper body narrowed and circled his navel.

He came into the room and stopped at the side of the bed. He'd been restless, as usual, and wide-awake when he'd heard Jolene screaming. Getting up the hill had only taken him a few seconds. Now, his eyes moved over her, taking in the rumpled quilt and the soft tangles of coppery hair that cascaded down her shoulders and back.

"I'm sorry," she said, bursting into tears because the dream had been so real. She'd seen Russell in her dreams. He'd been calling her name, but she couldn't reach him. No matter how fast she had run, he always remained just beyond her reach.

Luke didn't think about his reaction to Jolene's tear-stained face. He simply did what he'd been wanting to do for days. He sat down on the bed and pulled her into his arms, letting his body warm hers and knowing all the while that he was a damn fool for touching her at all.

Jolene clung to him like life itself, letting his natural heat end the icy chill that had claimed her during the night. She could hear his heart beating as she rested her cheek against his bare chest. His deep voice soothed her, telling her it was only a dream.

Unable to resist, Luke's hand moved to her hair, brushing it back from her face. It felt like warm silk. His fingers knotted gently in the soft curls. When she moved her head, trying to get closer to the warmth of his body, he felt her hair moving over his skin. It felt just as he had imagined it would, only more wonderful, more tempting.

Too tempting.

His hands stroked her back, soothing her trembling body as they pressed her closer, testing his tolerance to the breaking point. He charted the outline of her spine, letting his callused fingers explore at the same time he wanted to push her back on the feather mattress and learn very soft inch of her. The warm feathery breaths she was taking brushed over his skin, making his body burn with desire. He pulled back, thinking to untangle himself from the sensual web, but Jolene wouldn't let him. Her hands tightened and her body moved closer until there was nothing between them but heat and the thin cotton of her nightgown.

Luke was lost all over again. He cradled her face

in the palms of his hands, as he looked into the depths of her sapphire eyes. His thumbs wiped away her tears.

When their eyes locked, Luke lowered his head. Gone was rational thought. All logic had vanished, leaving only a burning desire that had him wanting her so badly he couldn't think at all. "Hush," he whispered. "It was only a dream."

Only a dream.

That's how Jolene felt. Like she was floating in some mystical fantasy. The room was a haze of moonlight and shadows. She could feel the strength of Luke's arms and the warmth of his body and the slow bittersweet pain that was making her shiver on the inside. Only this time it wasn't fear.

It was passion.

She'd never felt it before, but some elemental part of her recognized it for what it was. A deep female wanting that only this man could satisfy.

Still watching her face, Luke searched for something. Anything that told him she wouldn't pull away if he kissed her. When her eyelashes fluttered like butterfly wings, then closed, he pressed his mouth against hers. The kiss was more than a touching of lips, it was a burst of fire.

Jolene flinched, but she didn't push him away.

He pressed her back against the feather pillows and covered her upper body with his own. Loving the feel of her, the taste of her, the scent of her.

Jolene savored the hard pressure of his chest as it pinned her between the bed and his male body. His weight added to the strange sensations swirling wildly inside her, making her twist and turn in an attempt to get closer to the promise she sensed was waiting in his arms.

Luke combed his fingers through her coppery hair. He lost himself in the warm scented circle of her arms, in the soft whimpering sounds that were coming from the back of her throat. He could feel her breasts under him, feel their centers growing hard as he deepened the kiss.

His hands moved freely, stroking her back and arms, her shoulders, then slowly downward until he was cupping her breasts in his hands. She moaned again, but he drank the sound from her mouth. One kiss after another, slow and tender, hot and fierce, male and female, no beginning, no ending, just a hot searing pleasure that had his body hard and ready.

A hoot owl, perched in the tree outside the window, broke the silence of the night with a haunting call. Luke's common sense returned in a flood of guilt.

What in the hell was he doing?

He pulled back, as if Russell's ghostly hands had him by the throat.

Jolene's eyes opened. She didn't need Luke to tell her why he'd stopping kissing her. The answer was on his face. Regret and embarrassment flashed in his dark eyes as he came to his feet.

"I'm sorry," Jolene groaned, knowing she was the one who had brought Luke into the room. She was the one to blame, not him.

Luke stared down at her for a long moment. Her mouth was swollen from his kisses. He ought to be horsewhipped. Instead of offering Jolene comfort, he'd offered her lust. Instead of letting her cry out her grief for the man she loved, he'd kissed her and gone on kissing her until they were lying in the very bed where Russell should be sleeping.

Disgusted with himself, Luke turned and walked out of the room.

Jolene closed her eyes against the pain and humiliation she'd caused. She was so ashamed. No thoughts of Russell had crossed her mind once Luke's kisses had chased the dream away. Not one twinge of guilt or remorse had joined the hot sensations that were still flooding her body.

She pulled the quilt tightly around her. How had she forgotten the strict morality that had always been her measuring rod? Women didn't let men kiss them so boldly, certainly not men who weren't their husbands. She was in mourning for Russell, yet it was Luke's image that filled her mind and her heart.

How was she going to face him in the morning?

What was he going to think of her now?

Jolene turned over and buried her face in the pillow. This time her sobs were muffled.

Outside, Luke stood on the back porch, letting the night wind chase the fever from his body. He hated himself for doing the very thing he'd promised not to do. He wouldn't be surprised if Jolene met him in the kitchen in the morning with a loaded shotgun instead of a cup of coffee.

Beneath his self-targeted anger, Luke couldn't help but remember the way Jolene had felt in his arms. The warmth of her soft body, the taste of her as she'd returned his kisses, and the way she had twisted and curled under him like a kitten wanting to be stroked. She'd been pure sweet fire in his arms.

She was thinking about Russell, he told himself. *One minute she was dreaming about him and the next she was in my arms. It was a natural reaction. It was Russell she was kissing, not me.*

But Russell was dead.

And Luke was alive. Hard and hot and more alive than he'd been in years.

Damnation!

He'd have to apologize once the tension eased, but he didn't like the thoughts of saying he was sorry when the kisses he'd shared with the girl from Tennessee had been the sweetest ones he'd ever known. Wild, wonderful kisses that a man could cherish. *Moonlight and memories.* It was all he could allow himself to have, if he didn't want his conscience beating him to death.

Jolene cooked breakfast, but her thoughts were down the hill, in the bunkhouse, with the man who had kissed her breathless last night. She'd always been able to sort out her emotions before, even during the war when she'd been worried about her father and brothers and oftentimes frightened for her own safety. She had been able to dissect them rationally, label them, and by doing so, she'd understood them. But the things she felt this morning were different.

What she felt for Luke Maddock was hot and cold, bitter and sweet, maddening and strangely comforting. It was passion. It was hope. It was . . . love.

Jolene dared not say the word out loud for fear the promise of it would vanish as quickly as smoke up a chimney, but she held it deep in her heart. Did she love the gruff-speaking, hardheaded man who had met her stage? Could a woman fall in love that quickly with any man? If she could, Jolene was falling fast and hard.

By the time the biscuits were ready, Jolene decided if Luke thought her wanton or unworthy, there was little she could do about it now. She certainly wasn't going to hide in her room or pretend that he hadn't kissed her. One way or the other, they'd have to come to terms with what had happened between them. Sooner or later, they'd have to put their grief and their feelings for Russell behind them and move on. Their future, as either partners or lovers, or both, was yet to be decided.

Jolene's good intentions went flying out the door the moment Luke opened it and stepped inside. His dark eyes met her head-on, and she felt the same rush of pleasure she'd felt the previous night when he'd appeared in her doorway, wearing nothing but an ill-buttoned pair of pants.

Luke stared at Jolene's strained features for a brief moment, then busied himself pouring a cup of coffee. A kitchen that was soon to be filled with half a dozen hungry cowboys wasn't the place to sort out their differences. He mumbled a curt good morning, then took his cup and went back outside. The morning sun had cleared the hills that rimmed the valley. It's golden light silhouetted four riders.

"Looks like Morgan," Grizzly said, squinting his eyes to bring the approaching men into focus. "Wonder what's got him up so bright and early?"

"Trouble doesn't need a watch," Luke said, setting his coffee cup aside.

Jolene heard the men talking. When none of them came into the kitchen, she untied her apron and went outside, knowing something wasn't right.

Luke was standing just beyond the porch with the six Crooked Spur riders in a loosely formed semicircle behind him. They were all wearing guns and a questioning look in their eyes as four men rode toward the house.

The riders stopped a few feet from their welcoming committee. Jolene recognized one of them. It was Sanders.

The oldest of the group inched his horse forward. "Miss Chapmen," he said, tipping his hat. "Good morning. My name is Everett Morgan. I own the Lazy M. We're neighbors." He was well dressed and riding a Thoroughbred stallion. Lean with dark brown hair, sprinkled with gray at the temples, and brown eyes, he was a distinguished looking gentleman with a very southern accent. "I came to offer my condolences on the unfortunate death of your fiancé. And to welcome you to the valley."

Jolene forced herself to smile. Normally she would have returned his greeting with enthusiasm, but she didn't care for the company Mr. Morgan was keeping. Sanders was close enough to rub elbows with his boss. Something about Everett Morgan's eyes bothered her. It didn't take Jolene long to figure out what it was. He used them to look down on people.

"Thank you for coming by," she said, stepping off the porch.

Jolene kept walking until she was standing next to Luke. Everyone noticed the telling sign, but nothing was said until Everett Morgan smiled and inched his horse a tad closer.

"I detect a hint of the South in your voice, Miss Chapman. Tennessee?"

"Memphis," Jolene told him, unsure why anyone would come calling before breakfast and feeling uneasy because she could sense the tension hovering over the group of men. One spark of anger and guns were going to start exploding.

"You got a real reason for riding in here before the sun's had a chance to warm the air?" Luke asked, drawing Jolene back with his left hand until she was standing slightly behind him.

"I'm giving a party next weekend," Everett said, ignoring Luke's cold tone and smiling at Jolene. "A yearly celebration of sorts. Nothing as impressive as the parties I used to have in Louisiana but, I hope, as enjoyable. A barbecue. I'd be honored if you would attend, Miss Chapman."

Not wanting to prolong the tension, Jolene accepted the invitation. "I'd be pleased to come," she said. "We'll be there," she added, letting Morgan know that she would be escorted by at least six of the seven men standing around her. "Thank you."

Everett tipped his hat before riding off. The other men followed. All but Sanders. He started down at Jolene, letting his eyes roam over her like a pair of greedy hands.

"You got another invitation to extend, Sanders?" Luke asked.

His voice was as soft as the breeze ruffling the hem of Jolene's dress and as dangerous as the Colt resting against his right hip.

The foreman of the Lazy M bristled as if he'd been slapped. "One of these days, Maddock, you're going to push me too far."

The men behind Luke shifted their weight, as their hands inched closer to the guns they were wearing. Jolene didn't notice. She was too busy wondering if she was imagining the drawn Colt that seemed to appear out of thin air. Luke's gun was aimed at Sanders's questionable heart.

"They've got a saying where I come from," Luke said calmly. "Don't fork a horse you can't ride."

Jolene watched as Sanders mentally calculated the odds of winning against a man like Luke Maddock and a loaded Colt. Without a word, Sanders spurred his horse into a turn and sent him galloping down the hill.

Jolene watched, her breath trapped in her lungs, until the four riders disappeared over the crest of the hill.

Luke holstered his gun. "Are you all right?"

Jolene nodded, then gave him a contemplating look. "One of these days, you're going to pull that trigger, aren't you?"

"One of these days," he said.

Jolene shivered on the inside as Luke walked toward the bunkhouse. The thought of two grave markers on the lonely hilltop made her blood run cold.

Six

Jolene emptied the last bucket of hot water into the big brass tub, then latched the door of the spare bedroom. She didn't give a hoot what Luke Maddock thought about sashaying off to some damn party, she was going to enjoy herself. The last time she'd been to anything more than a church social had been before the war. She was overdue for a little entertainment.

Knowing her heart was ruling her head, Jolene had to admit that the main reason she wanted to go to Morgan's party was the possibility of being held in Luke's arms one more time. Of course, dancing with him wouldn't be the same as being cradled against his bare chest, but it was all Jolene could think about. Watching the way Luke moved, she knew he would be a graceful dancer.

After her hair was dry and tamed into an artful array of curls down her back, she donned a buttercup yellow dress. It had a round neck with white eyelet lace that hugged the upper rise of her breasts. The skirt was full and needed at least three petticoats to do it justice. While she got dressed, she refused to think about the cream-colored satin gown that she had brought with her from Tennessee. The month of June would come and go, and the dress would remain in the trunk. She and Russell had planned to marry on his birthday, but now the tenth day of June would hold only melancholy memories for her.

Jolene left the house by the front door. Luke and the men were mounted and waiting. All but Grizzly. He was driving the buggy that would deliver Miss Jolene Chapman to her first western party.

"Hellfire," Grizzly said through his teeth as he caught sight of Jolene. The stout foreman shook his head, then looked at Luke. "It's a good thing you're fast with a gun. That woman's pure trouble if I ever saw one."

The men responded with a reverent "Amen."

Luke gave them a scalding glance before he turned his attention back to Jolene. Didn't the woman have any idea what she was doing? It was a blessed wonder he hadn't shot someone already, what with every man on the place talking about their new boss from sunrise to sunset. Between them and her waltzing out of the house like a ray of sunshine, how was he supposed to control his temper?

Mindless to the thoughts rolling through Luke's head, Jolene climbed into the buggy with a smile on her face. Let the stubborn man act as if he didn't know her from Adam's cat. All he'd done was scowl and brood since the night he'd come into her room.

It didn't take long to arrive at the Lazy M. Moonlight was beginning to filter through the trees and the sound of fiddles and banjos filled the air. The front lawn of the impressive home was filled with people. Long wooden tables stacked with food and drink were set to the side of the house under the trees.

Before she could climb down from the buggy, Luke was there. Wordlessly, he held out his arms. Wanting more then his gentlemanly manners, but willing to bide her time, Jolene welcomed the momentary touch of his hands as they held her by the waist and lifted her free of the buggy's seat.

"Make sure you keep one of us in sight," he said, setting her feet on the ground. "There's enough liquor here to start a flood."

Nodding, Jolene straightened her shawl. Within minutes, the musicians stopped playing and Everett Morgan approached her. The woman he'd been dancing with was walking beside him, her hand resting casually on his bent arm.

"Good evening, Miss Chapman," her host said, smiling. "May I introduce my sister, Rosalind. Rosalind, this is Miss Jolene Chapman, our new neighbor."

The women exchanged greetings. Jolene saw some family resemblance but not enough to make her dislike Rosalind Morgan on sight the way she'd disliked the brother. Tall and slender with dark brown hair and light brown eyes, Rosalind was closer to thirty than twenty, but still a very attractive woman.

"I'm sure you know my partner," Jolene said, as Luke joined them.

The tall Texan tipped his hat as the musicians started playing again.

"Would you honor me with a dance?" Everett asked before Luke had a chance.

Knowing she couldn't decline the invitation without being blatantly rude to her host, Jolene allowed herself to be led toward the planked dance floor that had been constructed in front of the main house.

Everett Morgan was a perfect gentleman, but Jolene couldn't shake the feeling that he had a motive for his manners. When the music ended, her eyes searched the crowd for Luke. She spotted him standing beside a table stacked with beer kegs. Gene was standing next to him. Both men were looking in her direction, and Jolene suspected she hadn't taken a breath without them seeing it. They didn't trust Everett Morgan anymore than she did.

"I didn't know Mr. Morgan had a sister," Jolene remarked as she joined Luke and Gene. "She's very pretty."

Luke didn't agree or disagree, but Gene flashed her a smile that said she wasn't the only one who had noticed Rosalind's qualities. As she turned to look over the crowd again, Jolene saw Everett's sister approaching them.

"I've forgotten my manners, Miss Chapman," Rosalind said in a soft southern voice. "Would you care for some food? I was about to fill a plate for myself."

Once they had selected food for themselves, Jolene started preparing a plate for Luke. Rosalind hesitated, then reached for one of the clean plates neatly stacked at the end of the table. A few minutes later, with each woman carrying two plates, Jolene and Rosalind returned to where Luke and Gene were waiting.

"I could have fetched my own food," Luke said, taking the plate Jolene offered.

"You're welcome," she said, glaring at him. The man was beginning to make her angry.

"Let's sit down," Gene suggested. "I'm not much good at eating when I'm standing up."

They moved away from the beer kegs and toward a small table under the sprawling branches of a nearby tree.

"Everett won't like you takin' up with the likes of him."

Jolene whipped around to find Jake Sanders standing behind them. The foreman was glaring at Gene. A quick glance told her that Luke had emptied his hands, so he could go for his gun if the foreman kept making trouble.

"Mr. Hawkins is a guest," Rosalind pointed out.

"He's half a man," Sanders spit out the words.

Rosalind sucked in her breath.

"You've got a bad mouth, Sanders," Luke said, stepping forward. "It's time someone taught you a few manners."

The Lazy M foreman grinned like a jackal. "See, Rosie, the man even has to have someone fight his battles for him."

"Stop this, Jake," Rosalind beseeched him. "This is my brother's birthday party. I won't have you starting a brawl."

"Go back to the house," Sanders snapped. "Everett will back me up on this. He's got no use for the likes of—"

"That's enough," Luke said. "Let's take this to the barn. No use upsetting the ladies."

Jolene watched as Luke's hand went to his gunbelt. He unbuckled it and handed it to Gene. Sanders did the same, passing his revolver to one of the three Lazy M men who had joined him.

"Stay here," Luke told Jolene, adding a cold glare to make sure she knew he meant business.

She reached out and grabbed the sleeve of his shirt. "He won't fight fair."

"Then neither will I," Luke said before he walked away.

A small circle of people were gathering around the barn. Jolene looked for Everett Morgan. He was leaning against one of the white columns at the front of the house, sipping whiskey, and looking like everything was going according to plan.

Jolene gathered up the hem of her dress. Rosalind stepped in front of her. "Mr. Maddock told us to stay here."

"I've never been very good at taking orders," Jolene said. She looked at Gene, then smiled. "Come on. We're going to miss the fight."

As Jolene hurried toward the corral, she wondered if she should be in such a rush to see Luke get hurt. He'd defused the situation by taking off his gun, but she wasn't naive enough to believe that the upcoming encounter was going to be a mild one. The two men clearly hated each other. One of them was going to pay the price of that hatred, and she prayed it wouldn't be her partner.

A deadly silence circled the corral as the guests pressed closer to get a better look. Sanders took a moment to size up his opponent before charging Luke like a bull plowing through a fence. Luke side-stepped just enough to put the stouter man off balance. The foreman staggered, but he didn't fall. Then the fight started in earnest.

Luke took a punch that would have downed any other man, but he stayed on his feet. Someone in the crowd let out a whoop as Luke delivered a thundering round of punches to Sanders's thick midsection. Fists flew like flies around a picnic table. The foreman fell this time, supporting his bruised weight on his knees, while Luke stepped back to catch his breath. Jolene knew it wasn't over. Neither of the men could be counted victorious until one of them was unconscious in the dirt.

Someone shouted for Luke to watch out as Sanders came to his feet, wielding a wicked-looking knife that he'd concealed in his boot.

"I'm goin' to cut out your Yankee-blue heart." The foreman slashed the knife in a wide circle, causing Luke to suck in his middle and jump back.

Jolene held her breath as the foreman kept advancing. Luke didn't seem overly concerned that the odds had turned against him. He kept his eyes on Sanders while he moved in a narrow circle that kept him just out of the man's reach.

Wild with rage, Sanders lunged forward. Once again, Luke moved with the agility of a cat on a mantel. He took a short step to the side and hooked the foreman's leg with the toe of his boot. Stumbling forward, Sanders had too much weight behind him to stop the fall. Another quick move on Luke's part and the foreman was lying facedown in dirt with his arm bent behind his back and Luke's elbow pressed against his throat.

"That's all for now, Sanders," Luke said, breathing hard. "The next time you see me, don't except any mercy."

"Yippee!" Calhoun yelled as he jumped down from the corral fence and handed Luke a mug of beer to wash the blood out of his mouth.

"Gather up Jolene and let's get out of here," Luke said, grimacing as he moved. "I think the bastard broke my ribs."

"Jasper, get the buggy," Jolene called out as Luke came out of the corral.

He gave her a scalding look as she rushed to his side. "I ain't ridin' home in no buggy," he said, wiping the blood from the corner of his eye with the sleeve of his white shirt. "And I told you to stay put."

Jolene was too relieved to see Luke standing on his own two feet to be upset over his sharp tone. She knew he was in pain. His face was bleeding and bruised, and he was favoring his left side.

Grizzly was helping Luke on his horse, despite Jolene's insistence that he should ride in the buggy, when Everett Morgan approached them. Making sure her voice carried to anyone who might be listening, Jolene confronted their host. "If I were you, Mr. Morgan, I'd send Jake Sanders packing. Sooner or later, Luke's going to kill the man."

"Is that a threat, Miss Chapman?" Everett asked, feigning insult.

"Just a good piece of advice," she told him as she climbed into the buggy next to Jasper. "I'd take it, if I were you."

Seven

"You're better get inside," Gene told Luke. "That little lady is ready to bandage you up, while she's givin' you hell."

Luke was hurting too bad to argue.

Gene followed him into the kitchen. Jolene was already there, with an apron draped over her yellow dress and a basin of warm water setting on the table.

"Take off your shirt. And get rid of that gun," she said tartly, before looking at Gene. "Cut that old sheet into strips for me." She pointed at a stack of faded cotton. "I'll need to bind his ribs good and tight."

"Yes, ma'am," the drover replied. He helped Luke out of his vest and shirt, then picked up the scissors and began cutting.

"I want a drink," Luke said. "I keep a bottle in the desk drawer in the parlor."

Gene nodded, then made himself scarce. It was easy to see that Jolene's temper was ready to cut loose. Her hands were shaking so badly, she could barely open the tin of salve she'd found to put on Luke's cuts and scraps.

It didn't take long to fetch the whiskey. After Luke pulled the cork out of the bottle with his teeth and took a substantial drink, Jolene took the bottle away.

He didn't move as she added some whiskey to the warm water and began to clean his face. Once the

worst of the blood and dirt was gone, she emptied
the basin and refilled it with more warm water.
When she came back to the table, she looked into his
eyes. "You look like you've been rolling around in a
pigsty."

"More like a corral full of manure," Luke said,
grimacing when he tried to smile.

"Stand up," Jolene told him. "And stand still."

Luke did as he was told. It was apparent that
Jolene planned to wash the sweat and dirt off his
chest before she bandaged his ribs. And he was going to let her. Having her touch him in any way was
better than keeping her at a distance, and that's
what he'd been doing since the night he'd kissed
her.

Luke sucked in his breath as Jolene moved the wet
cloth over his bare chest. Her touch was as gentle as
moonlight, but he could feel it all the way to the
soles of his feet. It didn't hurt to breathe, because
he'd stopped breathing the moment she'd put her
hands on him.

Finally, when she was satisfied that he was clean
enough to be bandaged, Jolene dried his chest and
shoulders with the same gentle care she'd used to
wash them.

She hated the bruises that were already darkening
his skin almost as much as she loved the man who
was letting her touch him so freely. She smoothed
the drying cloth over his chest. "Does it hurt?"

"Not too much," Luke said.

What hurt was having Jolene standing so close he
could smell her. No matter how many times he reminded himself she was Russell's woman, he
couldn't stop thinking about how good it had felt to
hold her. Watching her dance at the party, seeing
her in another man's arms, had put his temper to
the test. He'd been primed and ready when Sanders
had tossed his insults. Pounding the other man into

the dirt had helped his temper, but it hadn't done anything for his sexual affliction. He wanted Jolene so much, he was aching.

When she was done drying his chest and shoulders, Jolene stepped back and looked up at him. "You're a stubborn man, Luke Maddock."

"So I've been told," he replied in a rough whisper.

Neither one noticed Gene putting down the scissors and exiting the kitchen.

"I'm stubborn, too," Jolene told him. "Tennessee stubborn, as my brothers used to say."

Luke's gaze was penetrating as he looked at her. Jolene felt something deep inside her warm. The small spark quickly turned into an uncontrollable blaze. She could feel it consuming her, heating her body until she felt a trickle of moisture dampen the valley between her breasts. She'd already acknowledged the desire she felt for Luke, but this was different. It wasn't a flash of lust. It was a long gentle burning that took her from the wishful daydreams of an innocent young girl to the uncharted realm of womanhood. If he touched her right now, she'd go up in flames.

Picking up one of the strips of cotton, she told Luke to raise his arms level with his chest. "Stand tall and suck in your breath."

Luke flinched with pain, but he did as she asked.

Jolene started wrapping his ribs. She wanted to kiss each bruise, but she didn't dare. The rousing sensation in her body grew each time her hands brushed his bare skin. "Just a couple more seconds," she said, knowing he was in more pain that he'd ever admit.

They were the longest seconds of Luke's life. If he thought resisting the urge to pull his gun and put a bullet in Sanders's mangy hide was difficult, it was nothing compared to the anguish of having Jolene brush up against him like a marmalade cat. Looking down he could see the coppery brightness of her hair. If he lowered his gaze, he could see the soft swell of her breasts above the white lace on her dress. Her hands felt like warm sunshine and his lower body was reacting in spite of the pain in his chest.

Jolene finally pulled the ends of the bandage tight and began tying a knot. "You can breathe now."

"Not damn likely," Luke grunted. "You've got me tied up tighter than a calf for branding."

"Sit down and stop complaining," Jolene said, now that the worst was over. "It serves you right for brawling like a little boy after school."

"I should have shot the bastard," Luke said, reaching for the whiskey bottle. "One of these days—"

"Not until those ribs heal," Jolene interrupted him. "And don't overdo the whiskey. Your head's going to hurt bad enough without it."

"Stop naggin' me." Luke turned the bottle up and took a long drink. The whiskey burned like fire, but he wasn't about to let some female tell him what to do, even if she was right. His head was already aching like a bad tooth.

"I think Rosalind Morgan is sweet on Gene," Jolene said unexpectedly.

"What!" Luke shouted, then grimaced. "If that isn't the dumbest thing I've ever heard. Being sweet on that woman could get a man killed."

"I still think it's sweet."

"Sweet," Luke repeated disgustedly. "In case you haven't noticed, Gene's not up to the kind of fight Morgan would bring his way."

"I noticed," Jolene snapped back. She emptied the basin of dirty water, then returned to the table. "That doesn't mean Rosalind Morgan can't like a man with one arm."

Luke stood up, whiskey bottle in hand. "Don't start playin' matchmaker," he warned her. "I've got enough trouble on my hands without you cookin' up a range war."

"I'm not cookin' up anything," she defended herself. "And stop yellin' at me."

Luke took another drink of whiskey. "I'm not yellin'. I'm telling you that love can tie a man in more knots than he can untie with two good hands."

Jolene's feelings had been tossed up, down, and around all evening. She had wanted Luke to tell her that she looked pretty in the yellow dress. All he'd done was glare at her. She'd wanted him to ask her to dance. But instead, he'd watched her from a distance. After that came the fight, then caring for his bruised ribs. She wasn't about to let the man stand there and tell her that love was a waste of time.

"We can discuss your low opinion of love some other time," she said curtly. "You need rest more than whiskey. I'll turn down the bed."

"What bed?"

"The only bed in the house big enough to hold you," Jolene said over her shoulder. She was halfway to the door. "I'll sleep on the cot in the back room."

Luke followed her down the hall. There was no way in hell he was going to sleep in Jolene's bed. "I don't need to be tucked in like a baby," he grumbled.

"I'm not offering to tuck you in," she said adamantly. "I'm trying to help you."

"I don't need any help going to bed."

The words brought on an uneasy silence as Jolene looked at him. Regardless of his stubbornness, she could see the pain etched on his face and burning in his eyes. When had she started to love this man? *What difference does it make?* she told herself. *You love him now.*

When Luke was settled, with his legs stretched out on the bed and his shoulders propped against a stack of feather pillows, Jolene looked aimlessly around the room, reluctant to leave him.

Luke was having similar thoughts. If the little lady didn't get her rump down the hall, he was going to come off the bed and show her that he wasn't hurt half as bad as she thought.

"Good night,' Jolene finally said. "If you need anything—"

"I've got everything I need right here," Luke said, holding up the bottle of whiskey.

He listened as her footsteps faded down the hall, then cursed under his breath. It was a long time before the bottle was empty, and Luke was asleep.

Eight

A week later Luke was cursing the fact that he'd taken off his gunbelt and challenged Sanders to a fistfight. If he had pulled his Colt and shot the no-good bastard, he wouldn't be suffering the torments of the damned by having Jolene fussing and pampering over him every minute of every day. The longer he stayed in the house, the more time they spent together. The more time they spent together, the harder it was to resist the temptation she represented.

Knowing he was at the end of his rope where the sassy redhead was concerned, Luke got up and got dressed. He was riding today and come nightfall he was bunking in with the rest of the men.

"Your ribs aren't completely healed," Jolene said the moment he walked into the kitchen.

Grizzly and Jasper were already up and sipping coffee at the table. The foreman looked from Luke's stern face to Jolene's determined one and decided he'd be wise to get out of the crossfire. Scooping a steaming biscuit out of the basket Jolene had just set on the table, Grizzly gave Jasper a sign that said get out while the getting was good. A scant second later, the screen door shut behind the two old cowhands.

"I'm mended enough to work," Luke said, ignoring Jolene's scowl and pouring himself a cup of coffee. "We're shorthanded. If we don't get those cows to Fort Worth by the end of June, we'll lose our contract."

Jolene stared at his back. She couldn't help the love ruling her heart. Luke was alive and standing in the kitchen, and she wanted him to stay that way. If Sanders had hated Luke before, he despised the Texan now. Russell was gone. She couldn't lose Luke, too. She wanted to share this house with him, to laugh with him and love with him, to sleep by his side and have his children.

Unaware that Luke's mind was wandering down a similar path, Jolene went about preparing breakfast.

Is this what Russell daydreamed about? Luke sat down at the table and watched Jolene as she moved around the room. *Did he think about the pure enjoyment of watching her move from place to place, and the way she hums to herself while she's working? Did he think about pulling her down on his lap and kissing her until she was clinging to him like ivy to a stone chimney? And holding her during the night? Did he think about spreading her hair over the pillow while he joined their bodies?*

By the time Grizzly came back into the kitchen, followed by the other riders, Luke's private thoughts had him strung tighter than a bowstring.

"Grizzly," Jolene said as she placed a platter of pancakes on the table. "Have one of the men saddle me a horse. If we're so shorthanded that Luke has to ride with bruised ribs, then you can use every hand you can get. I'll work cattle today."

Luke gave the foreman a look that said if Grizzly saddled Jolene a horse it would be the last thing he ever did.

Wisely, Grizzly reached for the maple syrup and pretended he hadn't heard the feminine order.

"You're not riding anywhere," Luke told her. "Stay close to the house like always."

"No."

The word echoed in the kitchen like the trumpets

of the Second Coming. Cowboys shifted in their
chairs while Luke came to his feet.

"Now look here, woman."

A skillet clanked down on the stove as Jolene's
hands went to her hips. "Don't 'woman' me, Luke
Maddock. I'm not some cowhand working for wages.
I'm your partner. That means I have just as much
right to saddle a horse and work cattle as you do."

"You're not riding the range," Luke said. If he
had used that tone on any of the men sitting at the
table, they'd be backed up in a corner by now.

Jolene didn't blink a blue eye.

"You've got no say over what I do or don't do,"
she told him.

Before Luke could say anything else, Jolene
stormed out of the kitchen.

"Got herself a temper, don't she?" Grizzly chuckled.

"Damn fool woman," Luke grumbled.

"She wouldn't be ridin' out if you'd give yourself
another day or two to heal. The boys and me can
handle things until then."

The look Luke sent Grizzly's way was colder than
a blue northerner. "She does her share cookin' and
cleanin'."

The foreman's wide shoulders moved in a questioning shrug. "Maybe she don't see it that way.
Some women ain't satisfied unless they're into everything."

Luke didn't comment. The only place he wanted
Jolene in was his bed.

The day went by in a flurry of bawling cattle and
Texas dust as they gathered up wandering steers and
guided them toward the main body of the herd. By
midday, Jolene was sweaty, dirty, and totally out-of-

sorts, but she didn't dare let on to Luke that she was anything but perfectly content sitting atop a horse.

I wasn't lying when I told him I was stubborn, she thought to herself as she maneuvered her gelding in front of a small calf that had gotten separated from its mother. *Luke may want to think that there's nothing between us but a ranch, but he's wrong. I can feel it every time he looks at me, and he'd been looking a lot lately.*

Late afternoon brought a brisk wind and tall billowing layers of dark threatening clouds. The soft rumble of distant thunder drew closer as the sky turned from blue to a forbidding shade of gray. Heat lightning shimmered against the thickening clouds as the cattle sensed the upcoming storm and became restless.

"I've got to get Jolene back to the house," Luke told Grizzly. The wind was whipping up dust, and the malcontented moans of cattle forced him to shout at the foreman.

Grizzly waved Luke on as he nudged his horse into a gallop and started yelling orders at the other five men who were trying to keep the cattle from scattering.

Jolene didn't argue with Luke when he told her to start riding for home. The rain started a few minutes later. It came in gusty sheets that soaked through their clothing in seconds. It was a damp relief from the sweltering heat of the day, but it wasn't long before she was shivering from the dramatic change in temperature. Heedless of the rain coming down like a liquid avalanche, Jolene kept the gelding galloping toward the comfort of the house Russell McClain had built.

"Follow me," Luke shouted as he rode next to Jolene.

"Where?"

"Line shack." He held on to his hat with one

hand while he turned his horse toward a small cluster of boulders.

Jolene followed. By the time they reached the one-room shed that served as a storage room during branding season and a warm place for a cold rider during harsh Texas winters, she was shivering so badly she had to clench her jaw to keep her teeth from chattering.

Luke scooped her out of the saddle. "Get inside. Now!"

The moment Jolene's feet hit the ground, she started running. The door gave way to her outstretched hand and she was inside, dripping on the dirt floor, while Luke tethered the horses.

Wrapping her arms around herself, Jolene stamped her feet. The rain that had leaked into her boots make a sloshing sound. A flash of lightning offered her enough light to see an oil lantern resting on a wooden supply box. She was looking for a match when Luke came running into the shack. He took off his hat and slapped it against his thigh, sending water in every direction.

He took the lantern out of her hand, put it on a small table, then opened the chest and withdrew a box of matches. Within seconds, amber light filled the room. One look at Jolene and Luke let loose with an explicit curse. The rain had soaked through her shirt and cotton camisole. In the soft glow of the lantern light, he could see the impression of her rain-hardened nipples. He stomped across the room and jerked a wool blanket off the end of the cot, tossing it at her.

"Get out of those wet clothes," he ordered. He turned his back, praying that the storm would pass before he lost the biggest battle of his life and stripped Jolene out of her wet clothes with his own willing hands.

Luke didn't have to see the clothes being peeled

away from Jolene's soft body, he could imagine it in his mind. With his feet braced apart and his eyes boring holes in the shed wall, he could envision each and every article of clothing falling away until there was nothing left but pure sweet woman. He took a long deep breath to still his racing blood, but it didn't solve the problem. Jolene had become a fire burning in his body, so hot and so deep, no amount of rain could quench it.

"What about you?" Jolene asked, once she'd stripped out of everything but her drawers and camisole.

Without answering, Luke walked to the chest and pulled out another blanket. He draped the blanket over his shoulders, then turned to look at her.

"I told you to get out of those wet clothes." He was angry because Jolene had insisted on riding with them that morning, and even angrier that another morning would come and go before he could get her back to the house. The storm had a long way to go before it rained itself out.

"I did," Jolene said shakily. She was so cold her bones were rattling.

"Take them all off," Luke said without preamble. "Your lips are turning blue. Do you want a dose of lung fever?"

Knowing fate had dealt him a losing hand, Luke began peeling off his vest and shirt. Unlike Jolene, he wasn't modest about it. The bandages she'd insisted on wrapping around his chest that morning came off like limp wet ribbons. He tossed them in the corner, then sat down and took off his boots and socks. While he unbuckled his gunbelt, Jolene managed to rid herself of the last of her clothing. She clutched the dripping undergarments with one hand and held the blanket together with the other.

While she was looking for a place to hang them, so they wouldn't be displayed like the flag on the

Fourth of July, Luke opened the chest and drew out
a bag of supplies, a dented coffeepot, and two tin
cups.

"For pity sake," he grumbled. "I've seen drawers
before. Just lay them over the chair with the rest of
your things and get on the cot. You need to get
warm."

"So do you," Jolene said shakily. Luke was acting
like she'd conjured up the storm using some sort of
female magic. It wasn't her fault water was coming
down in biblical buckets.

Jolene added her wet undergarments to the rest of
the clothes she'd draped over the back of the shed's
only chair while Luke put a pot of water on the small
miner's stove. Outside the storm was increasing
rather than decreasing. Thunder snapped like a
teamster's whip and lighting arced across the black-
ening sky in white streams of blazing energy.

She sat on the cot, resting her back against the
wall. Once her bare feet were tucked under the
coarse wool blanket, she looked at Luke. His upper
body was gleaming with moisture, accenting the rip-
ple of muscles as he moved around the room, making coffee and checking the supplies for anything
they could eat that didn't take a lot of preparation.

"Dry your hair," Luke said. He tossed her a towel
he'd found in the storage chest.

Undoing a wet braid, drying her hair, and keeping
a blanket around her nakedness was more than
Jolene could manage with only two hands. Seeing
her distress and knowing there was only one way he
could help her, Luke walked to the cot.

"I thought Missouri mules only came from Missouri," he complained as he gathered up her wet
braid of hair. Disgusted with himself for wanting to
strip the blanket away so he could warm Jolene with
his own body, Luke pulled a knife from his belt and

cut through the cantankerous ribbon with one sure swipe of the silver blade. "Stay put."

"Stop grumbling at me," Jolene said, then sneezed.

Luke gave her a thunderous look, then pushed her back on the cot and began rubbing her arms and legs through the blanket.

The rough fabric felt abrasive against her skin, but that didn't keep Jolene from moaning with pleasure. Luke's touch was warming her faster than the heat coming from the miner's stove. She closed her eyes, savoring the firm but gentle kneading of his fingers as they worked the stress and cold from her muscles. For the next few minutes the only sound was the battering of rain on the shed's roof and the crackle of thunder as the storm raged on.

Feeling both vulnerable and daring, Jolene freed her hand from the blanket and touched Luke's bruised chest. He flinched, then met her gaze. Spurred by days of remembering and the sound of the storm, reminding her that she might never have a moment like this again, Jolene abandoned her common sense and said what she was thinking. "Would you kiss me again?"

"You're treading on dangerous territory, Miss Chapman," Luke said in a rough whisper. "I'm not made of stone."

"I know," Jolene said, keeping her voice low. "These prove that."

Once again her fingertips traced a path around his discolored ribs.

Luke's control vanished.

He pulled her to him and lowered his mouth over hers in a deep hard kiss that left Jolene clinging to the blanket with one hand and Luke's bare shoulder with the other.

The kiss wasn't slow or hesitant. It was hard and deep and hot and Luke couldn't stop anymore than

he could remember all the reasons he shouldn't be
touching Jolene in the first place. Their mouths
mated in a wild exchange of breath and lips and
tongues as he shifted his weight and leaned back
against the wall, bringing her up and over his lap.

With a throaty moan, Jolene moved with him. She
twisted against his chest, wanting to get closer to the
lean hard body that offered her an exotic comfort
she couldn't explain or understand. She only knew
that Luke was kissing her again and that she didn't
want him to stop.

Luke couldn't get enough of her sweet mouth. His
tongue dipped and darted, tasting her as deeply as
he could. Heat coiled through him like the lightning
that was dancing through the darkening sky. It
wound tighter and tighter, until he thought his body
would explode if he didn't get closer, as close as a
man could get to a woman.

He raised his head and looked down at Jolene's
flushed face. Her eyes were bright with desire, and
he could see the pulse racing at the base of her
throat. The blanket fell away and he could see the
creamy perfection of her lush breasts, tipped with
dark pink nipples that were budding and hard and
begging for his mouth.

Although no words were spoken between them,
both Luke and Jolene knew that they could no
longer resist the simmering desire that had sparked
between them that first day in Fenton. Unable to do
anything else, Luke's hands reached inside the blanket, slowly caressing as they moved around her waist
and lifted her more snugly into his lap. He bit back
a groan as her body pressed against the rigid bulge
in his pants.

Jolene was doing some moaning of her own as
Luke's warm strong hands enveloped her breasts,
stroking and kneading them to fill his hands. He

traced their hardened crowns with his fingertips, making her flinch with a sweet need.

Distantly, in the far corners of her mind, Jolene knew she should be ashamed for allowing him such liberties, but she couldn't hold on to the thought long enough to make it materialize into the strength she needed to push him away.

His touch felt too right, too wonderful to be denied.

When Luke wrapped his hands around her waist and raised her up so his mouth could nibble and his tongue could tease the tips of her breasts, Jolene closed her eyes and arched against him, offering whatever he wanted. However he wanted it.

Luke enjoyed the creamy softness of Jolene's breasts until he was sweating with a desire that had to be satisfied. Slowly, seductively, he turned her again, lowering her to the mattress and pushing the blanket aside until he could see all the soft curves he had dreamed about for weeks. Her legs were long and slender, and she had a small mole a few inches to the right of her navel. He kissed the slight imperfection while his hands roamed slowly over her stomach and thighs, savoring the silky smoothness of her skin.

"You're beautiful," he said in a husky whisper.

Jolene wanted to say something in return, but she wasn't capable of speech. She'd never imagined a man's hands feeling so wonderful. Every sense she had was intoxicated, drugged by the sensual caress of Luke's callused hands.

Jolene jerked at the first gentle probing of his fingers, but Luke kissed her, melting away her resistance in a warm blur of sensations and colorless explosions that left her breathing raggedly and arching up to meet his exploring touch.

She stretched and moved against him like a cat trying to get closer to the gentle hands that made it purr with pleasure. There was no damp chill, no cold rain, nothing but the searing glide of Luke's hands as they learned her body's most intimate secrets. The slowly building ecstasy that was stealing Jolene's thought and turning her body into a stranger continued to build as Luke stretched out beside her. While his mouth kissed her, and one hand moved up and over every sweet curve he could reach, the other was unbuttoning his pants. The wet fabric resisted at first, but one by one the buttons were undone and he freed himself.

Jolene's eyes were still closed as he pushed his trousers down his hips and legs and finally away, letting them fall to the dirt floor. When he moved over her, pressing her into the mattress, she opened her eyes. Luke's features were strained from the same need that was tormenting and promising and making her shudder with desire.

At that moment, Jolene knew she'd never regret giving herself to Luke Maddock. No matter what he thought of her later, no matter what she thought of herself, she knew this moment had been preordained.

Luke watched Jolene's flushed face as he slowly joined his body to hers. Even in the dim twilight of the stormy evening, he could see the surprise in her eyes. "I won't hurt you," he said softly. "Just relax and let me show you how good it can be." Luke's fingers brushed through the tight copper curls at the junction of her thighs and felt the warm response of the woman who wanted him. "This isn't fear, sweet woman. It's passion."

Jolene wished he had used the word *love,* but she was too lost in the fiery need Luke's gentle caresses aroused to retreat now. "I love touching you," she said, letting her hands roam freely over the lean expanse of his chest, combing her fingers thought the crisp mat of hair that intrigued her more every time she saw it. Felt it. "You feel wonderful."

Luke sucked in his breath and prayed that he could last long enough to show Jolene just how wonderful it could be. He cradled himself in the warmth of her thighs and let her feel the force of his desire.

She moaned, and he shuddered as her hands began to move over him, learning the muscular contours of his shoulders and back. Delicately she felt the tight cording of the muscles along his spine. Holding his breath and willing his body not to betray him with a need that was quickly racing out of control, Luke slowly pushed against the defenses of her innocence. Jolene stiffened for a moment, then relaxed as his mouth found hers.

Luke forced himself to go slowly, to savor the smooth, silky acceptance of Jolene's body, to marvel at the intensity of their joining. His body vibrated with need as he moved gently, giving her time to adjust to him. He rained light kisses over her mouth and face, nibbling at the delicate skin of her earlobes and breathing soft reassuring words over her closed eyes. The more she relaxed, the deeper Luke sank into her delicious warmth until he was surrounded by her wet heat.

Wave after wave of pleasure moved over Jolene, washing her into a sea of sensual oblivion. There was the storm outside, but it wasn't raging half as strongly as the erotic tempest Luke was creating. She could hear his breathing coming harder and deeper as he moved over her, inside her, stealing everything she was and giving it back in hot waves of sensation that made her feel as if she were floating on a bed of clouds instead of lying on a straw tick mattress.

Luke abandoned himself to the fiery passion of Jolene's willing body. She moved with him, against him, her nails digging into his shoulders as her hips lifted to meet his deep thrusts.

"Come with me," Luke said, unable to stop the words that came with the tight tingling at the back of his spine. "Hold on and come with me."

Jolene didn't know what he meant. She didn't care. He was holding her so tightly she could barely breathe, but each breath was a sweet torment that came with the pleasure of feeling him inside her. Never in her wildest imagination could she have envisioned a joining so sweet, so hot, so totally consuming. It was a blissful surrender that gave back more and more as she let Luke guide her toward the nameless promise waiting just a stroke away, a kiss away.

When the moment came, it robbed Jolene of breath. Delicate shivers of ecstasy started deep in the center of her body, moving outward in tiny flickering tremors of heat and cold, making her shiver and shake until all she could do was cling to Luke.

He felt it, too, stealing his sanity for a long sharp moment as his body tightened and pushed deep, needing as much of Jolene as he could get. His hips rocked hard against her one last time before he surrendered to the pulsing sensations that left him weak.

They lay quietly together for a long time. Jolene kept her eyes closed as she relished the deep contentment of simply holding Luke's body next to hers. When he rolled to the side, gathering her in the circle of his arms, she went willingly.

There were no words. What could they say to each other?

Luke dealt with the guilt of having taken a woman he'd vowed to resist. But the regret didn't outweigh the pleasure that was still reverberating inside him.

The storm had settled into a long pelting rain that echoed off the roof and filled the air with the clean damp scent of the earth being refreshed. Luke pulled the wool blanket over them, then bent down and kissed Jolene again. She returned the kiss, smiling up at him.

When he started to say something, she pressed her fingertips against his mouth. "Don't say anything," she whispered, then kissed him again. "All I want to do is lie here and feel you next to me. Whatever has to be said between us can wait until the rain stops."

Luke didn't argue. He wasn't looking forward to reminding Jolene that she had come to Texas to marry another man, or the consequences they would both eventually have to face. Like his Tennessee lover, all Luke wanted to do was savor the sensation of her body pressing intimately against him. He stroked her tangled copper hair, loving the silky texture of it against his bare chest.

Delicious shivers threatened to steal Jolene's sanity once again as Luke continued the gentle conquering of her body. Light kisses turned into hotter, more demanding ones as the storm moved on its way, ending the magical time it had given them. The second time Luke claimed her, Jolene was twisting with passion, aware now of the blissful victory that awaited them.

Moving over her, Luke didn't hesitate this time but took her body in one deep fast thrust that left her gasping for breath. His movements were hard and determined as he forced her to explore the depths of her passion. He urged her on with exotic words that would have brought a blush to her face in the light of day. But Jolene didn't blush now, she gave Luke what he wanted, surrendering to his sensual commands. There was no holding back from him as his hands gripped her hips so he could drive harder and deeper into her. When the ecstasy came this time, it was an explosion that made her cry out his name.

A few minutes later, the rain stopped.

* * *

The promise he'd made to his friend gnawed at Luke's guts as he saddled the horses. He still had every intention of taking care of Jolene, but it wasn't the way Russell had planned for him to watch over her. He'd betrayed his friend's trust. It didn't set well on his mind, and it wasn't going to set well on Jolene's either, once she woke up and realized that she'd given herself to a man she didn't love.

Women didn't understand passion the way men did. They didn't accept that it could rule their senses and make them do things they normally wouldn't do. Like bullets, passion had a way of changing things in the short span of a second. Once unleashed, its results couldn't be undone. Jolene would never be an innocent virgin again, and Luke couldn't take back the pleasure he'd given her.

As soon as the cattle filled their bellies with the new grass the rain would bring, they'd start the drive to Fort Worth. The minute they got there, Luke planned on finding a preacher and putting a wedding ring on Jolene's finger.

It was the decent thing to do. And, truth be known, it was what he wanted.

The problem was that he didn't know what Jolene wanted. She'd been vulnerable since discovering that the man she'd loved since childhood was dead. Luke had installed her at the ranch, knowing full well that the attraction between them would eventually boil over and they'd end up just the way they had, naked and clinging to each other in the dark.

Still, he'd done it, and now there was nothing to do but pay the fiddler.

With the horses saddled and waiting, Luke stepped inside the line shack.

"Wake up, honey. It's time to go."

While Luke stood in the doorway with his back to her, Jolene got dressed. Her clothes weren't wet, but they still felt cold and clammy against the skin Luke

had warmed with his hands and mouth. She grimaced as she pulled on her wet boots.

"I'm ready," she said, letting him know that it was
okay to turn around and look at her.

It seemed oddly ironic for him to be offering her
privacy to dress when a few hours earlier he had
explored her body in a fiery adventure of touching
and kissing that had left nothing to his imagination.
The memory of just how thoroughly Luke knew her
now brought a blush to Jolene's cheeks.

She walked over to him, unsure as to how he
would receive the smile she offered.

"Are you . . . okay?" he asked hesitantly.

She nodded and smiled again. "I'm fine. Don't let
your conscience beat you into the ground. Nothing
happened that I didn't want to happen."

Luke gave her a bittersweet smile. "Do you think
I didn't want it to happen?"

"I'm not sure," she told him honestly. "You're not
an easy man to figure out."

"There isn't much figurin' left to do," he replied.
"As soon as we get to Fort Worth, we're getting married."

Jolene wasn't surprised by the unromantic proposal. She had known it was coming the moment
he'd turned his back so she could get dressed.
Rough Texas rancher or not, Luke was a decent
man, and a decent man married a women if he took
her virginity without the benefit of a wedding ring.
Knowing she loved him and that nothing would
make her happier than becoming his wife, Jolene
shook her head.

"I don't want or need a husband who doesn't love
me," she said bluntly.

Her blatant refusal pricked Luke's temper. "Taking
your virginity is reason enough to find a preacher,"
he said. "We're getting married come June."

"No, we're not," Jolene said each word with a cold

precision that sliced through her heart like a sharp knife. She'd agreed to marry one man without love; she wouldn't do it again.

Luke blocked her path as she tried to sidestep him and go out the door. "When we get to Fort Worth, you're going to put on that yellow dress and stand in front of a preacher, like it or not."

"You said we needed to get back to the ranch," Jolene reminded him calmly. "We can't go until you step out of my way."

"What if I gave you a baby?" he said impatiently. "I'm not going to let you birth a child of mine without a wedding ring on your finger. If you're carrying my baby, you *will* marry me."

Knowing there was no way she could avoid marriage if he had given her a child, Jolene made the only concession she was willing to make. "*If* there's a child, I'll marry you."

"Come here." He pulled her into his arms. The kiss he gave her was clearly meant to show her that he wasn't going to be put off by her stubborn resolve. He'd taken a virgin; now he'd take a wife. It was as simple as that to his way of thinking.

But nothing about Jolene's feelings for the tall Texan were simple. She returned the kiss, because she couldn't be touched by Luke without responding. But underneath her willing mouth and soft body was a heart that refused to be a wife of obligation and duty. As much as she longed for Luke's child, she hoped she hadn't conceived it. If she became his wife, she wanted to hear him repeat vows of love, not words of responsibility.

Luke kept Jolene in his arms for as long as he dared. When he set her away, her mouth was swollen from his kisses and her eyes sparkled like blue diamonds. He smiled smugly. "You'll marry me."

* * *

When they got back to the house, Luke took the time to change into some dry clothes. Setting his boots aside to dry, he pulled on a pair of socks and walked down the hall to the kitchen. Although no one had been bold enough to ask, he knew everyone was wondering where he and Jolene had ridden out the storm. Having the men curious about the hours that the two partners had been missing reaffirmed Luke's decision to put a ring on Jolene's finger as soon as possible. He didn't want gossip in the bunkhouse, and he'd personally shoot any man who spoke a disparaging word against the lady from Tennessee.

"You need to get some sleep," he said, finding Jolene in the kitchen.

"I'm not tired," Jolene told him. "And stop frowning. All I need is a hot cup of coffee and something to eat."

"You're going to fight me tooth and nail, aren't you?"

"I'm not fighting you at all," she said. "I'm being perfectly reasonable."

"You're being stubborn and you know it," Luke countered. "But I'm more stubborn than a little gal from Tennessee who thinks she can forget what happened last night."

Jolene kept her temper in check. Luke was goading her. Neither one of them was likely to forget what had happened in the line shack. She wasn't sure how Luke felt about her, but her instincts told her that the tender way he'd taken her innocence meant something. Even now, she could feel the haunting memory of his touch. The way she'd cried out when the pleasure had become so intense it had tossed her soul toward heaven couldn't be taken back.

"I'm not forgetting anything," she said. "I'm—"

"Stubborn and sweet and everything in between,"

Luke said, reaching out to caress her cheek. His hand left her face and found a wayward strand of copper hair. He twisted it around his index finger, watching her reaction. "Your hair is the color of a shiny new penny. Mine is as dark as sin. It's going to be interesting to see what our kids look like."

His blatant reference to children made Jolene think of a future she didn't want unless it contained more than Luke's bed. She'd been willing to marry Russell knowing his love alone would have supported their marriage. Now she was refusing to marry Luke because she loved him so much it hurt. It didn't make sense, but love wasn't logical. It was puzzling and passionate, with as many possibilities as there were people to feel it.

"The storm scattered the cattle," Jolene said, intentionally changing the subject. "What happens if we don't make the contract?"

"We'll survive," Luke told her. "But it takes cash money to pay riders, and without riders all we'll have is a valley full of unbranded cattle and no way to herd them to market next year."

"Is that Morgan's game? Does he want to force us into selling Crooked Spur?"

"Probably," Luke admitted. "But he's barkin' up the wrong tree if he thinks I'm going to stand by and let someone steal my ranch for ten cents on the dollar."

He looked at Jolene. She'd always been pretty to his eyes, but now she looked more lovely than ever. "Maybe he plans on letting Sanders put a bullet in my back, so he can marry my partner and get Crooked Spur for nothing."

Jolene went pale at the suggestion. "Don't say that. The thought of Everett Morgan touching me makes my skin crawl."

"Don't worry, honey." Luke's voice dropped to a

seductive whisper. "I'm not about to let another man have you."

The tone of his voice was a warm echo that reminded Jolene of the way he'd talked to her in the line shack, of the intimate instructions he'd whispered in her ear, telling her how to move and where to touch him so they both could enjoy each other to the fullest.

Luke watched her reaction and smiled. "Go on and fight me, honey, for all the good it will do you."

"Go to hell," Jolene said in a low seething whisper as her temper got the best of her.

Luke laughed.

Jolene's hand unfold so she could slap him silly. He grabbed her wrist in a gentle, but firm, grasp and brought it up to his mouth. He kissed the tender flesh of her palm as she struggled to pull away from him.

"You're all fire and vinegar," he said, clearly amused. "But I'm bigger and stronger, and a hell of a lot more determined to marry you than you are to keep your pride." He pulled her close, wrapping one arm around her waist while he continued kissing and nibbling at the sensitive flesh on the inside of her hand. "And I'm not Russell McClain."

"What's that supposed to mean?"

"It means I'm not some smiling-faced young man from Tennessee who's going to let a sassy, temperamental gal run him around in circles. If you had married Russell, you would have had him twisted around your finger in no time. I don't bend that easy."

Angry and embarrassed, Jolene said the first thing that came to mind. "Russell loved me."

She might as well have slapped him. Luke didn't need to be reminded that Jolene had given him her body while her heart still belonged to a dead man. "Russell's dead," he said. "He was a friend and a partner, but he's gone now, and I won't have you hiding behind his grave. I'm the man you asked to kiss you. I'm the man you slept with, and I'm the man you're going to marry. Get that through your pretty head once and for all."

Nine

It was late morning and Jolene wasn't feeling very enthusiastic about the future. How could she expect Luke to believe that she loved him without admitting that she'd let Russell believe the same thing not so long ago? How could she explain that she'd fully intended to be a good wife to Russell without admitting that she'd planned on deceiving him about her true feelings? No matter what words she used to explain her actions, she'd end up sounding selfish and coldhearted.

Jolene's breath unraveled in a long frustrated sigh as she got dressed. There was more to think about than her feelings for Luke and his feelings for her, whatever they might be. There was the very good possibility that they'd have trouble delivering the herd to Fort Worth, which meant the kind of trouble that was going to end with someone else getting killed.

Jolene's emotions did another somersault. Thoughts of passion and love were replaced with worries that weighed down her shoulders as she went into the kitchen. If time was on her side, she'd wait Luke out. After the herd was delivered to the army garrison and the trouble between Crooked Spur and the Lazy M was somehow settled, they could talk, and maybe by then she would have the courage to tell him that she'd never loved Russell McClain the way she'd let everyone assume she had.

But time wasn't catering to her wishes. Although she had no doubt that she loved Luke, she needed time to get to know him better. Time to break through the silent barrier he retreated behind whenever he didn't want to share his feelings. They both needed time to reconcile themselves to Russell's death and the aftermath of finding themselves partners. They needed time to learn to love and trust and laugh together. But the time wasn't there. Luke was determined that they marry. He felt bound by the promise he'd given Russell and the possibility that he might have fathered a child.

Jolene went out to the porch and sat in the swing. Her eyes focused on the land as she renewed her vow to Russell's memory. In the short time that she'd been in the valley, she'd come to love the rugged country dotted with cattle and towering pecan trees and bushy cottonwoods. She couldn't envision herself living anywhere else. Like Luke Maddock, Texas had reached into her heart and taken root.

She and Luke couldn't go on like this, with so much needing to be said between them, but no words being spoken.

Jolene made up her mind to talk to him after dinner. It would be the last night they'd have alone until they got to Fort Worth. With the decision made, Jolene was ready to start the daily chores, but the sound of a rider coming hard and fast kept her on the porch. Her heart stopped as she waited for one of the men to arrive with more bad news.

But it wasn't a man riding breakneck toward the ranch house.

It was a woman.

One look and Jolene knew that Rosalind Morgan had dashed away from the Lazy M with little thought to her appearance. Her hair was streaming down her back in dark tangles.

"Where's Mr. Maddock?" Rosalind called out as she jerked her horse to a halt that brought the animal up on its hind legs.

"What's wrong?" Jolene asked, seeing the fear on the other woman's face.

"Sanders," Rosalind said shakily, trying to catch her breath. "He and a group of men are riding against your herd. I came to warn you." She gulped down some air. "He shot Everett."

"My God!" Jolene came off the porch so quickly she almost tumbled into the dirt. "What happened?"

Rosalind slid out of the saddle, holding on to the stirrup to steady herself as she faced Jolene. "I was getting dressed when I heard Sanders and my brother arguing downstairs. It was awful," she added. "Jake was calling my brother a coward, saying he was too busy hiding behind his fancy manners and southern ways to get his hands dirty. Everett yelled back at him, saying he'd have no part of cold-blooded murder. They kept arguing, calling each other names. Then I heard a shot." A visible shudder ran through her body. "I ran downstairs and found Everett's body in the hall. He's dead."

Jolene offered her arm to the other woman. "And Sanders?"

"He gathered up the men and went riding out. I heard him bragging that this would be the last day Luke Maddock ran cattle in this valley."

Jolene shut her eyes for a moment, trying to block out the harsh reality that Sanders' boastful prophecy might well come true. "Go into the house," she said, running toward the barn. "I'll warn Luke."

Jolene's face was grim as she tallied the time it had taken Rosalind to ride from the Lazy M to Crooked Spur, plus the time it would take to reach Luke and the other men.

Once again, time seemed to be her enemy.

She saddled the small gelding with record speed, then went galloping out of the barn. *Please, God,* she prayed. *Don't put any more graves on the hill.*

Luke yanked hard on the reins, pulling his gelding back and around, before taking aim at one of Sanders's raiding men and pulling the trigger. The man fell off his horse and under the hooves of the stampeding cattle. Grizzly was riding not far from Luke. He whipped his rifle out of a deerskin scabbard, cocked the weapon, and fired. Another raider went down.

Through the thick dust being kicked up by the frightened animals, Luke could see two dozen men, circling the perimeter of the valley. Their guns were rattling off bullets in a sharp chatter that was joined by the heavier roar of rifles as the Crooked Spur riders abandoned their mounts and took cover in the rugged boulders that ran up and down the landscape like a rocky spine.

A dark anger rolled over Luke as he saw Sanders, flanked by two other riders. His nemesis was too far away to get a good shot, so Luke saved the bullet until it could get the job done. Outnumbered, Luke shouted for the Crooked Spur riders to keep their heads down and their guns loaded as he circled back the way he'd come. He sprinted his horse, running alongside the frightened cattle.

"Get to the rocks. Fast!" Grizzly shouted to Jolene when she came racing up beside him. "And keep your head down. You're too late to do anything but get in the way."

Jolene nodded, turning her mare toward a thick cluster of rocks and small trees. She scanned the landscape with anxious eyes, looking for a glimpse of Luke, but all she could see was the confusion of the herd and a cloud of dust thickened by the acrid smoke of guns being fired on a regular basis.

Then a few of the cattle split off to one side, and Jolene saw Luke. He was riding low in the saddle, toward the end of the valley. She let out a sigh of relief. But it didn't last long. Just ahead of her and to the left, where Luke couldn't see them, she saw Sanders and two other men.

Shouting for Luke and knowing that he couldn't hear her over the roar of guns and bawling cattle, Jolene kicked her horse into a gallop and rode toward him. She'd gone a few hundred yards, when she felt the sharp sting of a bullet rip through her upper arm. Her hand jerked with the painful impact and the gelding followed the lead of the reins, turning abruptly and almost colliding with a brawny steer that was running hell-bent for the creek.

Jolene screamed as her horse stumbled, then tried to regain its footing. It went down, and she was pitched out of the saddle. She hit the ground with a hard thump that knocked the wind out of her lungs. A painful second later, the world went black.

Luke felt Jolene's scream as much as he heard it. It vibrated through his body, turning his blood to ice and setting a fire in his soul that wouldn't be squelched until he'd put a bullet into Jake Sanders's murdering heart. Holding his mount steady with the firm pressure of his thighs, Luke leveled his rifle at the man riding toward him. Sanders let out a war whoop and raised his gun. Luke blocked out everything and pulled the trigger.

Sanders flinched, went stiff, and fell out of his saddle.

The raiders who hadn't taken a Crooked Spur bullet fled when their leader hit the dust.

Luke got to Jolene as fast as he could, coming out of the saddle and hitting the ground in a dead run. Unaware that he was cursing and crying at the same time, he gingerly lifted her into his arms and held her close, praying that the bullet that had dug a narrow furrow in her upper arm was the only injury she'd suffered. He'd seen her hit the ground. A head injury could do as much damage as a bullet.

"We'd better get the little gal home," Grizzly said, coming up behind Luke.

Luke was too numb with fear to do anything more than nod. The depth of his emotions kept him silent as the men forgot about cattle and rode behind him, each of them saying a prayer for Jolene's recovery.

Luke prayed, too. He prayed that God would let Jolene open her eyes. That she'd be able to hear him when he told her that he loved her. His grip was forceful as he whispered her name, hoping she could hear him. Hoping that he could penetrate her mind and heart with softly spoken words of love. Words he should have said before. Words that his pride had kept locked inside. Words that flowed from him now in soft fervent whispers as he cradled her in his arms.

Amidst the pain that made her arm burn like a torch and her stomach rock in motion to the horse's jerky steps, Jolene felt the soft kiss that Luke pressed against the top of her head. The roaring in her ears that had been deafening when she'd hit the ground had subsided enough for her to hear him talking.

"I love you, honey," he said. "God, I love you. Open your eyes and look at me. Let me see that you're going to be all right."

Jolene tried to do what he wanted, but her mind and body were still two separate entities. She strained to bring them back together, but the effort sent her plummeting back into the darkness.

Jolene felt like a thousand tiny soldiers were marching double-time between her temples. Memories came flooding back. Sanders's raid on the cattle. A bullet ripping her flesh. Her horse going down. Blackness and pain and the soft sound of Luke's voice.

She tried to move, but her body seemed weighted down.

The soft jingle of spurs told her that Luke was near the bed. She felt the cool touch of his hand as he checked her forehead for fever. Willing her eyes to open again, Jolene blinked and did her best to smile.

"Water," she mumbled the word.

Luke lifted her head and placed a glass to her mouth.

"Easy," Luke said. "You were shot."

"I know," Jolene replied in a raspy whisper. "Are you okay?"

Her vision was still too blurred to see the warm smile that softened Luke's worried features. "I'm fine. And you will be, too, as long as you don't move around too much. You've got a lump on your head the size of Texas."

"It feels bigger," Jolene grimaced.

"I'd be more worried about your bottom," Luke said sternly. "I'm going to set it on fire once you're out of that bed. What in the hell did you think you were doing, riding into a bunch of blazing guns!"

Rosalind laughed, then reached down and gave Jolene's hand a reassuring squeeze. "Isn't that just like a man? He'll sit by your bed, worried sick, then holler at you the moment you open your eyes."

Jolene didn't have a chance to reply. Luke was holding the glass to her mouth again and telling her to drink. Then he gently told her to rest.

When she opened her eyes again, moonlight was streaming through the open window of her bedroom. The house was silent and for a moment she ~~ought she was alone. She groaned as she tried to sit up. Luke's helping hands were there again, holding a glass of cold water while he instructed her to take tiny sips.

"How long?" she managed to ask before falling back against the pillows. Time hadn't mattered in the dark world that had been her universe since being shot and thrown from her horse. She'd relived her childhood. Her brothers had all been with her once again. Gerald and Wayne and Donnie, teasing her and threatening to tell Papa that she'd done one thing or another. Laughing and being alive again, if only in her dreams.

But most of all, Russell had been there, encouraging her to wake up, telling her that he'd always love her. Sometimes, his voice had changed, and it had been Luke, whispering his love. She'd clung to those moments, somehow knowing even in that dark world that he was waiting for her to open her eyes and join him again.

"You took a fever after Rosalind cleaned and bandaged your wound. You've been dreaming and mumbling in your sleep for the past three days."

What Luke didn't tell her was what she'd been saying. Sitting beside her bed and listening to her call out Russell's name had ripped his heart to shreds. If he'd had any doubts that Jolene still loved the young man from the Tennessee, they'd come to an end. The few times Luke's name had escaped her lips, it had been spoken more in pain than in memory.

"Morgan?"

"He's dead," Luke told her. "Along with Sanders and a dozen of his thievin' friends."

Words of passion and tenderness wanted to burst from Jolene's heart, but she was too weak to say them. It took all her strength to keep her eyes open. Willing herself to move in spite of the pain, she turned her head and looked at Luke. He needed a shave and his clothes looked to be the same ones he'd been wearing the day of the raid, but he was still the most handsome man she'd ever seen.

"Get some sleep," he said, coming to his feet. "It's the best medicine for you now."

"You, too," Jolene said. "You look tired. I'm sorry for causing you trouble."

Luke tucked the blanket around her. "Sanders caused the trouble, but it's over now. Sleep."

The gentle glide of his mouth over her forehead was the last thing she felt. Once again, sleep and dreams claimed her. But this time, Luke was laughing with her as they sat on the front porch of the house and watched their children playing in the yard.

So much for dreams, Jolene thought a week later. The gentle caress of Luke's lips over her forehead had been the last touch she'd received from him since the night the fever had left her for good.

The bullet wound and concussion had left her weak, but with Rosalind there to help, Jolene was getting her strength back on a daily basis. Today, she'd ventured out to the front porch. The men were loading the canvas-covered wagon that would serve as kitchen and supply store while they drove the herd north. Luke was nowhere in sight.

Jolene sank into the wooden rocker and looked out over the valley. She wondered if Luke still planned on them marrying. She wasn't pregnant. So he didn't have to feel obligated to put a ring on her finger.

"Would you like something to drink?" Rosalind said, opening the front door and stepping out into the late-morning sun.

Everett's sister had taken on a younger look since ꞏming to Crooked Spur. Jolene knew it was because of Gene Hawkins. Last night she'd seen them in the hallway. Gene had given Rosalind a kiss on the cheek before returning to the bunkhouse. Although Jolene was happy for them, she couldn't help but wonder if Luke would ever kiss her again. The longing to feel his arms around her was almost as painful as the bullet wound she'd suffered trying to warn him about Sanders.

Jolene gave Rosalind a weak smile and insisted that she was fine. The other woman seemed to know better.

"I don't know what has passed between you and Mr. Maddock, but I do know this," Rosalind said. "That man loves you."

"I love him," Jolene said aloud, finally verbalizing what she'd planned on telling Luke the night of the raid. But she'd never had the chance. Now she couldn't get close enough to him to say "boo."

"Have you told him?" Rosalind asked.

Jolene shook her head. "It's all so complicated. I came out here to marry Russell, but he was dead, and I . . . I never loved him the way I love Luke."

"Tell Luke how you feel," the other woman advised her. "One thing that I've learned recently is that we don't have time to keep our feelings to ourselves. I hated my brother for years. And I loved him at the same time. He was a selfish, narrow-minded man and I let him rule my life. I'm sorry he's dead, but I can't be sorry for finally being allowed to let my feelings out. I'm going to marry Gene," she added with a smile. "We'll be your neighbors."

"I couldn't ask for better ones," Jolene said, smiling in earnest this time. "He's a good man."

"So is Luke Maddock," Rosalind said. "Tell him how you feel. I know he loves you. All he needs to hear is that you love him, too."

* * *

Luke stepped into the kitchen, expecting to find Rosalind milling about the room. He stopped in his tracks when he saw Jolene spooning coffee beans into the grinder.

"What are you doing out of bed?"

"Getting my land legs back," she said, not turning around to look at him. "My arm still hurts if I move it too much, but I'm fine otherwise."

Luke couldn't take his eyes off Jolene as she moved slowly around the kitchen. She was wearing an apple green muslin dress with a scooped neck that showed too much of her soft skin. Her hair was brushed back and tied with a white ribbon.

"After dinner, I want you to take me out to Russell's grave," she announced.

"You're not up to a ride in the wagon."

"Then you can put me on your lap and take me there the same way you brought me back home after the raid," Jolene said casually. "I don't care how I get there. I'm going. And so are you."

Luke didn't argue. It was well past time for the dust between himself and Jolene to be settled. If she wanted to do it at Russell's grave, then so be it. If she was carrying his child, they'd be married, even if it meant tucking his pride in his hip pocket and letting her love a ghost while she slept in his bed.

Jolene said a silent prayer that Rosalind was right. If Luke did love her, then she had a chance to take the pain away. If not, she wouldn't stay in Texas. It would be like dying a little every day, sharing a ranch, but never sharing his heart.

Sunset was lingering over the valley when Luke brought his horse around to the back porch. He lifted Jolene into the saddle and got on behind her, keeping his arms close enough to steady her, but not so tight that she felt cradled in his embrace.

They rode in silence, each consumed with their own thoughts.

So near, yet so far, Jolene thought as Luke guided the gelding with a firm hand. The large tree draped over Russell's grave was a dark shadow against the warm shades of the late-evening sky. Luke dismounted first, then reached up for Jolene, being careful not to disturb the arm that was encased in a sling and resting against her chest.

Her breath came in hard and stayed for a long moment as she moved toward the lonely grave. "Hello, Russell," she said. "Luke is here with me."

Luke stiffened at the affectionate tone in Jolene's voice. It was like Russell was standing beside her, listening to every word. He felt more like a stranger than ever before, an uninvited guest who had stumbled upon two lovers. Bracing himself for what he thought would come next, he stood beside Jolene, hat in hand, while she talked to the spirit of the man from Tennessee.

Jolene lifted her head and looked up at the sprawling cottonwood tree. "It's so nice here," she said, her voice clear and strong. "Luke picked the perfect place for you. He misses you, you know. And so do I. So much it hurts." She wiped a tear from her eye. "You were my best friend. I could talk to you about anything. You could always make me laugh, no matter how bad I felt about things."

Luke watched her smile at the memories. His heart ached with the kind of pain that only love could inflict as he forced himself to listen to the words he wanted Jolene to be saying to him instead of to a dead man.

"Remember the day you left for Texas," she continued. "I knew then that you loved me." She stopped to wipe away another tear. "I was wrong not to tell you then, but I couldn't. You'd just come back from the war and the future was shining in your eyes.

I'd never seen you so full of life. I wanted to share in your dreams. I'd lost so many of mine. Three brothers and a father dead. So I kept the truth to myself and let you ride away thinking that I loved you."

Jolene took a deep breath, knowing Luke was clinging to her every word.

"I did love you, Russell," she went on. "Like a brother. You were and always will be my dearest friend. But I never loved you the way you loved me, the way I let everyone believe I loved you. When I found out you were dead, I was so ashamed. I should have written you. I should have refused your proposal, but Tennessee held nothing for me. I wanted to find my dream the way you found yours, so I came west."

She reached out and touched the wooden cross. "Forgive me. I promised myself every inch of the way to Texas that I'd never let you down. That I'd be a good wife. That I'd never let you regret loving me. And then you were dead. And I was left alone. Except for Luke."

Luke's mind was racing. What was Jolene trying to tell him? That she'd never really been in love with Russell? It couldn't be. Or could it. Had her passion been only for him? Could her heart be his as well? He felt the hope bubbling to the surface and with it a love so strong it brought tears to his eyes.

Jolene's soft laughter drifted over the lonely hillside. "He scared me the first time I saw him," she continued talking to her silent friend. "He was so tall and hateful looking, staring down at me like he wanted to truss me up like a Christmas goose and send me back to Tennessee. He's stubborn, but he's loyal to the friendship you shared, and he'd promised to take care of me. So he did. He brought me to the ranch and watched over me," she whispered. "But most of all, he loved me.

"And I love him," Jolene said, talking to her

friend but looking at Luke. Her eyes were bright with tears. "He's a good man, Russell. Brave and strong and he makes me feel safe. When I'm in his arms, I feel loved and cherished, like I've finally found my place in the world.

"If you can forgive me, if he can forgive me, then I want to go on loving him. I want to have his children and watch them grow up in this wild, wonderful country. I want to share his days and his nights, his tears and his laughter. I want to grow old with him, and one day, I want to be buried on this hilltop with him on one side of me and you on the other."

"Come here, woman," Luke said, wrapping her in his arms and rocking her back and forth while her tears wet the front of his shirt. "God, I love you," he whispered. "I wanted you that first day in town. Wanted you so bad that I couldn't breathe without hurting. Then I loved you and hated you because you belonged to Russell. Touching you was the sweetest pain I've ever known."

Jolene wrapped her good arm around Luke's waist and held on while he told her again and again that he loved her. That he'd never stop loving her.

Holding each other close, Jolene looked at the grave one last time. "He's the reason we're together," she told Luke. "And in my heart, I can't help but feel that he doesn't mind me loving you. Russell didn't have a selfish bone in his body. He always wanted me to be happy. I'm sure, he wanted the same thing for you. For both us."

"You make me happy," Luke said, leaning down to kiss her. "I'll spend the rest of my life taking care of you, just the way he wanted me to."

"We'll take care of each other," Jolene said. "And we're name our firstborn son Russell McClain Maddock."

"Are you pregnant?" Luke gave her a hopeful look.

"Not yet, but I have a feeling I will be before too long, so you'd better get a ring on my finger, Luke Maddock. Russell's liable to come back and haunt you if you don't make a decent woman out of me before the end of June."

"Don't worry, sweetheart. You'll be a June bride," Luke said, smiling as he scooped Jolene into his arms and headed down the hill. "That's a promise."